TROUBLE WAS CREEPING UP BEHIND HIM

Cole slipped his Colt from his holster, thumbed back the hammer, and pointed the barrel toward the blue Wyoming sky.

Something slammed into the back of his shoulder, knocking him to his knees before he could pull the trigger. The next instant, a man landed on his back, looping an arm around Cole's neck, bearing them both to the ground. Cole tried to drag a breath into his body, past the arm pressed against his throat but the grip was too tight. And he had been caught with little or no air in his lungs, so that his head was already spinning dizzily. A red haze seemed to be seeping into the edge of his vision.

Books by James Reasoner

Wind River
Thunder Wagon
Wolf Shadow
Medicine Creek
Dark Trail
Judgment Day

Available from HarperPaperbacks

JUDGMENT DAY

JAMES REASONER

HarperPaperbacks
A Division of HarperCollinsPublishers

HarperPaperbacks *A Division of* HarperCollins*Publishers*
10 East 53rd Street, New York, N.Y. 10022

Cover illustration by Rick McCollum

First printing: November 1995

Printed in the United States of America

HarperPaperbacks and colophon are trademarks of HarperCollins*Publishers*

❖ 10 9 8 7 6 5 4 3 2 1

For Oleta North and Patty Williams,
with thanks for letting us invade their stores.

JUDGMENT DAY

Cole Tyler heard the music playing as he stepped out onto the porch in front of the marshal's office. The stirring strains of a martial melody came from down the street in the center of Wind River's business district. A speaker's platform had been built in front of the Territorial House, the town's largest and best hotel. Cole had seen carpenters working on it the day before. He had no doubt that was where the town band was playing.

A well-built man of medium height who wore denim pants, Cole also sported a marshal's badge pinned to his buckskin shirt. He had held the job for more than a year, ever since he had arrived in Wind River on the first train to roll into the settlement on the Union Pacific rails. Before that he had been a civilian scout for the army, a buffalo hunter, and a wanderer in general, the kind of man who never stayed in one place for too long.

Wind River had changed all of that.

Cole's brown hair fell square-cut to his shoulders. He had keen gray-green eyes, clean-shaven jaw, and features that were too rugged to be called handsome despite their power. A Colt .44 revolver was holstered on his right hip, and a heavy Green River knife rode in a sheath at his left hip. He liked to think that town living had not softened him too much from his wandering days, and for the most part he was right. But he had grown fond of this settlement in the southern part of Wyoming Territory, about halfway between Rawlins and Rock Springs.

True, the landscape was a little bleak in these parts, and the town probably never would have existed if not for the railroad, but to the north, south, and west were ranges of snow-mantled mountains whose foothills contained many lush valleys where thriving ranches had been established. The biggest spread was Kermit Sawyer's Diamond S, northwest of the settlement. Sawyer had come up from Texas with a herd of half-wild longhorns and a crew of even wilder Texas cowboys and quickly made his mark as a Wyoming cattleman. Nearby was Austin Fisk's Latch Hook ranch, also quite successful now that the rustling threat in the area had been dealt with. The town itself had grown by leaps and bounds as it served the needs of the ranchers and the railroad alike. Its main street, Grenville Avenue, was the equal of any in the territory short of Cheyenne. In the months that he had been here, Cole had watched Wind River progress from a raw settlement that was half hell-on-wheels to a civilized community.

Soon the town would take one more step on the road of progress.

Wind River was going to elect a mayor.

Billy Casebolt stepped out of the solidly constructed stone building behind Cole and tilted back his battered old campaign hat. The middle-aged deputy was tall, lean, and grizzled. He said, "Sounds like we got a parade goin' on."

"Nope," Cole said. "It's not a parade. If I had to guess, I'd say it's a political rally."

Casebolt grimaced. "I can't figure out for the life of me why folks had to go and ruin things around here with a bunch of politics."

"Somebody's got to run things," Cole said with a shrug. "Wind River's getting too big to just muddle along the way it's been doing."

"Yeah, but Miz McKay's pretty much run things all along. Once she's the mayor, how's that goin' to be different?"

"Because the people will have elected her. She'll have the power of the electorate behind her, like Michael said in his last editorial in the paper."

Casebolt snorted. "Still sounds like a lot of foolishness to me."

"Maybe so, but there's no going back. Once there's a change like this, it's here to stay."

Casebolt didn't look convinced, and Cole couldn't very well blame him. Cole shared a lot of the deputy's sentiments. Like Casebolt, he remembered when this part of the country had been wild and untamed but still a rich, bountiful wilderness.

That was before land developers William Durand and Andrew McKay spread around enough bribe money to find out just which route the Union Pacific would follow as the transcontinental railroad was built. Durand and McKay had bought up most of the land around here and started their town, so that Wind River was waiting when the UP arrived. Both men were dead now, leaving McKay's attractive widow, Simone, as the leading citizen and owner of much of the town. And Wind River had prospered under her leadership, Cole thought, there was no denying that.

But Simone had promised that her election as mayor would bring even more changes, and that had Cole a little nervous. The town had survived riots, cattle stampedes, Indian trouble, bloodthirsty outlaws, and a lot of assorted uproar during its relatively brief existence. But maybe Billy Casebolt was right.

Cole wondered if Wind River could survive politics.

Simone McKay looked out over the crowd gathered in front of the speaker's platform and felt her heart thudding almost painfully in her chest. She had never been a speechmaker; that had been Andrew's job, back when he was alive. Now the time had come for Simone to speak for herself.

It wasn't as if she was facing a bunch of strangers, she thought. She had friends here, and plenty of them. Michael Hatfield, the sandy-haired young editor of the *Wind River Sentinel*, was waiting to jot down notes while she made her remarks, so that he could write a story about the speech for the next edition of the paper. Dr. Judson Kent, the tall, bearded, distinguished-looking Englishman who was the community's only physician, stood near Michael, a reassuring smile on his face as he waited for Simone to speak. Jeremiah Newton, the massive, moon-faced blacksmith and preacher, was also in the crowd, and Simone knew he was one of her most ardent supporters.

She looked around for Cole Tyler but didn't see the marshal. Cole had taken the lawman's job only because Simone had asked him to track down her husband's killer, but in the months since then the two of them had grown closer. Cole had some romantic interest in her, Simone knew that, but she had been careful not to allow things to go too far. As attracted as she was to the marshal, she couldn't let herself become distracted from the goal she had sought for so long.

The town band stood to one side of the speaker's platform, their brass instruments shining brightly in the afternoon sun. As the musicians finished playing, Nathan Smollett, the manager of the town's bank, who was sitting on the platform with Simone, stood up and moved to the lectern that had been placed in the center of the platform. He looked out at the crowd and said loudly, "Good afternoon, ladies and gentlemen. It is truly an honor and a privilege for me to stand up here and introduce the lady who is about to speak to you this afternoon. I may not have known Mrs. McKay for as long as some of you have, but I am already well aware of the fact that a finer, more upstanding woman could not be found in all of Wyoming! She is more than qualified to lead this town as it takes its proper place in the wave of progressiveness sweeping across our fair territory! Ladies and gentlemen . . . I give you Mrs. Simone McKay!"

Applause flowed from the crowd and broke over the platform like a wave. Simone stood up, her heart pounding even harder, and moved toward the lectern. She put a smile on her face as she looked out at the people waiting to hear what she was going to say. She hoped she wouldn't let any of them down.

The banker was clapping as hard as anyone when he stepped aside from the lectern. Simone nodded to him, then looked at the crowd again. Smollett drew back and sat down in his chair, still applauding.

Simone let the reaction run its course, holding up her hands for quiet only when she sensed that she was about to get it anyway. As the applause died away she said in a loud, clear voice, "Thank you. Thank all of you . . . and thank you, too, for those kind words, Mr. Smollett." She turned her head and nodded to the banker again, then brought her attention back to the spectators. "I'm glad all of you came here this afternoon to hear what I have to say. My message is a simple one: Wind River must move forward with the times, and if our town is to do that, we must not look back." Simone had no need for notes. She knew what she was going to say; she had gone over it enough times in her head. "This community had somewhat humble beginnings. Many of the buildings were only temporary, intended to last only until the railhead of the Union Pacific moved on. Other such settlements have been born, lived their brief time in the sun, and then died, leaving no permanent mark on the land or the people who lived there. But Wind River is different!"

Her voice rang out strongly, and more applause came from the crowd. Simone paused, basking in their approval.

"From the beginning, Wind River was meant to be different. My late husband, Andrew McKay, wanted this town which he founded to be a model for all other frontier towns."

She said nothing about William Durand, her husband's partner, who had died in disgrace as an outlaw, blamed far and wide for Andrew McKay's murder. There was no need to remind these people of the turmoil that had marked the settlement's early days. Many of them remembered it all too well.

"From the very first days of this community's life, we have had a newspaper, edited and published quite ably by Mr. Michael Hatfield," Simone said as she gestured at the young journalist. Michael blushed, but it was clear that he enjoyed the attention. Simone continued, "And we have also been blessed with the services of a fine physician, Dr. Judson Kent. Our law enforcement has been in the capable hands of Marshal Cole Tyler and Deputy Billy Casebolt, two exceptional public servants. Our own Brother Jeremiah Newton has attended to our spiritual needs and will soon be building the town's first church. As soon as it was possible, a bank was opened, under the management of Mr. Nathan Smollett. The record of progress is undeniable. Wind River has lived up to the promise that was my husband's legacy!"

Simone felt good now. She was enjoying this. It was all right with her that she would not be required to give speeches very often, since there was no one running against her for the position of mayor, but at least this one had gone well. She smiled, listened to the applause, then went on, "I am pleased to announce today that Wind River will soon be taking yet another step forward. A teacher has been hired, and by the time he arrives next year, a school for our children will have been built!"

That brought more applause. When Simone lifted her hands for silence, she said, "So you can see, my friends, that Wind River is well on its way to being a highly respected—and respectable—community. As I said before, we cannot look back. For the sake of our town . . . for the sake of ourselves . . . for the sake of our children, we must only look forward! There is no room in Wind River for the forces that would drag it back into a morass of frontier hooliganism! There is no room for ruffians, for thieves, for all the violent, immoral elements who unfortunately remained behind when the railhead departed. We must drive them from our midst, we must—"

An angry shout suddenly came from the back of the crowd. "She's talkin' about closin' down the saloons!"

Simone leveled a finger in the direction of the man who had called out. "That is exactly what I'm talking about!" she said. "The saloons, the gambling dens, the dance halls, the parlor houses . . . There is no room for them in Wind River anymore!"

She had lost some of the crowd. The muttering she could hear told her that. But many of the listeners began to applaud again, and more than that, some of them started to cheer.

Another voice bellowed, so loudly that the words overwhelmed the rest of the clamor, "Don't let that woman tell you how to run your life! She ain't the boss of this town yet! Vote for a man who says live and let live! Vote for Hank Parker!"

Simone stared thunderstruck at the man who had shouted. This development had taken her completely by surprise. There hadn't been any talk about anyone running against her, certainly not the burly, one-armed proprietor of the Pronghorn Saloon, Hank Parker. The wheels of her brain spun rapidly as she searched for a way to deal with this unexpected disruption.

In the meantime, Dr. Judson Kent had turned toward the man, who happened to be standing near the medico. "I beg your pardon," Kent said stiffly. "*What* did you say?"

"Well, I don't beg *your* pardon, sawbones!" shot back the man, who was roughly dressed and appeared to be either a railroad worker or a miner. "I said we ought to all vote for Hank Parker! He won't try to push us around!"

Several more men took up the cry, shouting Parker's name. Kent grabbed the shoulder of the man he had spoken to and said sharply, "Here now! That'll be enough of that. Have the decency to let Mrs. McKay speak."

"That bitch can go to hell!" the man shouted. "Get your hands off o' me, you Limey bastard!"

He swung a knobby fist at Kent's head.

The doctor saw the blow coming but wasn't able to move aside in time. The man's fist cracked against Kent's bearded jaw, jolting Kent backward into the crowd. Instantly men sprang to Kent's defense, grabbing the man who had hit him, but that individual had allies, too. Men yelled curses, women cried out, and punches were thrown right and left. What had been an enthusiastic political rally turned into an out-and-out brawl in a matter of seconds.

Tight-lipped, Simone watched the chaos from the speaker's platform. Her hands tightened on the sides of the lectern. She had seen this sort of thing happen before, when the celebration to welcome the first train into Wind River turned into a melee. All-too-vivid memories of that day came sweeping back into her mind. That was the day her husband had died. Someone in the milling, violent crowd had slipped out a gun and fired a fatal bullet into Andrew McKay's body. William Durand had been held accountable for the murder, once Cole Tyler had exposed the rest of his villainy, but Simone didn't like to think about that. She didn't like to remember anything about that day. Her hands clenched into fists, and she lifted them to her mouth, shuddering. She was barely aware that Nathan Smollett had jumped up from his chair and hurried to her side. The bank manager put an arm around her shoulders and tried to steer her away from the lectern. Simone let herself be led.

It couldn't be happening all over again, she thought. She wouldn't allow it.

Cole heard the commotion that broke out from down the street and hurried in that direction, Billy Casebolt at his heels. Both of the lawmen had still been lounging on the porch, enjoying the peaceful afternoon. Cole had been able to hear Simone's voice as she made her speech, even though he couldn't make out most of the words. That was all right with him. He just liked hearing her talk.

But then the peace had been shattered by a lot of yelling and screaming, and Cole had come up out of his chair to break into a run. He had heard the sound of too many big fights not to recognize one now.

The street in front of the speaker's platform was filled with knots of struggling men. Some members of the crowd were running away from the platform, trying to escape the fracas, but most of the men who had been listening to Simone's speech only moments earlier were now throwing roundhouse punches and grappling with each other. Through gaps in the mass of people, Cole could see the raised platform. Red, white, and blue bunting had been draped across the front of it. Simone was at the rear of the platform, Cole noted, out of harm's way with Nathan Smollett at her side.

Well, at least that was one thing he didn't have to worry about, he thought. He reached the edge of the brawl and grabbed a man's collar, slinging him to one side. Another man, either not noticing or not caring that Cole was a lawman, swung a wild punch at his head. Cole ducked under the blow, stepped in, and hammered a fist into the man's midsection, doubling him over. Cole shoved the man out of the way and continued to wade into the mob, yelling, "Stop it! Stop fighting, you damned fools!"

Nobody paid any attention to him, which came as no surprise to Cole. Once the fighting frenzy had seized a group of men like this, it was difficult to break them free of it. To do so took a shock of some sort. Cole slipped his Colt from its holster, thumbed back the hammer, and pointed the barrel toward the blue Wyoming sky.

Something slammed into the back of his shoulders, knocking him to his knees before he could pull the trigger. In the next instant a man landed on his back, looping an arm around Cole's neck and bearing them both to the ground. Cole tried to drag a breath into his body past the arm pressed against his throat, but the grip was too tight.

And he had been caught with little or no air in his lungs, so that his head was already spinning dizzily. A red haze seemed to be seeping into the edges of his vision.

He drove his left elbow up and back, smashing it into the body of the man holding him. Over the sound of his blood roaring in his ears, he heard a grunt of pain. Cole struck again, and the pressure on his throat eased. He gasped for breath, and the redness in front of his eyes receded a little. It didn't go away entirely, though. He was too angry for that.

Cole arched his back, throwing his assailant completely off him. The man landed in the street beside him, then tried to roll over and get back to his feet, but Cole didn't give that a chance to happen. He lashed out with the gun still in his right hand and clipped the man on the side of the head. The blow was hard enough to make the man slump to the ground face first, stunned.

A pair of gunshots ripped through the air, but they didn't come from Cole's revolver. He pushed himself onto his knees and swiveled his head to look over his shoulder. Billy Casebolt had fired the shots, Cole saw. Tendrils of smoke still trailed from the muzzle of the deputy's old Griswold & Gunnison revolver as he lowered it. Casebolt had done what Cole had intended to do: fire a couple of shots into the air to get the crowd's attention.

He had it. Men were frozen, fists cocked in readiness to strike another blow, and all eyes were turned toward the deputy. "Hold it!" bellowed Casebolt. "Everybody just stand still! The next tarnal idiot throws a punch, I'll ventilate him!"

Cole pushed himself to his feet, and Casebolt's anxious gaze swung toward him. "You all right, Marshal?"

"I'm fine," Cole told him. "Thanks, Billy."

Cole went to the edge of the speaker's platform, the crowd parting before him now. The look on his face and the heavy gun still in his hand made people want to get out of his way. When he reached the platform, he put his free hand on it and vaulted lithely onto the plank floor of the structure. Simone came toward him.

"Thank goodness you got here, Cole," she said in a low voice. "I thought this was going to turn into another riot."

"It almost did," he said. "Are you hurt?"

She shook her head. "All the fighting was down in the street."

"Good," Cole said with a curt nod. He turned and faced the crowd. "What in blazes happened here?"

"I can answer that, Marshal," Michael Hatfield said. The young newspaper editor bent to pick up his notebook from the street. Obviously it had been knocked out of his hand during the melee, and he looked at its ripped, stomped-on pages in disgust for a second before he glanced up at Cole again and went on, "Some men didn't like what Simone had to say, so they started disrupting her speech. They were yelling about how people ought to vote for Hank Parker for mayor. Then one of them threw a punch at Dr. Kent."

Cole's eyes sought out the tall figure of the medico. "Judson? Are you all right?"

Kent was brushing off his coat with one hand while he held his bowler hat with the other. The headgear was barely recognizable. Kent sighed as he looked at it, much as Michael Hatfield had regarded the damaged notebook, then nodded in reply to Cole's question. "My jaw may be a bit sore tomorrow, but so, I dare say, will be the jaw of the man who accosted me."

"You mean you punched him back, Doc?" asked Casebolt.

"I most certainly did. Just because I'm a doctor doesn't mean that I'm absolutely lacking in knowledge of the manly art of fisticuffs."

"Well, good for you," Casebolt told him. "Wish I could've seen it."

"Never mind about that," Cole said, impatience creeping into his voice. "What's this about voting for Hank Parker?"

"That's what some of the men in the back of the crowd were urging, Marshal," Nathan Smollett spoke up as he came forward on the platform. "They were the ones who started the fight, too."

"Point 'em out," Cole said grimly.

"I'd be glad to." Smollett's eyes swung toward the crowd still gathered in the middle of Grenville Avenue, but after a moment a frown appeared on his face. "I . . . I don't believe I see any of them, Marshal."

"What about you, Mrs. McKay? Did you get a good look at the fellers?"

"I saw several of them," Simone replied, "but I don't see them now."

"That's correct, Marshal," Kent put in as he looked around. "The man who assaulted me and fomented that disturbance seems to have disappeared along with all his cohorts."

"Likely they lit a shuck when they saw the law comin'," Casebolt said.

"Could be," Cole agreed. He holstered his Colt and looked down the street toward the Pronghorn Saloon. "But I reckon I know where to find them . . . or at least the man who sent them."

It was clear the speechmaking was over for the day. Cole and Casebolt dispersed the crowd, not bothering to arrest anyone for disturbing the peace, not even the men who, in their enthusiasm, had attacked Cole. The marshal had no doubt in his mind that the entire fracas had been planned, and the spectators had been goaded into the near-riot just as the handful of agitators had wanted.

Cole didn't particularly care about tracking down the men who had started the trouble, either. He just wanted the gent they worked for.

A few minutes after the crowd had broken up, Cole slapped aside the batwing doors across the entrance of the Pronghorn and strode into the saloon, trailed by Billy Casebolt. The lanky deputy had detoured by the marshal's office and picked up a scattergun from the rack on the wall. The greener was in Casebolt's hands now, and his thumb was looped over the hammers in readiness.

As soon as Cole came into the saloon, he spotted Hank Parker standing at the end of the long hardwood bar. Parker was tall and powerfully built, and his bullet-shaped head was shaved clean. He wore an expensive suit, a white shirt, and a silk cravat with a diamond stickpin in it. The left sleeve of his coat and shirt were pinned up. Parker had lost that arm during the Civil War, leaving it on the dark and bloody ground around Shiloh church. Using his heavily muscled right arm, though, he could still wield a bungstarter with the best of them.

Cole had known Parker for several years and had never liked the man. Parker had run a succession of tent saloons, moving from settlement to settlement along with the railhead of the Union Pacific, until he reached Wind River. Then, for some reason, he had decided to settle down here. He had been successful, too. The Pronghorn was Wind River's largest saloon. Parker had tried to change his image, dressing like a businessman instead of the ruffian Cole knew him to really be. You could put an Easter bonnet on a pig, the marshal thought as he walked toward Parker, but it was still a pig.

Parker grinned at him. "Afternoon, Marshal. What brings you here? Like a drink?"

"No, thanks," Cole said.

"You sure? I've got the best whiskey in Wind River. You know that."

It was true enough. Parker was willing to pay to have prime-quality goods brought in, instead of brewing up vile rotgut full of gunpowder and strychnine like most of the other saloons. The move had paid off, too, because cowboys, miners, railroad workers, and sodbusters from miles around came to the Pronghorn to wet their whistles. Cole wasn't in the mood for whiskey at the moment, however, no matter how good it was.

"I didn't come here to drink," he snapped. "I'm here because there was nearly a riot down the street a few minutes ago when Simone McKay tried to make a speech."

Parker shrugged. "I heard a little commotion, but I didn't pay any attention to it. I'm a businessman, Marshal. I've got a saloon to run."

"I hear you're also a candidate for mayor."

"You mean the word's gotten around town already?" Parker asked, his features twisting into a grin. "I just decided to run earlier today."

"You sent those men to ruin Mrs. McKay's speech."

The grin dropped off Parker's face. "The hell I did. You can't prove that, Marshal, and you don't have any right to accuse me of it."

Cole looked around. There were only half a dozen customers in the saloon right now, but it was the slowest part of the afternoon. Cole didn't recognize any of the men, which didn't mean anything. Wind River had long since grown past the point where he knew practically everybody in town.

"Why don't I just go get Mrs. McKay and Nathan Smollett and Dr. Kent and Michael Hatfield?" Cole suggested. "I want them to take a look at these gents to see if they recognize any of them."

Parker waved his hand casually. "Sure, go right ahead. But these boys have all been in here for at least an hour. They didn't start any fight out in the street."

Cole and Casebolt exchanged a quick glance, and the same knowledge was in the eyes of both lawmen. Parker wouldn't have agreed so readily unless he was confident of what he was claiming. Cole felt certain none of the men currently in the Pronghorn had had anything to do with the brawl. But that didn't mean Parker was in the clear.

"You, there," Cole said, catching the eye of one of the men drinking at the bar. "Did anybody else come running in here during the past half-hour?"

The man shook his head. "No, sir, Marshal. I ain't seen nobody like that."

"Me, neither," one of the other men chimed in without being asked. The rest of the customers began shaking their heads.

"There you go, Marshal," Parker said smugly. "You heard it yourself, from half a dozen impartial witnesses."

"Impartial my hind foot!" Casebolt burst out. "All these fellers are scared of you—"

"That's enough, Billy," Cole said. He looked intently at Parker and went on, "Maybe I can't prove it, but we all know what happened out there in the street and why. Are you really running for mayor?"

"You're damned right I am! Simone McKay's talking about closing down all the saloons if she's elected. What am I supposed to do, just stand aside and let her reform me right out of business? Let her ruin the whole town so that she and a few of her friends can act high and mighty?"

Cole's mouth tightened into a thin line. As much as he hated to admit it, Parker had a point. Simone's main backing came from a group of citizens intent on reform, which wasn't a bad thing in itself. But if it was carried too far . . . if all the saloons and the other places that some people considered unsavory were forced to close . . . then the settlement would be damaged. Parker was only interested in protecting his investment in the Pronghorn, of course, but at the same time, he was right about what Simone's plans might mean for Wind River.

"I don't care about any of that," Cole said, ignoring the misgivings he felt deep down. "I just don't want any more trouble in my town. You run a clean campaign, Parker, instead of paying some rannies to cause problems for Mrs. McKay—or you'll have to campaign from a jail cell."

Parker slipped a fat cigar from the pocket of his coat and put it in the corner of his mouth. "I didn't pay anybody to do anything," he said. "All I did was start spreading the word that I was running for mayor. If some of my supporters got carried away, you can't blame me for that." His teeth clamped down on the cigar, and he growled around it. "And another thing . . . you're a public official, Tyler. You can't take sides in this election. I'm a citizen just like Mrs. McKay, and I got just as much right to run for office." He gave a humorless chuckle. "Besides, if I'm elected, this won't be *your* town much longer. You'll be out on your ass so fast you won't know what happened."

Casebolt edged forward, the barrels of the greener coming up a little. "Marshal . . . "

Cole held out a hand. "Back off, Billy. Parker can spew all the hot air he wants to. He hasn't been elected yet, and I've got enough faith in the people of Wind River to figure he won't *ever* be elected." He looked at Parker again and added, "Just remember what I said."

Parker took the cigar out of his mouth. "Oh, I'll remember, Tyler. You can count on that."

Cole jerked a thumb at the entrance of the saloon, and out of habit, he and Casebolt backed out of the place. When they reached the boardwalk and turned toward the marshal's office, Casebolt said angrily, "I'd like to put both barrels of this here scattergun through that baldheaded son of a—"

"He's right, Billy," Cole said.

"Right? How in tarnation do you figure *that*?"

"We can't prove he had anything to do with those men starting the fight. And he's entitled to run for mayor against Simone if he wants to. Just like the people here in Wind River are entitled to vote for him if that's what they want."

"Hell, nobody in this town is that addlebrained. You said so yourself."

"Yeah," Cole agreed, but he wished he could be certain of that. Unfortunately, in politics there was only one thing that could be counted on: Damned near anything—no matter how far-fetched—could happen.

There was a faint red glow in the night sky over Jeremiah Newton's blacksmith shop. Jeremiah had a fire going in his furnace, and the ringing of hammer against metal could be heard through the open doors of the squat, blocky stone building.

Inside the building, Jeremiah bent over his forge, working the bellows with his foot to produce more heat as he hammered a horseshoe into shape. A long, thick canvas apron covered him from shoulders to knees. He could have done this work anytime; there was no rush on the shoes. But he had found that working with his hands left his mind clearer to concentrate on the things that were really important. He did some of his best praying and thinking while he was working at his forge.

The art of the blacksmith had been born in ancient Mesopotamia, in the fabled city of Ur. Later on, the Hittites had discovered the secret of smelting ore to produce the near-mystical gray metal known as iron. Jeremiah was well aware of the history and lore of his profession, and he took pride in it. But his true calling was spreading the word of the Lord, and soon he would be able to do that from the pulpit of Wind River's first real church.

That is, he clarified to himself, if that heathen Hank Parker didn't ruin everything.

There was a beautiful wooded knoll just southwest of town where Jeremiah intended to build the church. The only problem was that Hank Parker wanted to buy the land, too. Parker's goals were less than holy, however. If he got his hands on the knoll, he intended to build some stockyards on its lower slopes. He had even talked of building a slaughterhouse and rendering plant on top of the knoll. Jeremiah didn't know enough about such things to be sure if Parker's plans were practical or not; all that mattered was that Jeremiah had plans of his own, plans that he was certain had been divinely inspired. The thought of blood and offal covering the ground where the church ought to be made Jeremiah strike that much harder as he hammered out the horseshoe.

He stopped what he was doing and grimaced. His anger had gotten the best of him, and he had ruined the horseshoe he was gripping with a pair of tongs. Now he would have to heat it up again and reshape it.

His nerves were stretched taut, and he knew why. He had sent off a letter to the company in the East that owned the knoll where he wanted to build the church. In that letter had been his best offer on the property. Jeremiah knew from talking to one of the clerks at the Union Pacific depot that Hank Parker had also written to the Eastern company at about the same time. No doubt Parker had made an offer on the land, too. Since then, more than two weeks had passed, and there had been no word. That wasn't an unreasonable amount of time to wait for a response, of course. Logically, Jeremiah knew that.

Logic had little to do with what he was feeling these days, however. He had to know what was going to happen, and he had to know soon. Otherwise he was afraid he would go mad.

Jeremiah put his hammer aside and worked the bellows harder, building up the fire and directing more heat into the forge. His attention was on his work, and he didn't hear the men who came into the blacksmith shop behind him. He didn't know he was no longer alone until one of the men said, "Hey! Preacher!"

Jeremiah stiffened and looked over his shoulder. He saw half a dozen men standing just inside the entrance of his shop. All six of them had bandannas pulled up over the lower half of their faces and tied behind their heads. They were all wearing holstered guns, but none of the weapons had been drawn.

Straightening slowly and turning to face them, Jeremiah said, "Good evening to you, brothers. What can I do for you?"

"What do you think, big man?" asked one of the masked men.

"Well, I doubt that you're here to have any black-smithing work done," Jeremiah said. "And there's no money here, so you can't be planning to rob me. The only other answer is that you've come to discuss the Lord, and your faces are hidden because you're ashamed of the fact that you're sinners." Jeremiah smiled. "There's no need to be embarrassed about that. The Good Book says that all have sinned and come short of the glory of God."

"Yeah, that's right, preacher," another man said as he sauntered forward, and Jeremiah recognized his voice as that of the first man who had spoken. "We're sinners. But we're not ashamed of it. In fact, we're here to tell you to forget about building a church in these parts. Nobody wants one."

"Ah, but that's where you're wrong, brother. The good, God-fearing people of Wind River want a sanctuary, a place where they can bring their problems and turn them over to the Lord."

The spokesman drew his gun, a smooth, efficient gesture. "Your problem's going to be lead poisoning if you don't give up on the idea of a church, preacher. We're here to show you just how misguided you really are. Now step away from that forge."

Jeremiah shook his head. "I don't think so."

The masked man lifted his gun. "You figure I won't shoot you? Hell, preacher, that'd solve all the problems right quick. Now move—or die."

Jeremiah could read the truth in the man's eyes. He wouldn't hesitate to pull the trigger of that gun if Jeremiah didn't follow orders. But Jeremiah had no intention of doing that. He had faith in the Lord . . . and in his own strong right arm, which was halfway behind him. His fingers closed around the handle of the heavy hammer he had set aside a few minutes earlier. With no warning, he whipped the hammer around one-handed— an impressive feat of strength in itself—and sent it spinning toward the intruders.

A couple of them let out surprised yelps, and all of the men jumped frantically out of the way of the hammer, which was heavy enough to break bone and pulp flesh. Jeremiah lunged right behind the throw, heading toward the man who had a gun out, since he was the greatest threat. The blacksmith's long, powerful fingers closed around the gunman's wrist and jerked the weapon aside. As he twisted his wrist, bones crunched together, and the masked man screamed thinly as the gun slipped from suddenly nerveless fingers.

Hearing the rapid shuffle of feet behind him, Jeremiah thrust the first man away with a hard shove, then pivoted with surprising speed and grace for a man of his size. His left arm swung around in a sweeping backhand that found the jaw of the man rushing toward him. The man was knocked backward by the blow. His booted feet tangled with each other, and he lost his balance, sitting down so hard that the breath was knocked out of him.

Two more of the men were lunging at Jeremiah. He met them with an angry roar and open arms, grabbing them and slamming them into each other so that their heads knocked together sharply. Both men went limp and folded up on the floor when Jeremiah released them.

Unfortunately, the maneuver, as effective as it was, took time . . . time that Jeremiah didn't have. Another man had gotten behind him and slashed at his head with a drawn gun. The impact staggered Jeremiah, and the gunsight tore a gash in his scalp above his left ear. He caught his balance, twisted, and snapped a punch at the man who had just hit him. The blacksmith's massive fist caught the man on the nose. Blood spurted over Jeremiah's knuckles, and the man went backward as if he had been lassoed and jerked off his feet.

The sixth man snatched up a short, thick length of wood from the pile Jeremiah used to feed his furnace and rammed it into the blacksmith's back, just above the kidneys. Pain shot through Jeremiah, pain so intense that it blinded him for a second. The man hit him again with the piece of wood, this time on the head. Jeremiah went to one knee and put a hand on the floor to keep himself from falling.

One of the other men had recovered somewhat by now, and he leaped onto Jeremiah's back and began hammering blows at him. Jeremiah went down, sprawling on the floor with his furious assailant on top of him.

The first man, the one whose wrist Jeremiah had twisted to make him drop his gun, stepped up, holding his injured limb with his other hand. His feet were free, though, and he used one of them to kick Jeremiah in the head. The rest of the men were recovering now, and they followed suit. Even with Jeremiah's overwhelming size and strength, six-against-one odds were too tough to buck. His attackers crowded around him, stomping and kicking.

After a while, the blows crashing into him didn't hurt anymore. Jeremiah was beyond pain. All he could do was lie there numbly and wait for the ordeal to end. He felt consciousness slipping away from him and wondered idly if the men would kill him. The matter no longer seemed that pressing, one way or the other. He had no fear of death.

His lips moved, but no sound could be heard over the thudding of the kicks. The words were clear enough in Jeremiah's head, however.

The Lord is my shepherd . . .

Cole Tyler wasn't prepared for the bloody apparition that came shambling into the marshal's office later that evening. He had been doing a little paperwork—the bane of all lawmen, he had discovered since pinning on a badge—when the door opened and Jeremiah came a step or two into the room. The big blacksmith was swaying, his features bruised and covered with blood, and he looked like a man about to fall onto his face. Cole muttered, "What the hell—!" as he came up out of his chair and hurried around the desk to grasp Jeremiah's arm and steady him.

That arm was as thick and hard as the trunk of a young tree, but at the moment there was little strength in it. Jeremiah let Cole lead him over to a chair in front of the desk. The piece of furniture groaned in protest as Jeremiah's great weight came down on it.

"What in God's name—no offense, Jeremiah—happened to you?" demanded Cole as he came around in front of the blacksmith and leaned over to study his wounds.

"Some men . . . came to my shop," Jeremiah said, struggling to get the words out through thickly swollen lips. "Wore masks . . . "

"Outlaws?"

Ponderously Jeremiah shook his head. "Didn't try . . . to rob me . . . just . . . beat me up . . . "

That was quite an accomplishment in itself, Cole thought. Jeremiah could hold his own in just about any fight. "How many of them were there?"

"Six. They had guns but . . . didn't shoot."

"You're probably lucky," Cole said. "Did you see any of their faces?"

Again Jeremiah shook his head. "Had bandannas tied around them . . . tight. Didn't recognize their clothes . . . or their voices."

"Well, you just stay put right there," Cole told him. "I'll go fetch Dr. Kent. I'd send Billy, but he's gone down to the cafe."

Jeremiah reached up and caught hold of Cole's sleeve as the marshal started to turn away. Even injured like this, strength was returning to the big man's grip.

"They . . . wrecked my forge . . . ," he forced out. "Broke my tools . . . tore up the bellows . . . "

"Why in blazes would anybody do that?" Cole asked.

"Said they wanted to . . . teach me a lesson. Wanted to convince me . . . not to build . . . church . . . "

An anger even greater than what he had felt when he first saw Jeremiah flared inside Cole. He knew all about the letter Jeremiah had sent to that company back East, and he knew that the blacksmith had a rival for the land where he wanted to build the church.

"You know what that likely means," Cole said. "You know who was probably behind this attack on you."

"Yes," Jeremiah said. "Hank Parker . . . "

Once again, however, there was a little matter of proof. Jeremiah hadn't gotten a good look at any of the men who attacked him and would be hard pressed to identify them. They hadn't claimed that Parker had sent them. The conclusion was obvious, but Cole knew what would happen if he went down to the Pronghorn and confronted the saloonkeeper. Parker would just insist that he knew nothing about the attack on Jeremiah, and there would be no way to prove he was lying.

Just because Cole knew all of that didn't mean he had to like it, though.

He was still seething a half-hour later when Judson Kent finished stitching up the gash in Jeremiah's scalp. "That should take care of it," Kent said. "Your other injuries, though painful, are largely superficial. I want you to rest as much as possible for a few days, Jeremiah. You'll probably have a frightful headache in the morning, and there's always the possibility of a brain injury when there have been sharp blows to the head."

"My skull's plenty thick, Brother Kent," Jeremiah said. "I don't think I have anything to worry about . . . except my shop."

Billy Casebolt, who had come back from the cafe munching on an evening snack of one of old Monty Riordan's biscuits, put a hand on Jeremiah's shoulder. "No need to fret about that. The way folks around here feel about you, I reckon everybody'll pitch in and get your place back in order 'fore you know it."

"That's right," Cole said. "Do you want to press charges, Jeremiah?"

"Against who? I can't prove Parker had this done to me."

Cole shrugged. "Maybe not, but somebody ought to at least have a talk with him."

"It wouldn't do any good," Jeremiah said. "I'll take care of the talking, Cole . . . but I thank you anyway."

"You're going to talk to Parker? I don't know if that's a good idea."

"Not Parker," Jeremiah said with a shake of his head. "That wouldn't help."

"Then who are you goin' to talk to?" asked Casebolt.

Jeremiah looked up at the three men standing around him and said, "Why . . . God, of course."

In the big house on Sweetwater Street, at the western edge of Wind River, Simone McKay paced restlessly. From time to time she paused to run her fingers through her thick dark hair in a nervous gesture. She wore a silk dressing gown that had been purchased in one of the finest shops in Philadelphia a few years earlier; she had always liked the smooth feel of the fabric against her skin. But tonight she took little comfort from it, or anything else.

She wasn't sure what had caused this mood to come

over her. All she knew was that ever since she had dined alone, earlier in the evening, she had been unable to settle down. The cook had gone on to bed, leaving Simone alone in the parlor, not an unusual set of circumstances. Simone had tried to read but had not been able to concentrate on the book that was open on her lap. She had turned pages, then realized to her annoyance that she had no idea what was written on them. Putting the book aside, she had tried to calm herself with some needlework, but that hadn't helped, either. She found herself on her feet, walking from the parlor to the dining room to the kitchen and back again. She lit a candle and moved through every room on the first floor of the house. It was as if she was searching for something—or some*one*, she realized.

That was ludicrous. She knew she was alone in the house except for the servant woman, who by now was doubtless sound asleep in her room on the third floor. Simone's bedroom was on the second floor, and she told herself she ought to go up there and lie down. Perhaps that would make her feel better.

But she knew it wouldn't. She knew that no matter what she did or how long she stayed up there, sleep would not come to her. She couldn't have said how she knew that, but the knowledge was certain in her mind.

"This is ridiculous," she said aloud as she paced through the parlor for perhaps the sixth time this evening. "I'm acting like some sort of flighty schoolgirl."

"You're as beautiful as a schoolgirl," a voice said behind her.

Simone froze, utterly unable to move. Her heart pounded heavily in her chest, and her throat was suddenly dry and tight. She knew that voice. She *knew* it.

Even though she hadn't heard it in over a year—and had never expected to hear it again . . .

"Of course, you were always beautiful," the voice went on. "You'll never change, will you, Simone? Simone? Don't you hear me? Turn around, darling."

There was an unmistakable tone of command in the words. Simone forced herself to swallow painfully, then her stiff, unwilling muscles began to slowly turn her. At first she saw only the familiar, luxurious furnishings of the parlor, and for a dizzying moment she thought he wasn't there at all, thought that she had imagined the entire episode.

Then she saw him standing in front of the fireplace, as tall and handsome as ever, his suit impeccable, his cravat just right. The light from the lamps in the room even glittered on his stickpin and cuff links. He smiled at her.

Her husband. Andrew McKay.

Who had been dead and buried for over a year.

"What's the matter, Simone? Aren't you glad to see me?"

Somehow, her stunned brain formed words, and she dragged them out of her mouth. "Andrew . . . you . . . you're dead."

"Yes. I am."

"But . . . but that's impossible! That would mean you're a . . . a . . . "

"Ghost?" The corners of his mouth quirked ironically as he smiled. "I suppose you could call it that. I don't really know. Such distinctions just aren't that important where I am now."

"Are . . . are you in heaven?" It was a ludicrous question, Simone knew, but she was curious.

"Heaven? No, I don't think so."

"Then . . . ?"

Andrew shook his head. As he did so Simone noticed that she could see right through it to the stones of the mantel over the massive fireplace behind him. "No, I'm not in hell, either," he said and chuckled. "Though I must admit, I was a bit surprised when I got here and found that the place wasn't ablaze. You know as well as I do, my dear, that my life was rather . . . unsavory at times."

"I don't want to think about that," Simone said stubbornly. Her voice shook a little, and she didn't like the sound of it.

"Of course you don't. I don't blame you. No one likes to think about their past misdeeds and the fact that they may someday catch up to us. But that's not why I'm here."

"Wh-why *are* you here?"

"To ask a favor of you. I think that's reasonable enough, don't you, after everything we shared together in life?"

Simone made herself swallow again. "A . . . a favor?"

"That's right." Andrew gestured around himself, and as Simone's eyes followed his hand, she saw the wall through it. As long as he stood still he seemed to be substantial, but whenever he moved, he took on a hazy, semi-transparent quality. "Despite the fact that my surroundings are not unpleasant, I feel a . . . a pull, I suppose you could say. I need to move on, Simone. The place where I am now was meant to be only a temporary stop." He smiled. "A depot, you could say, like the Union Pacific depot in Wind River. How is our little town, by the way?"

"It . . . it's fine," Simone said, feeling ridiculous again to be answering such a question from a ghost. "Can't you see what's happening here from . . . from wherever you are?"

"I'm afraid not," Andrew replied regretfully. "At least not under normal conditions. We can contact someone who is still on the other side, of course, as I'm contacting you now, but believe me, that's not as easy as it sounds. In fact, it's a bit of an ordeal. But I have to do it if I'm ever going to move on and be at peace."

Simone's mouth tightened into a thin line. She had

figured this out now. She had gone insane, of course. She had lost her mind, so the best thing to do was just to play along with this fantasy so that it would be finished as soon as possible. Her voice was stronger and calmer as she asked, "What is it you want me to do?"

"It's quite simple, really," Andrew told her. "I want you to find out who killed me. My spirit can't rest until my real killer is brought to justice."

Simone stared at him. That request was one of the last things she had expected, but she knew she shouldn't be surprised. Nothing else about this ghostly encounter had made sense so far.

After a moment she found the words to speak again. "Your killer has been brought to justice, Andrew. I shot William Durand myself."

"William!" exclaimed Andrew. "William didn't kill me. He may have planned to double-cross me eventually, I wouldn't doubt that for an instant. After all, I planned to do the same to him, remember? But I'm absolutely certain he didn't kill me. I saw him on his way through here, and he told me he didn't do it."

"You saw him?"

"Yes, and it's impossible to lie on this side. That's one of the odd things about it. Damned frustrating at times. But as I said, William told me he didn't shoot me, and he was rather put out with *you* because you shot him. That was all we had time to talk about, because he was here for only a short time." Andrew sighed. "I'm afraid poor William was definitely on his way to someplace warm."

Simone's head was swimming. She felt as if she might pass out at any moment. The strain of trying to stand there calmly and talk to the ghost of her dead husband was almost too much. Knowing that she had to bring this to an end as quickly as she could, she said, "All right. I'll do what you ask. Tell me, what do you remember about that day?"

"It's all quite vivid. I remember the band playing, and I remember the speech I was making after the train rolled in, and then that fight broke out. . . ." He shook his head, turning transparent again for a second. "It was a brawl, really. I was worried about you, afraid that you might get hurt in all the commotion. I recall turning around and seeing that the crowd had already gotten between us. I started pushing my way through, trying to reach you . . . and that's all I remember until I woke up here. I assume someone shot me during the confusion of the melee?"

"That . . . that's right. Oh, Andrew, I . . . I'm so sorry!" A sob racked her. She lifted her hands and buried her face in them.

"There, there, dear, it's all right. It's not your fault." He grimaced. "I wish I could put my arm around you, I really do. Here, perhaps if I try . . . "

She stiffened again as she felt *something* brush against her shoulders. For an instant it felt just like his arm, the way it had felt when he drew her into his embrace. A huge shudder went through her, and then she gasped for breath as the featherlight touch vanished.

"I'm afraid that's the best I can do," Andrew said softly. "And I really must be going. I wish I could stay with you longer, Simone. I hope that somehow, someday, we'll be together again. Goodbye, Simone. Goodbye . . . "

She kept her eyes screwed tightly shut as the voice faded away.

Simone could not have said how much time went by before she opened her eyes again. But when she did, the parlor looked perfectly normal. There were no spectral visitors standing in front of the fireplace. Everything looked as if Andrew had never been there.

Of course he hadn't been there, Simone told herself. He was dead, and there was no such thing as a ghost. The stress of running for mayor and trying to lead the community into the future had simply been too much for her for a moment or two. That was all it had been.

She couldn't tell anyone about this. If word got out that she was seeing things, her chances of being elected—even running against a boor such as Hank Parker—would be damaged. She wouldn't say anything about this to anyone, not even Cole Tyler or Judson Kent. Simone smiled. She hated to think how Cole and Judson would react if she told them she had been talking to her husband's ghost. They were two of the most levelheaded men she knew. Surely they would think she had lost her mind.

She went to a small cabinet, opened it, and took out a bottle of brandy and a glass. After what had happened this evening—or what she *imagined* had happened—she deserved a drink.

The liquor was a jolt of smooth fire as she sipped it. She felt its warmth spreading through her, and with it came a calm resolve. She would put this episode behind her and never allow herself to even think of it again.

Then, abruptly, her fingers tightened on the glass until she thought it would shatter in her hand as once again she seemed to feel the touch of a phantom hand on her shoulder. She whirled around—

There was nothing there.

The empty glass fell from Simone's hand and thumped to the thick rug under her feet. Her heartbeat was racing again. Eyes wide, she whispered, "Andrew . . . ?"

The only reply was silence.

Billy Casebolt was right about how the people of Wind River would react to the attack on Jeremiah. By the next morning, word had gotten around town about the outrage, and more than a dozen able-bodied men showed up bright and early at the blacksmith shop offering their services to Jeremiah, willing to do whatever was necessary to set the place to rights.

Visibly moved by their generosity, Jeremiah put the men to work, and by late that afternoon, the major damage to his forge had been repaired. His hammers needed new handles, since the old ones were all broken, and Simone McKay donated the items from the general store she owned. She also provided the canvas Jeremiah needed to repair the bellows. Amateur carpenters replaced the shelves inside the shop, which had been torn down by the vandals. When Cole stopped by the place a little before dusk, Jeremiah was thanking the men who had shown up to help.

"I hope all of you will be as eager to lend your strong

right arms to the cause of the Lord when it comes time to raise the roof of the new church, brothers," he told them.

"You're still going to build a church, Jeremiah?" asked one of the men. "I heard that was why those gents jumped you last night. They were trying to discourage you, weren't they?"

"They don't know me very well, do they?" Jeremiah said, drawing grins from the other men. "The Lord's told me to build Him a house of worship here in Wind River, and that's what I intend to do. And I don't care who wants to stop me."

"That's a mighty fine sentiment, Jeremiah," Cole said from the doorway of the shop, where he stood with one shoulder leaning against the jamb. "But you'd better keep your eyes open, or the warning might be worse next time. There might not even *be* a warning, just a bullet in the back."

"The Lord watches over His servants."

"I don't doubt it for a minute," Cole said, "but be careful anyway."

One of the men said angrily, "I think we ought to go down to the Pronghorn with some tar and feathers and teach Hank Parker a lesson. We all know he's to blame for what happened to Jeremiah."

Cole straightened, but before he could say anything, Jeremiah responded, "I'd ask you not to do anything like that, brother. More violence isn't going to help matters. If there was any proof that Hank Parker was behind the attack on me, the law would deal with him."

"That's right," Cole said. "We haven't had any vigilante justice around here since I've been marshal, and I intend to keep it that way. Don't worry, I'll be keeping my eye on Parker. If he moves against Jeremiah in the open, he'll regret it."

"The marshal's right," another of the men said. "Besides, once Mrs. McKay's elected mayor, she's going to run Parker and his kind out of town, so it'll be safer here for honest, God-fearing citizens like us."

That brought nods of agreement, and a couple of the men said, "Amen!" Cole didn't say anything. He still wasn't sure Simone was on the right track with her idea of banishing Parker and his ilk from Wind River, but he didn't want to get into a political argument right now. He waited until the men had all left, then said to Jeremiah, "If you have any more trouble, let me know right away. How's your head?"

Jeremiah grinned. "As I told Brother Kent, the Lord blessed me with a thick skull. It hurt some when I got up this morning, just like the doctor said it would, but I'm feeling much better now. Hard work and the companionship of good men can do wonders."

Cole just nodded, lifted a hand in a casual wave of farewell, and moved on. He was unsure what to hope for. He didn't want to wish for any more trouble to befall Jeremiah, but on the other hand it would be nice to catch Hank Parker in the act sometime, instead of just having to suspect him of mischief.

If Parker was behind the trouble—and Cole had no doubt that he was—sooner or later he would overplay his hand.

And when he did, Cole intended to be waiting.

Waiting was exactly what he was doing the next morning about eleven o'clock. Hank Parker had nothing to do with Cole's current chore, however. There was a westbound train due this morning, and as usual, one of the town's lawmen was on hand at the station to greet it and see who got off. Today it happened to be Cole lounging against one of the posts that held up the roof over the depot's platform.

He had left Billy Casebolt in the office a little while earlier. The deputy had been trying to clean out the coffeepot, a task that Cole was more than glad to leave to him.

The whistle on the big Baldwin locomotive blew when the train was still half a mile out of town. Cole listened to the shrill sound becoming louder, and he could also hear the rumble of the engine and the hum of the rails as the train approached. He leaned out a little to peer along the tracks and in the distance saw the thick black smoke rising from the diamond-shaped stack. There were a few passengers on the platform waiting to board, mostly traveling men with their worn suits and heavy sample cases. Cole looked at the drummers and shook his head. A life such as they led would drive him crazy in a week. Not to mention what those tight, stiff collars would do to a neck accustomed to a soft, open-throated buckskin shirt. Cole smiled faintly, glad that he had always been able to lead the sort of life that made him happy most of the time.

Of course, nobody was satisfied *all* the time, he reflected. He had waited for long months, hoping Simone McKay would show some sign of returning the interest he felt in her. So far it hadn't really happened. She was friendly enough toward him, and there had been a time or two when he had thought she might be ready to carry things beyond that, but somehow the opportunities had never materialized. It was like every time she caught herself moving too far out of her shell, she retreated a little again. It was damned frustrating, Cole thought.

And here lately he had found himself thinking more and more about Rose Foster, the pretty strawberry blonde who ran the Wind River Cafe. Rose had had some trouble in her past, the sort of trouble that had made her leery of getting too close to anybody wearing a tin star, but that was behind her now. She was making a fresh start.

Maybe Rose's fresh start ought to include him, too, Cole mused as the Union Pacific locomotive rolled into the station and past the platform. He'd have to give that some more thought, he told himself, but right now it would have to wait. He concentrated instead on the people who got off the train.

The first few passengers to climb down from the train on steps put in place by the conductor were most likely salesmen, like the men waiting to get on. Several families followed. Cole was on the lookout for tinhorn gamblers, gunslicks, and other troublemakers of that ilk, and he was pleased to see that nobody like that was disembarking at Wind River. All the passengers seemed to be completely normal and innocuous, in fact.

Then the young woman in the red dress appeared on the rear platform of one of the passenger cars and started down the steps, and Cole straightened out of his nonchalant stance. This woman was worth a closer look.

She was young—seventeen, eighteen, no more than that—but obviously already mature. Although she was slender, the red dress fit snugly enough to show that her curves were those of a woman. Her traveling outfit was expensive, and its stylish cut softened somewhat the impact of its bright color. A small hat of the same shade sat on her hair, which was thick and dark as a raven's wing and piled on her head in an intricate arrangement of curls. Her features had a faintly exotic cast to them, and she was made even more striking by the small dark beauty mark just to the right of her mouth. Her eyes were dark, her gaze keen and intelligent as she glanced around the platform and then started toward the double doors that led into the lobby of the station.

She was followed by another woman who might have seemed more attractive if her companion had not been so lovely. This woman was much older, in her early fifties perhaps, but still quite handsome. She had obviously lived a life of comparative ease, probably back East, because a frontier woman of similar years had usually had most of her vitality drained by hardship by the time she reached this woman's age. Her traveling gown was as expensive as her companion's but much more sedate, befitting a woman of her age and standing. Soft brown hair touched lightly with gray peeked out from under her hat. She went into the station behind the young woman in the red dress.

The two women seemed to be traveling alone, and Cole wondered who they were and why they had come to Wind River. He started toward the station lobby, intending to see what they were doing inside, but before he reached the open double doors, the woman in the red dress appeared again, and this time her dark eyes fastened on him immediately.

"Are you Marshal Tyler?" she demanded.

Her sudden appearance and her attitude took Cole a little by surprise. He nodded and said, "Yes, ma'am, I am. What can I do for you?"

"I asked the clerk inside where I could find the local authorities," the young woman said, not really answering Cole's question, "and he said he thought you were out here on the platform."

"Yes, ma'am. Do you need some help from the law?"

The older woman came out of the lobby in time to hear Cole's question. She smiled and said, "What my granddaughter and I really need, Marshal, are some directions. We're looking for someone."

"I'll be glad to help if I can, ma'am," Cole said. "You are . . . ?"

"I'm Mrs. Margaret Palmer," the older woman said. "And this is my granddaughter Brenda."

"Brenda Durand," snapped the woman in the red dress.

Cole's eyes widened in surprise. He couldn't help the reaction. Durand was still a well-known name in these parts. William Durand, in partnership with Andrew McKay, had founded Wind River. Then he had entered into an alliance with a notorious outlaw called Deke Strawhorn, an alliance which had ultimately led to the kidnapping of Simone and Delia Hatfield, Michael's wife. The resulting shootout had cost both Strawhorn and Durand their lives. Durand had been gunned down by Simone McKay, in fact, avenging her husband's murder.

Those memories flashed through Cole's mind as he looked at the young woman, and he hoped he was wrong in his guess as he asked, "Any relation to a fella named William Durand?"

"There certainly is," the young woman said. "William Durand was my father."

Simone was at her desk in the office of the Wind River Land Development Company, record books spread open before her. Her features were drawn more tightly than usual as she tried to force her mind to focus on the numbers written in the journals. Weariness wrapped around her like a shawl thrown across her shoulders, and her eyes felt gritty, as if the sockets were lined with sand. Even though she'd had no more ghostly visitations from her late husband, she had not slept well the previous two nights. The lack of rest was catching up to her.

What she needed, she had decided this morning, was something else to think about, something to get her mind off what had happened in the parlor of her house a couple of nights earlier. Providing material to help Jeremiah Newton repair the damage done to his shop in the attack on him was a distraction, but only a fleeting one. So was brooding about the campaign being waged against her by Hank Parker, but that wasn't enough to make her forget, either. She had come down here to the office and started poring over the company's books as part of her continuing effort not to think about her spectral visitor. So far she hadn't found anything except plenty of evidence that the enterprise founded by her late husband and his partner was thriving.

But she had known that already, and in frustration she slapped one of the books closed. A second later, footsteps in the corridor outside her office made her look up in annoyance. She had given the clerk in the front room strict orders that she was not to be disturbed.

From the look on the man's face as he poked his head in through the half-open door, he was reluctant to disobey her command, but something was compelling him to do so. He said quickly, "I'm sorry to bother you, Mrs. McKay, but Marshal Tyler is here to see you. He said it was important."

Simone's stern expression relaxed slightly. "That's all right, Ben. Send the marshal in."

"Well, ah, he has some people with him. A pair of, ah, ladies . . . "

Simone couldn't help but be curious whom Cole might be bringing here to her office. She said, "Do you know these ladies?"

"No, ma'am," the clerk replied in a low voice. "I never saw them before. They look like they might've just gotten off the westbound train."

Simone glanced at the banjo clock on the wall. It was half past eleven in the morning, she saw, and she recalled that a westbound did indeed pass through Wind River at eleven today. She nodded and said, "All right, Ben. Send Marshal Tyler and the ladies in."

The clerk's head disappeared, and a moment later the door opened all the way. Cole came into the office first, stepping aside so that he'd be out of the way of the young woman who followed him. An older woman entered last.

"Good morning, Simone," Cole said as he nodded to her. "There's somebody here I'd like for you to meet."

Simone nodded politely to the two women. "Hello," she said. "I'm Mrs. McKay. What can I do for you?"

Without introducing herself, the young woman in the red dress said, "I believe you have something that belongs to me, Mrs. McKay."

"Oh?" Simone murmured. As far as she could remember, she had never seen either of these women before. "And what might that be?"

"Half of this town," the young woman said flatly.

Cole moved forward smoothly as Simone stared at her visitors in surprise. He said quickly, "You'd better hear her out, Simone. This is Miss Brenda Durand and her grandmother, Mrs. Palmer."

Simone might as well not have heard anything after the mention of Brenda Durand's last name. She looked at the young woman for a long moment, then said hoarsely, "Durand?"

"That's right. William Durand was my father."

For several long seconds, Simone said nothing. She was as stunned as she had been when she first heard her husband's voice again in the parlor of the big house on Sweetwater Street. Finally, though, she was able to speak, and she said firmly, "That's impossible. William Durand left no heirs when he—" Her voice broke.

"When you killed him," Brenda Durand said sharply. The older woman put a hand on her shoulder, as if to hold her back. Brenda shrugged it off and continued,

"You are the one who shot him, aren't you, Mrs. McKay? You killed him and then took everything he owned."

"That . . . that's not the way it was," Simone managed to say. The iron control she normally imposed on herself was rapidly slipping away.

"Listen, Miss Durand, I was there when the man you say was your father died," Cole said. "If Mrs. McKay hadn't shot him, I would have about two seconds later. He had turned outlaw, and he and his partners took Mrs. McKay and another lady hostage when the men were trying to get away from the law. I'm sorry to have to tell you these things, but that's the way it was."

Simone came to her feet. Cole's intervention had given her a moment's respite, and she had recovered some of her self-possession in that time. She said, "I mean no offense, Miss Durand, but what proof do you have that you are who you say you are? I always understood that William Durand was unmarried and had no children."

The older woman stepped forward and said, "Please, Brenda, let me talk to Mrs. McKay for a moment." To Simone, she went on, "My name is Margaret Palmer, Mrs. McKay, and I can assure you that William Durand was indeed married to my daughter Nancy. He . . . left her a few months before Brenda here was born. But we have this birth certificate. . . ."

She opened her bag and took out a piece of paper that she extended across the desk toward Simone. Simone hesitated, then took the paper and looked at it. The document was a birth certificate from Baltimore, Maryland, stating that a daughter, Brenda Elizabeth Durand, had been born to William Howell Durand and Nancy Palmer Durand on May 16, 1852. As far as Simone could tell, everything about the certificate looked authentic.

"I had a look at that paper, too," Cole said, "before I

brought the ladies over here. It looked like the genuine article to me."

"It is," Margaret Palmer said. "I can swear to that, Mrs. McKay. I was with my daughter when Brenda was born." Her voice shook a little. "Just as I was with her a week later when she died of complications from the birth."

"I'm sorry," Simone murmured. She handed the document back to Mrs. Palmer. "But I'm afraid I still don't understand—"

"What I'm doing here?" Brenda cut in. "It's simple: I've come to claim my birthright. What was my father's is now mine."

Simone felt a tiny flame of anger kindle to life inside her. "That's ridiculous! Surely you don't expect me to hand over half of Wind River to you. Your father—if that's who he really was—forfeited all his rights to any of this town when he murdered my husband!"

Brenda took a step forward, and for a second Simone thought the young woman was going to lunge across the desk at her. Then, with a visible effort, Brenda controlled herself and said, "Show her the letter from Judge Evans, Grandmother."

"Judge Abercrombie Evans?" Cole asked, sounding surprised.

Mrs. Palmer nodded as she took another piece of paper out of her bag. "That's right. Do you know him, Marshal?"

"I don't reckon we've ever met, but anybody who's been in this part of the country for very long has heard of Judge Evans. There's not a better-known lawyer this side of San Francisco."

"Nor as esteemed a legal mind," Mrs. Palmer said as she handed the second document to Simone.

"The man's just a lawyer, not a judge anymore," Simone said crossly.

"Nevertheless, you can see from that letter that it is his considered legal opinion—an opinion he is prepared to argue in court on our behalf if necessary—that whatever William Durand's misdeeds and crimes may have been, they in no way affect his ownership of legally acquired assets."

"He took over my husband's half of the company after he killed him," Simone shot back.

"And as I understand it, those assets fell back under your control when William Durand died," Mrs. Palmer said calmly. "Yet, *you* killed *him*."

"It was never proven in court that my father had anything to do with your husband's death," Brenda said. "Maybe it ought to all be mine."

Simone bristled again. Cole moved in front of the desk, his hands up, the palms held out. "Why don't we all just settle down until we can sift through this?" he said. "Simone, let me see what Judge Evans has to say."

"All right, but you're no lawyer," Simone said as she handed over the letter from the renowned attorney who practiced in the territorial capital of Cheyenne.

Cole pored over the letter for a few minutes while Simone and Brenda glared at each other and Mrs. Palmer stood calmly to one side. When he finally looked up from the paper, he said slowly, "Well, it looks to me like Miss Durand here has a case. Once William Durand and Andrew McKay were both dead, it made sense that all of their holdings would go to Mrs. McKay, because we didn't know anything about Durand having an heir. But according to Judge Evans, the law is pretty plain in a situation like this: Durand's half of the partnership should have gone to Miss Durand here."

"That means I own half of this land development company," Brenda said smugly.

Simone felt like screaming. "It's impossible," she said, her voice trembling a little. "This is my company, my town." She was aware that Cole was watching her with a strange expression on her face, but she couldn't help it. On top of everything else that had happened, this was just too much for her to cope with.

"Not anymore."

Cole glanced at Simone again, then once more moved so that he was between the two women. "How did you find out about all this?" he asked Brenda.

"I saw a story in the newspaper back in Baltimore about your town, Marshal," Margaret Palmer replied instead. "It mentioned William Durand's name, and I thought I should investigate. My husband left me fairly well-off financially when he passed away, so I hired a detective to come out here and find out everything that had happened. Once I had read his report, I told Brenda about it. She's lived with me ever since she was a baby, you know. She never knew her mother—or her father."

"And now I never will," Brenda said. "He's dead."

"He deserved to die," Simone said through clenched teeth.

Before they could snipe at each other any more, Margaret Palmer went on, "Brenda and I decided that we should investigate further. Through our attorney in Baltimore, we contacted you, Mrs. McKay."

Simone frowned. "I never heard of either of you until today."

"No, but you've heard of the B & D Investment Corporation, haven't you?" Brenda asked. "We bought some land from you."

"My God!" Simone exclaimed, her eyes widening. "You're the B & D Investment Corporation?"

"That's right. We wanted to find out just what you were

doing out here with my father's company, and doing business with you seemed to be the easiest way. You got a good price for that piece of land you sold us, Mrs. McKay. I imagine you've made a lot of money since you took everything over."

Simone sat down. This . . . this obnoxious little girl owned the property that Jeremiah Newton and Hank Parker were feuding over! It was hard to believe, but she was coming to accept it. Regardless of the legality of the other claims Brenda Durand was making, that knoll southwest of town had been purchased legally, and the sale would stand up in any court in the country. As for the rest of it—

"Surely you don't think you can just waltz in here and I'll hand over half of everything to you?"

"You don't have any choice," Brenda said.

"But you're just a child!"

Mrs. Palmer said, "Since Brenda *is* still underage, I will help her manage her estate, of course. I'm her legal guardian."

"Why didn't you ever try to find out where her father was before you saw that newspaper story?" asked Cole.

"Well . . . to be honest with you, Marshal, neither of us wanted to know. I . . . I never thought William Durand was a very good husband to my daughter, and that was confirmed when he abandoned her while she was with child. He was always looking for some easy way to make money, and he didn't care if it was honest or not. After Nancy died, I decided that Brenda and I were well rid of him."

"But all that's changed now," Brenda said.

Simone made a small noise of contempt. "Of course it is, now that you think you can cash in on his death."

Once again Brenda looked as if she wanted to physically attack Simone. She put a thin smile on her face, however, and said, "You can say whatever you want, Mrs. McKay. None of it changes the facts of the matter. Half of this town—or at least half of the part you still own—is mine. And half of the proceeds from anything you've sold off since my father's death are rightfully mine, too."

Simone's head was spinning. "I can't think about this anymore," she said. "Get out of my office."

"Half of this office is mine," snapped Brenda.

Simone took a deep breath. "I'm going to wire Judge Evans and get an opinion from him myself. Until then, just steer clear of me."

Brenda looked as though she wanted to say something else, but her grandmother stopped her with an outstretched hand. "We'll give you some time to become accustomed to the situation, Mrs. McKay. In the meantime, we'll be at the hotel. The Territorial House, I believe it's called?"

"Read your detective's report," Simone said bitterly. "It probably tells all about the hotel."

"It does," Brenda said. "And we'll only be paying half the normal rate, too. Come on, Grandmother."

She stalked haughtily out of the office, followed by Mrs. Palmer, who said as she left, "Thank you for your help, Marshal. Goodbye, Mrs. McKay."

Simone didn't look up from the desk.

When the two women were gone, Cole asked worriedly, "Are you going to be all right, Simone?"

"Of course I am," she said dully. "This is all some sort of misunderstanding. Wind River is *my* town. I'm going to be the mayor. It's *my* town. . . ."

She didn't hear his sigh, didn't notice when he left the room.

Rose Foster was pouring a cup of coffee for a customer at the counter when Cole walked into the Wind River Cafe that evening. A smile appeared on her face when she looked up and saw him. Cole returned the smile and sat down on one of the empty stools. There weren't very many, since the cafe always did a good business around suppertime.

"Good evening, Marshal," Rose greeted him. She was still holding the coffeepot, using a thick pad of leather to protect her fingers from the hot handle. She reached for an empty cup on the shelf behind her, put it on the counter in front of Cole, and poured some of the strong black brew into it.

"Thanks," he told her. Rose knew his habits by now, knew that he usually had a cup of coffee about this time of the evening, even on those nights when he had already eaten supper in the dining room of the boarding house where he rented a room.

"Can I get you something to eat?"

Cole shook his head. "No, thanks. I've already filled up on Abigail Paine's chicken and dumplings. But this coffee sure does finish off a meal mighty nice."

Rose smiled again, and Cole thought how pretty it made her look. With her strawberry-blond hair and fair complexion, she was a real beauty, especially now that fear no longer haunted her green eyes. The trouble that had dogged her trail all the way from New Orleans was over, and never again would she have to worry about it catching up to her. That knowledge had made a world of difference in the way Rose Foster looked at the world.

She was looking at him differently these days, too, Cole sensed, and he couldn't help but return her interest. Billy Casebolt had been trying to play matchmaker for the two of them for quite a while, even before the problems from Rose's past had resurfaced, but Cole suspected that had more to do with the cooking skills of old Monty Riordan, the cafe's biscuit-shooter, than with any genuine urges to play Cupid. Cole didn't care about that. All that mattered was that things had changed between him and Rose, and both of them knew it. Neither of them was quite sure what to *do* about it, but Cole was confident they'd figure it out sooner or later.

Nobody along the counter or at any of the tables covered by red-and-white checked cloths was demanding attention at the moment, so Rose lingered and said, "I heard about that girl who came in on the train today, the one who claims to own half the town. Is she telling the truth?"

Cole sipped his coffee and shrugged. "As far as I can tell, she's really the daughter of William Durand. And the best lawyer in the territory has already gone on record as saying that her claims are legitimate. Simone sent off some wires earlier in the day, trying to get it all sorted out, but it looks to me like things are going to be changing around here."

Rose shook her head. "I hope it all works out. Mrs. McKay and I aren't what you'd call close—a lady like her doesn't eat in a place like this, you know—but I wouldn't wish any trouble on her. I never much liked that Mr. Durand, either, when he was my landlord."

"He never bothered you, did he?" Cole asked sharply.

"No, but I always felt like he wanted to. It's been a lot nicer dealing with Mrs. McKay."

"You shouldn't be able to tell much difference, even if Simone does have to turn over half of her holdings to Brenda Durand. Somebody's still got to run things, and I reckon that'll be Simone." Cole paused, then added, "Although you can't ever tell. I got the feeling Miss Durand wouldn't mind being the boss around here."

"Well, I feel sorry for Mrs. McKay. First she has to worry about Hank Parker running against her for mayor, and now this."

Cole nodded slowly. He was more than a mite worried about Simone, too. She hadn't looked or sounded like herself after Brenda Durand's visit to the land development company. Simone had been through a lot since coming to Wind River, and although Cole had always been impressed by her strength, anybody could be pushed too far, no matter how strong they were.

He hoped Brenda Durand's arrival in town hadn't been enough to push Simone right over the edge.

Simone stood by the sideboard in the parlor and tried to pour brandy into a glass. Her hands were shaking so badly that she had to give it up as a bad job. She thought about wrapping both hands around the bottle, lifting it to her mouth, and drinking straight from the neck. But that would have been unladylike, and she had been raised to always be a lady.

Instead she picked up the piece of paper she had laid down beside the bottle. It was a yellow Western Union telegraph, the kind familiar to anyone who sent very many messages over what the Indians called the singing wires. The clerk from the Western Union office at the depot had brought it over to the land development company late that afternoon. The telegram was from Judge Abercrombie Evans, and it confirmed what the attorney had written in the letter Margaret Palmer had shown to Simone. Brenda Durand was William Durand's legal heir and as such entitled to one half of the assets held by the company that had been formed by Durand and Andrew McKay.

Simone wondered how much Mrs. Palmer and Brenda had paid Evans to get him on their side. It didn't really matter, of course. What was important was that Evans was friends with every sitting judge in the territory. That was why he seldom if ever lost a case; none of his poker-playing cronies wanted to rule against him.

No, fighting this through the legal system was out, Simone knew. She was beaten before she even got started. All of her work, everything she had sacrificed . . . all for nothing.

Well, not exactly nothing, she told herself. She was still *half*-owner of the land development company, the hotel, the newspaper, and most of the other businesses around here. Half of a thriving town was better than nothing.

But the fact that it wasn't *all* hers anymore was galling. She wasn't sure if she could live with that or not.

"Will there be anything else tonight, ma'am?"

The voice of her cook and housekeeper came from the door of the parlor, making Simone turn around sharply.

The white-haired Irishwoman looked startled at the expression on her mistress's face and took an involuntary step backward. With an effort, Simone softened her features a little and even twisted them into the semblance of a smile.

"No, there's nothing else. You can go on to bed."

"Thank you, ma'am," the servant said. She backed out of the parlor and disappeared up the stairs, but Simone had noticed the strange look the woman gave her before she left.

She's just like everyone else, Simone thought. *She thinks I'm going crazy, too.*

Simone looked down at her hand when she became aware that she was still holding the telegram. She had crushed the paper a little between her fingers, and now she finished the job of crumpling it. As she turned around and tossed the ball of yellow paper into the cold ashes of the fireplace, she wished there were a fire burning so that she could have seen the hateful telegram consumed. On a warm summer evening like this, of course, there was no need for a blaze.

She heard a footstep behind her and thought the servant had returned. "I told you I didn't need anything else," she snapped at the woman.

"But I need something, Simone."

Her hands flew to her mouth and pressed tight against her lips. She let out a quiet moan.

"What's wrong, Simone?" Andrew asked. "Why don't you turn around and look at me? I won't hurt you. I'd never hurt you."

Her movements were jerky as she made herself turn to face him. He looked just as he had the other time, tall and handsome and *real*. She found herself staring at the front of his shirt and vest, searching for the bloodstains that had been on those clothes that day on the platform at the railroad station.

The day Andrew McKay had died.

His shirtfront was white and unmarred, though, and the brown tweed vest was as neat and clean as it had ever been. Wherever Andrew was, Simone supposed that the evidence of their passing had been erased from those who were there. In most cases, that was probably merciful.

"Have you found out who killed me yet?" asked Andrew.

"I . . . I've been busy," Simone replied, knowing even as the words came out of her mouth how feeble they sounded.

Andrew looked disappointed. "I hoped I could leave here soon and travel on to where I'm supposed to be. I know it may be worse, but I still have to do it."

"I understand, and I want to help you, but things have come up. . . ." Simone's voice trailed off. She couldn't allow herself to think about what was really going on here. She couldn't admit that she was having a serious conversation with a ghost. She knew that if she did, her fragile grip on what was left of her sanity might slip away. She found herself explaining, "There's this young woman . . . who wants to take the town away from me. . . ."

Andrew frowned and stepped toward her, moving so abruptly that for an instant he almost flickered out of existence entirely before seeming to solidify again. "What? Wind River is yours by rights. William and I are responsible for the settlement being there in the first place, and you're the only legal heir of the partnership—"

"Durand had a daughter," Simone said.

"What?"

"He had a child, even though he abandoned her mother and never even saw the little girl. She's his heir."

"Damn! I never thought to ask William about that when he was passing through here. The subject never came up." Andrew shook his head, making him hazy for a moment. "I'm sorry, Simone. I honestly thought that you'd be left well off if anything ever happened to me . . . and I suppose you really are. Owning even half of a town like Wind River makes you a rich woman!"

"I know that," Simone said testily. She didn't need a ghost to tell her what she had already realized. "I just can't believe that this girl showed up out of the blue like she did. It's not fair."

"It wasn't fair that someone shot me, either," Andrew reminded her. "Like I told you, Simone, I really need your help."

"And I'll do what I can," she said with a sigh, not even thinking about how ludicrous it was for her to be explaining her troubles to a ghost as she went on. "But you have to understand the strain I'm under. I'm running for mayor, you know."

"You are?" Andrew sounded a bit surprised. "That's a wonderful idea. I wouldn't really have expected it from you."

"You never expected half the things I'm capable of, Andrew," she said. "I was always more than just your ornament."

"Of course you—"

"You never realized how many of the schemes you and William thought you came up with were really my ideas," she went on. She began to pace back and forth across the rug on the parlor floor. "I was always there behind the scenes, pushing you when you needed it, nudging you in the right direction. And you never gave me credit for it, not once!"

"I'm sorry, Simone," Andrew said, an edge of desperation

coming into his voice. "I certainly never meant to hurt you or ignore what you were doing to help us. But that's all in the past, and now I have this other problem—"

Simone stopped, whirled around to face him, and screamed, "The hell with your problem! I'm losing everything I've worked for! I won't even be mayor if I don't win this election!"

Andrew seemed to be fading, even though he wasn't moving. He said, "You'll be all right, Simone. You can do whatever it takes, I know you can."

Her bosom heaving with emotion, her fists clenched at her sides, she nodded curtly and said, "Damned right I can."

"I'll even help you if I can. But you've got to help me. I . . . I can't stay across the line anymore now. I've got to go back. Help me, Simone . . . help me get where I need to be."

"I'll do what I can," she promised again. The turmoil that had gripped her a moment earlier was fading. The tension within her eased. "Don't worry, Andrew."

She could barely see him now. When he had vanished after his first visitation, she had kept her eyes closed, but this time she watched with keen interest as his figure became dimmer and dimmer. His lips were moving as he said something, but she couldn't make out the words any longer. Finally, after several long seconds ticked by, he was gone.

Simone heard footsteps on the stairs. "Miz McKay?" a voice called tentatively.

She sighed. The housekeeper had heard her screaming at Andrew and probably thought that she had lost her mind. Simone went to the door of the parlor and smiled up at the woman, who stood halfway down the staircase wrapped in a woolen robe.

"It's all right," Simone said. "I was just practicing one of my campaign speeches."

"Oh." Clearly the woman didn't believe her. "I just heard a bit of a commotion, ma'am, and wanted to make sure you didn't need me."

"I'm fine," Simone assured her. "I'm sorry I disturbed you. You can go back to bed."

"Oh, 'twas no bother, ma'am. If you're sure you'll not be needin' me . . . "

"I'm certain. Good night."

"Good night, ma'am." The woman retreated up the stairs.

Simone went back to the sideboard, and this time her hands were rock steady as she picked up the glass and the bottle of brandy. She poured a drink and tossed it back, savoring the warmth of the liquor in her belly.

She knew what she had to do now–ghost or no ghost. That didn't matter; neither did Brenda Durand's unexpected arrival. Let the girl grab half of the town. It wouldn't matter because she wouldn't have any real power.

Power was all that counted, when you got right down to it. Money was just a means of acquiring it, and there were other ways. Simone had run things around here for more than a year, and she was going to continue giving the orders. She was going to be the mayor of Wind River, damn it, and between that and the wealth she still controlled, no one would ever be able to tell her what to do. *She* was in charge. The first step was winning that election, no matter what sort of stunts Hank Parker tried to pull.

Her lips curved in a smile. She almost hoped he *did* try something else.

If he did, he would soon find out what a big mistake he had made. . . .

Hank Parker scratched a lucifer into life and held the flame to the tip of the long cigar clenched between his teeth. He puffed on the cigar until it was burning properly, then shook out the match and dropped it in the bucket of sand next to his desk. Parker took the cigar out of his mouth and leaned back in his chair. There was a big smile on his face.

The election for mayor was less than a week away. He had waited until fairly late to throw his hat into the ring, but it hadn't taken him long to make up some ground on Simone McKay. The women in the settlement were solidly behind Simone. However, there were a lot more men than women in Wind River, and nearly all of them stopped into the Pronghorn for a drink at one time or another. Parker had bought a lot of rounds since announcing that he was running for mayor. That was all right; he could afford the whiskey.

What he couldn't afford was for Simone to be elected so that she would have a chance to carry out all her promises.

Most of those campaign pledges had to do with forcing Parker and those like him out of business. Hell, she wouldn't really be satisfied until all of those she considered unsavory elements had left town completely.

Parker didn't intend to let that happen.

The door of the office in the back of the Pronghorn opened, and one of the saloon's bartenders came in. He was carrying a canvas pouch. As he placed it on the desk he said, "There you go, boss. That's tonight's take so far."

Parker grunted in approval. He balanced his cigar on the edge of a heavy glass ashtray, then pulled a fat gold watch from his vest pocket, flipped it open, and saw that the hour was after midnight. The Pronghorn never really closed down, but the bulk of the night's business was over. There were probably still a few men at the bar who would drink until they passed out, and there might still be a poker game going on, but that was the extent of the activity in the big room on the other side of the office door. Parker pulled the pouch containing the night's receipts closer to him and said, "All right, Bud. You can go home."

"G'night, Mr. Parker," the bartender said as he left the office.

Parker just grunted again. He had the pouch open, and as soon as he was alone and the office door was closed again, he upended the pouch and poured out its contents on the desk.

Most of the money was in coins, but there were a few bills and even a single nugget of gold. Parker's grin widened as he picked up a handful of coins and let them slip through his blunt, thick fingers to clink back onto the pile. He never got tired of hearing that sound, and the mere thought that someone wanted to take it away from him was enough to make his jaw tighten in anger and resolve.

A soft knock on the door make Parker look up sharply. "Who is it?" he growled.

"It's me again, boss," came the voice of Bud, the bartender who had just brought the money into the office. "There's somebody out here who wants to see you."

"Tell 'em to go away," Parker called through the door, not caring whose feelings he might hurt by such a brusque response.

There was a moment of quiet, and Parker thought he heard some whispering on the other side of the door, even though he couldn't make out any words. Then Bud said, "The lady claims it's mighty important that she sees you, Mr. Parker."

A lady, eh? Parker frowned. He liked women as much as the next man, but he'd never made a fool of himself over one, never let himself be led around by the nose like some gents. Still, he was curious who this female was who wanted to see him, so he said, "Wait a minute," and started stuffing the coins and bills back into the canvas pouch. When he had the money cleared away and the pouch locked in the middle drawer of his desk, he stood up and went over to the door. He grasped the knob and swung it open.

Bud was standing just outside the office, a nervous look on his thin face. "Sorry, boss," he said immediately, "but she insisted it was important and said she had to see you—"

Parker looked past the bartender at the young woman who stood there. He knew right away that he had seen her before, but he couldn't place her. She was eighteen or twenty, pretty in a coarse sort of way, with long, straight pale hair that hung down on both sides of her face. She wore a tight dress that clung to her smallish breasts and rounded hips. Parker frowned as he tried to recall who she was.

"You don't remember me, do you, Mr. Parker?" she asked with a smile.

"Sorry—" he began, then the name popped out of his memory. "Becky, isn't it? Becky Lewis?"

"That's right," she said with a nod. "Thanks for letting me talk to you."

He remembered her now. She was a soiled dove, one of the women who had worked in the backstreet cribs. She had never worked directly for him as one of his girls, but he had seen her a few times in the old tent saloon he'd had before building the Pronghorn. As he cast his memory back he couldn't recall what had happened to her. She just hadn't been around anymore.

Now she was back, and for the life of him, he couldn't figure out why she was paying him a visit.

But there was only one way to find out, so he inclined his head toward the office behind him and said, "Come on in." Glancing past Bud, he saw that the crowd in the saloon was as sparse as he expected at this hour. The sole bartender left behind the hardwood could handle it without any trouble. "Go on home like I told you, Bud," added Parker.

Bud nodded and hurried away as Parker stepped aside to let Becky Lewis enter the office. He closed the door firmly behind her and gestured toward the chair in front of the desk.

"Have a seat. What brings you back to Wind River, Becky?"

"How did you know I was ever gone, Mr. Parker?" she asked as she sat down. "I didn't work for you, after all."

"No, but I had my eye on you," Parker lied. She had been just one more pathetic whore as far as he was concerned, of no more interest to him than any of her sisters. He wanted to indulge his curiosity, though, so he went on,

"I was thinking about offering you a job when you up and disappeared."

"I didn't just up and disappear," she said. "I was paid to leave town."

Parker went behind the desk and started to sit down in the big leather chair. "Paid?" he repeated in surprise. "Who paid you to leave Wind River?"

"Simone McKay."

Parker froze, halfway into the chair. His eyebrows lifted. He truly was surprised now. He put his knuckles on the desk and leaned forward. "Simone McKay paid you to leave town? Why the hell would she do a thing like that?"

"Because I was carrying her husband's baby," Becky said.

Parker let out a little exhalation of breath, like he had been punched in the belly. He sat, coming down in the chair harder than he had intended. His heart had started to thud faster than usual in his chest. To calm himself down, he picked up his cigar, drew in a lungful of smoke, and slowly blew it back out. "Interesting," he said, trying not to reveal just how very interesting this revelation was to him. "But what's that got to do with me?"

"I was over in Rawlins and heard that you were running for mayor of Wind River. I thought you might want to know about what Mrs. McKay did, so I caught a ride with some freight wagons that were headed in this direction. I didn't have enough money for a train ticket."

This was starting to make sense now, Parker thought as he nodded. Like all whores, Becky Lewis was after money. She had traded a few nights of letting a bunch of freighters use her on the trail for the chance to cash in on something she knew.

And that knowledge might well be worth something, Parker admitted to himself. But he wasn't going to let

Becky see how eager he was. Keeping his face expression-less, he said, "You must have thought I could use what you told me against Mrs. McKay in the election campaign. You figured I'd pay you for telling me about it."

She pushed back one of the wings of blond hair that had fallen forward over her face. "I got a right," she said. "The McKays ruined my life."

As if that life had been much to brag about in the first place, Parker thought. He puffed on the cigar and said, "Go on." He could tell the girl wanted to talk, and he was going to let her do just that.

"He was Mr. High and Mighty Land Developer," she said, her voice taking on a tone of bitter anger. "But that didn't stop him from coming to see a poor girl who'd decided that selling her body was the only way she was going to be able to live. Then when he got me in the fam-ily way, he swore the baby wasn't his. Didn't want a thing to do with me then, no, sir!" She sniffed in righteous indignation. "I tell you, I sure didn't shed any tears when Mr. Andrew McKay got himself killed. I figured it served him right."

"What about his wife?" asked Parker. "How did she find out about all this?"

"That doctor fella told her, I reckon. I went to see him when I realized I was going to have a baby. I told him about McKay. It was about that time that man Durand turned outlaw and kidnapped her. Once she got back safely to town, though, after she'd shot Durand, she came to see me and gave me enough money to get out of Wind River and start over somewhere else with my baby. She didn't want anybody knowing what sort of man her hus-band really was." A sly smile appeared on Becky's face. "She didn't know how much I really knew. I could've taken her for a lot more money. But I figured I'd do like she said and make a fresh start. I had enough for that. Thought I'd just raise my baby and try to be respectable for a change."

So Judson Kent had known about Andrew McKay's connection with this soiled dove, too, Parker thought. And Kent was one of Simone's biggest supporters now. That knowledge could come in handy as well. It wouldn't look good if he revealed that the town's doctor had helped a whore blackmail Wind River's leading citizen.

He still didn't have all the story, though. He asked, "What happened? How come you didn't do like you'd planned and start over somewhere?"

"I would have," Becky said miserably, "but the baby . . . I lost the baby. I was only six months along when she tried to come. I was in Laramie then. The midwife said there wasn't nothing she could do, said it wasn't my fault, that it just wasn't meant to be. But I knew better. I was being punished for the sinful life I'd led. Don't you reckon that's what happened, Mr. Parker? I was trying to live a better life, but the Lord just couldn't let it go. He had to get back at me for what I'd done in the past."

Parker shrugged, feeling uncomfortable. "I don't know anything about things like that," he snapped. "You want to talk about that, you'd best go find that damned black-smith who fancies himself a sky pilot. But maybe you'd rather talk about how much what you've told me is worth."

Becky's face, which had softened momentarily with remembered grief, hardened again. "Damn right," she said. "It ought to be worth plenty. Once you tell everybody how Mrs. McKay paid a whore to leave town because the girl was carrying her husband's bastard, a lot of people won't vote for her."

Nodding slowly, Parker considered what she had said.

It was true that this information might damage Simone's reputation somewhat. But there was another side to it as well.

"Not necessarily," he said harshly. "Think about it. What did she really do? She tried to protect the good name of her dead husband. You think folks are going to condemn her for that? Hell, if I raise a stink about this, some people might vote for her just out of pity!"

Becky began shaking her head. "No. No, that's not what would happen—"

"It might," Parker cut in. He reached in his pocket and pulled out a double eagle. "Here. I reckon that's all your story's worth to me." He flipped the twenty-dollar gold piece across the desk to her.

Becky's hand shot out and closed over the coin. The movement was obviously instinctive. But her face was set in a look of anger and frustration, and she protested, "That ain't fair! It's worth a hell of a lot more than twenty dollars!"

"Not to me," Parker said coolly. He had always driven a hard bargain, and he didn't intend to change now.

Becky's eyes narrowed, and a cunning cast came over her features. "There's more," she said.

Parker's hand clenched into a fist and thumped down hard on the desk. "Don't try to sell me a pack of lies, girl! I'll boot your rump out of here so fast you won't know what happened!"

"It's the truth!" Becky insisted as she flinched back against the chair in the face of Parker's anger. "I wouldn't lie to you, Mr. Parker, I swear it!"

"No little whore makes a fool out of Hank Parker." He saw the look of genuine fear in her eyes and relished it. "If you've got something else to say, spit it out."

"I . . . I can make her get out of the election for good. She won't even run for office."

That was more like it, Parker thought, again being careful not to show the reaction. If the girl knew something that he could use to force Simone out of the race entirely, he had to have that knowledge. He leaned back and said around the cigar, "Tell me about it."

"It . . . it has to do with her husband's death."

"That's old news," Parker said. "William Durand shot him during that brawl at the railroad station."

Becky shook her head. "No, he didn't." Her voice grew stronger, took on conviction. "Durand didn't kill McKay. I was there that day. I saw who did."

Parker's teeth clamped down so hard on the cigar that he bit through it as he realized what she was about to say. Most of the cheroot fell on the desk. He ignored it, spit out the butt still in his mouth, and leaned forward eagerly, unable to stop himself. "Say it," he hissed.

"Simone McKay killed her husband," Becky Lewis said with a smile. "I saw her do it."

Parker surged to his feet, the expression on his face so fierce that Becky stopped smiling and cringed back again. "Tell me what you saw," he ordered. "Everything, damn it!"

"I . . . I told you, I was there on the platform when the first train came in. I saw the fight start, and then I . . . I tried to get out of there before I got hurt. But I was still there when Andrew McKay tried to push through the crowd to get to his wife. I was about ten feet away from her, and all of a sudden there was a little clear spot between the two of us. I saw her take a pistol out of her bag—"

"What kind of pistol?" Parker broke in. He had to be certain about this. There couldn't be any doubts.

"I don't know," Becky said with a shake of her head. "I don't know anything about guns. It was just a little pistol, you know, with a barrel about this long." She held up her hands with the fingers about three inches apart.

Parker grunted. That description could fit any number of pocket pistols, but at least it made sense. He would have known Becky was lying if she'd said Simone had hauled a full-sized revolver out of her bag. "Go on," he said.

"She had the pistol up close to her body, so it was hard to see. But I saw it, all right. And then her husband pushed a man out of the way and came up to her. He was looking back over his shoulder at something, though, and I don't reckon he ever saw what she did. She stuck the barrel of that pistol right up against his belly and then pulled the trigger."

It could have happened that way, Parker realized. In the confusion of that melee on the platform, it sure could have.

"She jammed the gun back in her bag and stepped away from him before he even had a chance to fall down," Becky went on. "Then as soon as she had a little distance between them, she started screaming and crying about how her husband had been hurt. She didn't know I'd seen what she did. I got the hell out of there."

Parker's pulse was hammering in his head. "Why would she kill her husband?" he asked.

"Well . . . think about it. McKay died, and Durand got everything. Then Durand died, and it was Mrs. McKay who wound up with the whole town. Maybe that was what she planned to have happen all along. Maybe Durand really played right into her hands when he kidnapped her. She was able to kill him and blame her husband's murder on him."

It could have happened that way, Parker thought.

"Why didn't you go to her right away and demand money to keep quiet about what you'd seen?"

"I was *scared* to," Becky said. "I had just seen her murder her own husband in cold blood." She laughed hollowly. "You think I wanted to get on her bad side?"

Parker considered for a moment, then nodded. Becky wasn't the kind of woman who possessed an abundance of either brains or courage. But she was smart enough to have found a way to cash in.

"So you blackmailed her over the fact that McKay had gotten you pregnant, but not over his murder?"

Becky shrugged. "I figured she wouldn't try to kill me over what her husband did, and I was right. She was happy just to pay me off and get me out of town."

"And you protected yourself even more by approaching her through Doc Kent." Parker smiled thinly. "That was smart, Becky, pretty smart."

She glowed at his praise. "Thanks. I thought so."

"But now things have changed." Parker began to pace back and forth behind the desk. "Things didn't work out like you wanted, so you've come back for more. Now you don't have to get Simone to pay you off, though. You figured you'd come to me."

"It's worth a lot, isn't it?" Becky asked eagerly. "You can use what I told you to make her drop out of the election. You can be mayor of Wind River, Mr. Parker, and nobody will ever bother you again." She paused, then added, "Besides, you can blackmail Mrs. McKay yourself now. All I want is my fair share."

"And for me to protect you, so that Simone doesn't know who told me all about it."

Becky inclined her head in acknowledgment of that point.

"Yeah, pretty smart." Parker stuck his hand in his pocket again, and this time when he brought it out he was holding several bills. He extended them across the desk.

Becky came to her feet and snatched the money out of his fingers. Her desperation was pretty pathetic, Parker thought. But he had to admire her cunning, and although he could have doublecrossed her, he decided to play along for a while. "That's not a payoff," he said. "Take that money and buy yourself something decent to wear and a few good meals. You're working here at the Pronghorn now, and I like my girls to look nice."

She gazed at him with wide eyes. "You mean it, Mr. Parker?"

"Sure. I got a feeling you and I are going to get along just fine, Becky." He came around the desk and held out his hand toward her again, empty this time. "Simone McKay doesn't know it yet, but this just turned into the worst day of her life."

Becky hesitated, then took his hand. His fingers closed on hers and pulled her toward him. He figured they needed to do something to seal their bargain. His mouth came down hard on hers.

Cole was surprised when Simone showed up at the marshal's office the next morning. Not so much that she was there, he thought; the two of them were friends, if nothing else, and it wasn't unusual for her to drop by. What surprised him was how good she looked, rested and radiant with seemingly a new outlook on life.

"Well, I'm glad to see you smiling again," Cole said as he stood up to greet her with a smile of his own.

"I decided there was still plenty to smile about," she said. "After all, in less than a week I'm going to be the first mayor of Wind River."

"I hope so," said Cole.

"I *know* I will be. I'm not going to allow myself to think anything else."

"Now you're talking." Cole grinned. "Have a seat, and we'll talk about what it'll be like when you're the mayor of this town."

Simone surprised him again by shaking her head. "There'll be plenty of time for that later. Right now I have something else I need to do, and I want you to go with me."

"I reckon I can do that. Where are we headed?"

"I'm going over to the Territorial House," Simone said. "I want to see Brenda Durand and her grandmother."

Cole couldn't stop himself from frowning. If Simone was in this good a mood, he wondered, what had she decided to do about the problem of Brenda Durand?

"I want to have a witness when I talk to them," Simone went on.

"Well, that's encouraging, I guess," Cole said. "At least you're not planning to shoot both of them, or you wouldn't invite the marshal along."

"Shoot them?" Simone repeated. She laughed. "Of course not. I've come to the conclusion that I can't fight them."

"You're going to give Miss Durand what she wants?" Cole was surprised again. He hadn't figured Simone would give up without a fight, even if it was one she had little chance of winning.

"I'm not going to stand in the way of anyone claiming what's legally theirs. Besides, I have more important things on my mind, like the election next week."

Cole nodded slowly, pleased to hear that Simone was going to be reasonable where Brenda Durand was concerned. That situation could have gotten real ugly real fast, he reflected, and he might have wound up in the unenviable position of having to take sides. He was glad that evidently it wasn't going to come to that.

"I'll be happy to go with you while you talk to them," he said. "We can go over to the hotel right now."

"That's fine with me."

They were just leaving the marshal's office when Billy Casebolt came whistling down the boardwalk. The deputy lifted a finger to the brim of his hat and said, "Mornin', ma'am. Mighty nice day, ain't it?"

"Indeed it is, Deputy," Simone agreed with a smile. "And it's going to be even better."

"If you say so, ma'am." Casebolt started to move past them toward the door of the office.

Cole stopped the older man with a hand on his arm. An idea had occurred to him. "Why don't you come with Mrs. McKay and me, Billy?"

"Sure," Casebolt replied with an indifferent shrug. "Where're we goin'?"

"Over to the hotel to see Miss Durand and Mrs. Palmer."

Casebolt's eyes widened. Cole had told him the whole story of Brenda Durand's visit to Simone's office the day before. Obviously he expected that more fireworks were imminent between the two women. He asked, "Are you sure that's such a good idea, Marshal? I mean, hadn't somebody ought to stay here at the office in case folks come lookin' for us?"

"We're just going over to the hotel," Cole said. "If there's a big commotion, we'll hear it. Come on, Billy. Simone needs some witnesses, and I reckon both of the town's lawmen will do just fine."

Simone nodded. "Cole's right, Deputy Casebolt. I don't want any question later about what goes on in this meeting. I think you should be there as well."

"Don't look like I've got a whole lot of choice," Casebolt said uneasily. "There ain't goin' to be no hair-pullin' or caterwaulin', is there?"

Simone laughed. "I promise I'll behave myself, Deputy. You'll be safe enough."

"It ain't me that I'm worried about," mumbled Casebolt, but he fell in behind Cole and Simone as they crossed the street and then moved down the boardwalk toward the hotel.

They found Brenda and her grandmother in the hotel dining room. Both women were dressed more simply this morning, but their clothes were still expensively elegant. They looked up in surprise from their breakfast as Simone, Cole, and Casebolt approached. .

"Good morning," Simone said before either of the other women had a chance to speak. "I was wondering if I might talk to you ladies for a moment."

"What do you want?" Brenda asked bluntly.

Margaret Palmer was more diplomatic. "Of course, Mrs. McKay," she said. "Please, join us."

"I've already eaten breakfast," Simone said, "but I wouldn't mind a cup of coffee."

"You and your deputy are welcome as well, Marshal," added Margaret.

There were two vacant chairs at the table. Cole held one of them for Simone, then took the other while Billy Casebolt snagged a chair from an empty table, reversed it, and straddled it. Cole might have said something to him about his lack of manners, but neither of the newcomers to Wind River seemed to mind. In fact, there was a smile on Margaret Palmer's face as she looked at the lanky deputy.

A waitress hurried up, and Margaret told her, "We'd like coffee for our friends."

"Yes, ma'am. Good morning, Miz McKay."

Simone smiled at the young woman. "Good morning, Erica."

"I'll be right back with that coffee."

Brenda watched the waitress's retreating back and commented, "She's certainly anxious to please. She wasn't that happy to see *us*." She shot a glance at Simone. "But then, I'm not her boss . . . yet."

"And you won't be," Simone said. Brenda frowned and started to speak, but Simone went on first. "I have something here I want to show you." She opened her bag and took out a bundle of papers.

Brenda was still anxious to say something, but her grandmother stopped her this time. "Let's allow Mrs. McKay an opportunity to show us what she wants to," Margaret said.

"All right, but nothing's going to change my mind," Brenda replied crossly. "Half of this town is still going to be mine."

"Not quite half," Simone said. She spread out the documents between the plates so that both Brenda and Margaret could see them. "This is the partnership agreement between my late husband and your late father, Miss Durand."

"So you're not disputing the fact that William Durand was my father?"

"I'm not disputing anything," Simone told her. "I'm prepared to honor your claim."

"Well! That's a surprise. I guess you must have realized you couldn't win."

Margaret said softly, "It's not ladylike to gloat, dear."

"However, I want everything delineated very clearly," Simone went on. "The newspaper, this hotel, and several other pieces of property were owned outright by my husband, as you'll see here in the agreement." She used a slender finger to point out the pertinent clauses. "Therefore, you're not entitled to any share in those assets."

Brenda sniffed. "All right. I don't like it, but I suppose you're right about that part of it. Everything else, though—"

"Everything that was originally held jointly by Andrew

McKay and William Durand will now be held jointly by the two of us as their heirs," Simone declared. "That's as fair as I can possibly be about it."

"Fairness is all we want, Mrs. McKay," Margaret said.

"Of course, I will continue to be in charge of the day-to-day operations of the Wind River Land Development Company, as well as managing the other joint holdings."

"Now wait just a minute—" Brenda began. Once again her grandmother silenced her with a gracefully lifted hand.

"You're much more familiar with the details of the estate than either of us," Margaret said to Simone. "Such an arrangement as you propose seems agreeable . . . at least for the time being."

Simone nodded. "I hoped that you'd be reasonable about this, Mrs. Palmer. Now, every six months I'll go through the books and calculate Brenda's share of the profits, which I will then send to you in Baltimore. I assume a bank draft will be satisfactory?"

"No, indeed," said Margaret.

Cole saw a glitter of anger in Simone's eyes. He grimaced. This had all been going so well, better than he had expected. Now the deal looked like it might fall apart over some trivial point. . . .

"How do you want the money?" Simone asked bluntly.

"We intend to open an account in Brenda's name at the bank right here in Wind River."

"Here? What good will it do you to have the money in the bank here when the two of you are in Baltimore?"

"We're not going to *be* in Baltimore," Margaret said.

"That's right," Brenda put in. "We're going to stay here in Wind River."

Billy Casebolt let out a low whistle of surprise. Cole felt like doing pretty much the same thing himself, but he reined in the impulse. As for Simone, she stared across the table at Brenda and Margaret in disbelief. For a long moment, no one said anything.

Except for the young waitress, who came up to the table with a tray on which rested a coffeepot and three cups. She said brightly, "Here you go, folks." Oblivious to the tension pervading the atmosphere, she poured coffee for Simone, Cole, and Casebolt, then freshened what was in the two cups already on the table.

Simone waited until the woman was gone, then said slowly, "Why in heaven's name do you want to stay in Wind River?"

"There's nothing *wrong* with the town, is there?" Brenda asked. "The way you seem to think it's *your* town, you ought to want people to settle here."

"Brenda wants to be here so that she can see what's being done with her inheritance, Mrs. McKay," Margaret said. "I think that's a perfectly logical desire. There's no real reason we have to go back to Baltimore. We can make a life for ourselves here just as easily." She lifted her cup to her lips, sipped from it, and smiled. "Besides, we've already made arrangements to have all of our things shipped out here. I'm certain we can find a suitable house."

Simone regarded the older woman intently for a moment, then said, "You're awfully sure of yourself, aren't you?"

"My granddaughter and I knew that we were in the right, that's all. And you've already agreed with that conclusion, Mrs. McKay."

Simone sighed. "So I have."

Margaret continued. "Besides, I find your frontier citizens to be so . . . colorful. So interesting." Once again she looked at Billy Casebolt and smiled.

Cole had to look down at the floor to keep from showing off the grin that had suddenly appeared on his face. The reasons that Margaret and Brenda had given for wanting to remain in Wind River made sense, all right. Margaret had indicated that she was fairly well-off, but Cole doubted if she was rich. Brenda, on the other hand, was— at least now that Simone had agreed to share the assets of the original partnership with her. If he had been in the same position, he would have wanted to stay where he could keep an eye on his holdings, too.

But he could still sympathize with Simone . . . and with Billy Casebolt. Unless he missed his guess, Cole had seen the beginnings of a romantic interest on Margaret Palmer's face when she looked at the deputy. Why a lady like Mrs. Palmer would take a shine to a scruffy character like Casebolt was beyond Cole, but he recalled that old saying about how love was blind. He figured that sometimes it was hard of hearing and didn't have much of a sense of smell, either.

"Well," Cole said, looking up and managing to keep his expression fairly solemn, "now that things are all settled, I think it'd be nice if somebody showed Mrs. Palmer and Miss Durand around town. Billy, why don't you do that?"

"Wait just a doggoned minute—" Casebolt began.

"I think that's an excellent idea," Margaret said. "Have you lived in Wind River for very long, Deputy . . . Casebolt, is it?"

"That's right, ma'am, Billy Casebolt. And I been here in Wind River ever since the town got started. I was the constable, back before Marshal Tyler took on the law job."

Margaret smiled at him. "Then I'm sure you'll be the perfect person to point out all the community's salient features."

Casebolt glanced at Cole, who said, "Mrs. Palmer means show 'em the sights."

"Oh," Casebolt said with an uneasy nod. "Yeah, I reckon I could do that."

Brenda asked, "Do you know a man named Jeremiah Newton?"

"Brother Jeremiah? Sure, we know him. He runs the blacksmith shop right down the street."

"We have some business to conduct with him. He made an offer on that land purchased by the B & D Investment Corporation," explained Margaret.

Simone looked interested. "You're going to sell him the land he wants for his church?"

"That's right," Brenda said. "Does that give you a little bit better opinion of us, Mrs. McKay?"

Cole saw Simone's lips thin slightly in response to Brenda's comment, but she was nothing if not polite as she said, "Just because we had a business disagreement doesn't mean I have a low opinion of you or your grandmother, Miss Durand. If you were in my position, you might have reacted the same way."

Brenda shrugged. "Maybe."

"And I am glad you're going to sell the land to Jeremiah. I'd much rather see him have it for his church than for Hank Parker to get his hands on it."

"Hank Parker," repeated Margaret. "He's the saloonkeeper who's running against you for the position of mayor, isn't he?"

"You *have* kept up with what's going on around here, haven't you?"

"This is going to be our home. Naturally we learned as much about it as we could before we came here, and since arriving yesterday we've also looked around closely. You have an excellent newspaper here, by the way. It's full of information about the town."

"I'll be sure and tell Michael Hatfield you said that. He'll be glad to hear it. He's the editor."

"Yes, I know," Margaret said. "I read his editorial about

the upcoming election in the latest issue. It's no surprise that he endorses you."

"I don't tell Michael what to write," Simone said crisply.

"No, of course not. But a progressive newspaper editor is hardly going to support a man like Parker, is he?"

Billy Casebolt stood up and put his chair back where he had gotten it. "If you folks are goin' to talk politics, I reckon it's time I left. I'll come back by in, say, half an hour and take you ladies on that tour of the town."

"That will be fine, Deputy," Margaret told him. "Or should I call you Billy?"

Casebolt swallowed hard. "You call me whatever you want, ma'am, just don't call me late to supper."

Margaret smiled. "Oh, I would *never* do a thing like that . . . Billy."

Cole looked down at the floor again and grinned. Simone might be a bit put out by the upheaval caused by the arrival of Brenda Durand and Margaret Palmer, and Billy Casebolt was clearly uncomfortable about the interest Margaret was showing in him, but as far as Cole was concerned, he didn't mind them being here.

As long as they were around, things were going to be a mite more interesting in Wind River.

8

Jeremiah was at work in his shop later that morning when he looked up to see Billy Casebolt coming into the low-ceilinged stone building. Two women were with him, strangers Jeremiah hadn't seen before. Both of them were well dressed. One was young and very attractive, the other considerably older but still an undeniably handsome woman. Casebolt lifted a hand in greeting and said, "Howdy, Jeremiah. Got some ladies here who want to talk to you."

"Hello, Brother Casebolt," Jeremiah said as he turned away from his forge. He nodded to the two women. "Ladies. What can I do for you?"

"It's we who can do something for you, Mr. Newton," the younger one said. "I'm Brenda Durand, and this is my grandmother, Mrs. Margaret Palmer. We're here in connection with some land you want to purchase from the B & D Investment Corporation."

Jeremiah's eyes widened in surprise. "I don't understand, ma'am. . . ."

"*I* am the B & D Investment Corporation, Mr. Newton," Brenda Durand went on. "And I'm going to sell you that land you want. I understand that you're going to build a church on it?"

Jeremiah's heart was pounding heavily. He had just about given up on hearing anything from the Eastern company that owned the knoll. Now, without any warning, the young woman who was evidently the owner of that company had shown up here in his shop, telling him that he was going to get what he wanted. Surely he had to be imagining this. For one thing, Brenda was too young to be the owner of such a corporation. . . .

"The lady's tellin' you the truth, Jeremiah," Casebolt said. "Reckon it comes as a pretty big surprise, don't it?"

"I . . . I can't believe it. . . ."

Margaret Palmer opened her bag and took out a piece of paper. "We've taken the liberty of preparing this deed to the property, Mr. Newton. As you can see, the price we've specified is somewhat different from the offer you made us in the letter you wrote."

Jeremiah forced his hand to reach out for the document. His big, work-roughened fingers closed over the paper. He looked at it for a second, then glanced up at the women. "But this is only half of what I offered for the land!"

"Consider the other half a donation to your church," Brenda said. "You'll be putting the property to good use."

"Yes, ma'am, I intend to, but you ought to make a fair profit. . . . Why, Hank Parker might be willing to pay you three times this much!"

"From everything we've heard about him," Margaret said, "we would prefer not to do business with a man like Mr. Parker. You, on the other hand, are well known as one of Wind River's finest citizens, Mr. Newton. And since

Brenda and I intend to make our home here, we want to do something for the community."

"You sure have," Jeremiah said as he looked at the deed, still hardly able to believe what he was seeing. "And you'll be welcome in the church anytime, ladies, anytime."

Casebolt slapped a hand on Jeremiah's broad shoulders. "Looks like we're goin' to have a real church around here after all, don't it?"

"The Lord provides, Brother Casebolt," Jeremiah said fervently. "Never doubt that. The Lord provides."

Even Jeremiah was surprised at how quickly things moved after that. Since the price Brenda Durand wanted for the land was only half of what Jeremiah had intended to pay, there was plenty of money left in the church's account at the bank to buy lumber. He had more than enough volunteers willing to lend their time and abilities to the task of building. Just as people had pitched in to help him repair the damage to his blacksmith shop, they were eager to be part of the church's construction. Not wanting to be outdone in generosity by Brenda, Simone donated enough kegs of nails from the general store to build *two* churches.

Two days after Brenda's first visit to the blacksmith shop, about half the men in town descended on the knoll and spent the day working under Jeremiah's direction. Their women came along, too, spreading blankets on the ground and filling them with picnic baskets. Wagons full of materials rolled up the slope and were cheerfully unloaded. By midmorning, the air in Wind River rang with the sound of hammering.

Hank Parker stood just inside the doorway of the Pronghorn Saloon, listened to the sound, and scowled darkly. When he had first heard that Jeremiah Newton was going to get his hands on that knoll after all, Parker had hurried to the hotel in an attempt to change the minds of Brenda Durand and her grandmother. The women had refused to see him, wouldn't even give him a chance to argue the matter.

Parker didn't like being beaten in anything, didn't like it one little bit. Jeremiah might have won this hand, he told himself, but the game wasn't over yet, not by a long shot. He had already decided how to take care of Newton. Besides, Parker had other, more important things on his mind these days, and the thought of that put a grim smile on his lips. His plan to deal with Simone McKay would soon be in motion.

And then he would have taken the first step in utterly destroying Simone's ambitions and putting this town firmly in his own iron grip . . .

That evening Jeremiah stood alone in the fading light of dusk and looked up at what God—and the people of Wind River—had wrought in a single day.

The framework of the church was nearly complete. The flat land on top of the knoll had been cleared, a foundation of stones and heavy beams had been laid, and the walls had gone up steadily as the sun moved from east to west. The ceiling joists were in place, and some of the roof beams had even been erected. It was amazing how much had been accomplished in such a short time.

The people had thrown themselves into the work heart and soul. Michael Hatfield, Judson Kent, and Nathan Smollett had volunteered, and hands that usually wielded a pen, healed the sick, and counted money occupied themselves for long hours instead with hammering nails.

Cole Tyler and Billy Casebolt had been there, and some of the cowhands from Kermit Sawyer's Diamond S spread had shown up, led by Sawyer's *segundo* Frenchy LeDoux and young Lon Rogers. Rose Foster had provided basket after basket of food, and the other women of the town were equally generous. Simone had surprised Jeremiah by arriving in a plain dress and sunbonnet, and she had spent the day pouring lemonade and coffee for the workers. Brenda and Margaret had joined her, and although Jeremiah sensed there were some hard feelings between Simone and Brenda, they cooperated cheerfully in this effort. Truly, the day had been blessed, Jeremiah thought as he stood there.

Everyone else had gone back to town when the light began to fade, but Jeremiah hadn't been able to bring himself to leave. He stepped up onto the bare flooring of the church and walked along the row of wall studs, surrounded by the sharp, clean smell of fresh-cut wood. A warm evening breeze sprang up. He breathed deeply of it.

In another week or two, the church would be ready for services to be held in it, he knew. He went to the center of the building and turned around, seeing the lights of the town clustered not far off. When he tilted his head back, he saw pinpoints of light in the darkening sky above as stars began to pop out.

He had never been happier or more fulfilled in his life.

That was when he heard the quick rush of feet behind him.

Turning, Jeremiah spotted several shadowy shapes lunging toward him. He let out a surprised exclamation, then heard the hiss of something moving quickly through the air. He threw an arm up just in time to block the blow as one of the men attacking him swung a heavy piece of lumber at his head.

The board cracked from the impact but didn't break. Jeremiah wasn't sure if the same thing could be said of his arm. Pain shot along it to his shoulder, blinding pain that was replaced a second later by utter numbness. He staggered back, trying to catch his balance. A roar of rage burst from his throat. He was being attacked again, this time in the confines of what should have been a holy place. He lowered his head and threw himself forward to meet the attack.

His powerful body bowled over a couple of the shadowy figures. "Watch it!" one of the other men called harshly. "He's like a damn bull!"

Jeremiah swung his good right arm in a sweeping backhand that knocked another man off his feet. But there were at least half a dozen of them—probably the same men who had wrecked his shop, he thought fleetingly—and three of them were still on their feet. They had all grabbed up boards from the piles of lumber stacked here and there throughout the structure and were using them as weapons. Jeremiah felt one of the boards jab into his midsection. He slapped it aside, but pain and sudden sickness made him bend forward. Another length of lumber came crashing down across his bowed shoulders, the board splitting in two from the force of the blow. Jeremiah stumbled forward. His left arm still dangled uselessly from his pain-numbed shoulder, but he put up his right hand and more by accident than design caught one of the boards as it was swung at him. He wrenched it out of the grip of the man wielding it and swung around in a circle, lashing out with the lumber. His assailants had to fling themselves backward to avoid having their skulls cracked by the board.

He couldn't defend himself in all directions at once, however, and the three men he had knocked down when the fight began were on their feet again. One of them leaped onto Jeremiah's back and locked an arm around his neck. With his other hand, the man palmed out a revolver and chopped at Jeremiah's head with the barrel of the gun. The blow sent stars pinwheeling through Jeremiah's head that were a hundred times brighter than any of the real stars in the sky above. He shook off the man who had just hit him, but more blows fell from the boards. Jeremiah's feet went out from under him, and he slumped to his knees. One of the makeshift clubs slammed into the back of his head.

He was vaguely aware of pitching forward onto his face. Splinters from the rough plank flooring dug painfully into his cheek, but they were a minor annoyance compared to the other pains that washed over him. For the second time in less than a week, he was kicked and stomped to the edge of senselessness.

"That's enough," one of the men ordered after a couple of savage minutes. Jeremiah could barely hear the words. They seemed to be coming from far, far away. "Leave him there and get on with the rest of it."

What else could they do? Jeremiah wondered fuzzily. They had already beaten him within an inch of his life—again.

The answer came a few seconds later as the sharp, unmistakable reek of kerosene stabbed into his nostrils. It was enough to bring him back from the brink of unconsciousness. He let out a groan and tried to push himself onto his hands and knees.

"Look out!" one of the men said. "He's gettin' up!"

Jeremiah's strength gave out. He slid back down, once again scraping his face as it hit the floor.

Another man laughed. "No, he's not. And he'll never get up once we're through here. Splash plenty of that stuff around. I've got a lucifer right here."

Lucifer, Jeremiah thought, misunderstanding in his agony. So Satan was behind this. He should have known. The Devil didn't want the Lord's word spread in Wind River. He had to get up, Jeremiah told himself. He had to get up and smite Satan. . . .

Suddenly there was a whooshing sound, and Jeremiah felt waves of heat batter him. The crackling of flames filled the air around him. He heard laughter . . . the laughter of Lucifer and all the imps of hell. The evil sound faded, drowned out by the roar of the fire.

This was all wrong, Jeremiah thought. He was a good man, a man of God. He shouldn't be in Hades.

But there was no mistaking the flames and the heat and the sound of a soul screaming in eternal torment. Screaming and screaming and screaming . . .

His throat was raw from the screams and the smoke that filled the air as he burst through the wall of flame that had only shortly before been the framework of the church. Where he had found the strength to get up and move, he never knew. All he could guess was that the hand of the Lord had reached into the inferno and touched him, leading him through the fire to safety. His clothes were ablaze, so when he felt himself falling, he let himself go, rolling over and over on the ground until the flames were out.

Then he lay there, shuddering, as the church was consumed and the hellish glare from its destruction filled the night sky over Wind River.

Cole was on his way to the Wind River Cafe for some supper when he saw the red glow in the sky to the southwest of town. Instantly a tingle of apprehension shot through him. Fire was one of the greatest enemies of people who lived on the frontier, and judging from the way the sky was lit up, this was a big blaze.

And it was coming from the direction of the partially completed church, he realized with a shock.

Cole was almost at the cafe, so he burst into a run toward it, the aches in his muscles from the long day's work forgotten in the face of this threat. Knowing there would be quite a few men in Rose's place, he slapped the door of the cafe open and shouted, "Fire! Fire at the new church!"

That brought a few shouted questions, but most of the cafe's patrons leaped to their feet and ran out, right behind Cole. He was hurrying back down the street toward the marshal's office, yelling a warning along the way. Men, women, and children spilled out of the buildings along Grenville Avenue in his wake. The commotion gripped the entire town in a matter of moments.

Cole paused as he reached a spot where he could look between two buildings and see the gentle knoll rising to the southwest of the settlement. His fears were confirmed by what he saw. The huge blaze was on top of the knoll, right where the church was being built. He could even see some of the framework silhouetted against the flames, like the skeleton of a corpse that was being burned.

"Jeremiah," Cole breathed.

He raced across the street to the blacksmith shop, urgently calling Jeremiah's name. Cole didn't remember seeing Jeremiah since everyone had come back to town. In fact, Cole didn't remember him leaving the knoll. Jeremiah might still be up there, trying to fight the fire by himself or maybe even trapped in that inferno.

There was no time to waste in wondering how the fire had gotten started. Once Cole was satisfied that Jeremiah wasn't at the blacksmith shop, he hurried even more. Billy

Casebolt met him at the door of the marshal's office and asked anxiously, "What in tarnation is goin' on?"

"The new church is on fire," Cole told him curtly, "and I can't find Jeremiah. He may still be up there."

"Lordy!" exclaimed Casebolt. "Let's go!"

"You fetch Doc Kent!" Cole ordered. "I'm getting up there as fast as I can."

Casebolt nodded and loped off toward the doctor's office.

People were already streaming out of the settlement toward the burning church. Many of them were carrying buckets, Cole saw as he ran down to the livery stable where he kept his big golden sorrel, Ulysses. To save time, Cole just slapped a harness on the horse and led it out of the barn, then swung up bareback. Ulysses responded instantly to the pressure of Cole's heels and the shouted command from the marshal. The sorrel launched into a gallop that sent it racing along Grenville Avenue and then up the slope toward the blaze, passing the running townspeople along the way.

Ulysses had more sand than any horse Cole had ever known. The big sorrel had stood fast through countless gunfights and battles, had outraced Indian ponies to carry Cole to safety, had been as staunch a friend and companion as any frontiersman could want. But even Ulysses shied away from the pillar of flame as Cole rode closer and closer to the fire. Waves of heat swept over man and horse, and choking clouds of smoke and cinders clogged Cole's throat. Finally, as Ulysses fought him more and more, he gave up and slid down from the horse's back. He slapped Ulysses on the rump and called, "Go home, boy!" knowing the sorrel would return to the stable. Then he turned and approached the burning church on foot, holding his left arm up over his face in an attempt to shield his features from the heat.

That didn't help much. Cole was forced to stop and tie his bandanna over his nose and mouth to block the cinders and ash that threatened to gag him. He stumbled ahead, bellowing, "Jeremiah! Jeremiah, where are you?"

There was no answer, at least none that Cole could hear over the crackling tumult of the conflagration. Saving what had been built of the church was impossible, he saw. The fire was too well established. Much of the framework that had been erected during the day was already destroyed. Cole squinted against the stinging smoke that hung in the air and searched for the body of his friend. He didn't see Jeremiah anywhere around the church.

And if Jeremiah was inside, there was no hope for him. Cole knew that. All that he and the people of Wind River could do now was try to stop the fire from spreading.

There was a small creek at the bottom of the slope. Cole turned away from the blaze and ran to meet the first of the people from the settlement. He called out orders, setting up a bucket brigade. Soon a double line of men and women stretched from the creek to the top of the knoll. Cole took the position closest to the fire, since it was the most dangerous. After a couple of moments that seemed longer, a sloshing bucket that was three quarters full of water was thrust into his hands. He turned and flung the bucket's contents onto the flames. The water didn't seem to make a bit of difference.

But Cole turned and handed the empty bucket to the man at the head of the other line. It would be passed back to the creek, refilled, and started up the knoll again. Cole already had a second bucket in his hands, and he dashed that water onto the fire, too. Then another and another and another . . .

Eventually the blaze would be under control. And when it was . . . when the ashes had cooled enough . . . Cole knew he would have to go in there.

He was afraid he already knew what he was going to find.

• • •

Hank Parker chuckled as he heard the shouting in the street outside the Pronghorn. As a man stuck his head into the saloon and yelled, "The new church is on fire! Come on, boys!" Parker turned to the bar and motioned for his bartender to hand him a glass and a bottle of the good stuff.

The bartender complied, saying, "What do you think, boss? Should we go fight that fire?"

Parker glanced over his shoulder. Most of the saloon's customers were rushing out to join the crowd heading up to the knoll . . . the knoll that should have belonged to him, Parker thought. He shook his head. "They'll have plenty of people for their bucket brigade. They don't need our help."

The bartender looked uneasy about that decision, but he nodded and stayed where he was behind the bar. Parker splashed whiskey into the glass, lifted it to his mouth, and tossed back the drink, savoring its warmth in his belly.

Whiskey might be warm, but he was willing to wager it was a lot hotter where Jeremiah Newton was right about now.

Hank Parker had not killed anyone since the war except some outlaws when he was riding with one of Cole Tyler's posses. He had been ruthless about getting what he wanted, but he had always stopped short of murder—until now. Threats and intimidation had been more his style. But he was tired of people getting in his way. He wanted Jeremiah Newton disposed of, and it had been surprisingly easy to pay those hardcase drifters to see to it. In the process, the church would be destroyed, so that Parker wouldn't have to go to the trouble of tearing it down later so that he could build his stockyards and slaughterhouse out there. Everything was going to work out just fine. He roused himself from his reverie, realized that quite some time had passed, and poured himself another drink.

Behind him, one of the percentage girls let out a scream.

Parker's head snapped up so that he could see what was going on in the long mirror behind the bar. A bloody, soot-covered apparition had appeared in the doorway of the saloon, swatting the batwings aside. A bellow of rage came from the thing's throat, and for a couple of horrifying seconds, Parker didn't realize what he was looking at.

But then, as he turned to meet the charge, he recognized Jeremiah Newton. The big blacksmith was still alive, and even worse, he was lurching toward Parker, his massive arms outstretched and his hands aimed right at the saloonkeeper's throat.

With a curse, Parker twisted aside and then met the attack with a lunge of his own. The two big men came together like a pair of bull buffaloes fighting for dominance over the herd. Their collision seemed to shake the entire building.

They were pretty evenly matched. Jeremiah was heavier, but Parker's reach was a little longer. However, Parker had only the one arm to Jeremiah's two. Jeremiah's left arm wasn't working very well, though, and blood was welling into his eyes from a gash on his forehead. He was already so battered that the only thing keeping him on his feet was his rage. Parker sensed that, and he slammed his rock-hard fist into Jeremiah's face again and again, keeping the blacksmith from wrapping him up in a bear hug that might prove fatal.

If the fight had been between just the two of them, it might have gone on until one or both of them dropped from exhaustion. As it was, the odds swung quickly to Parker's side as the bartender and two of the men he employed to break up trouble in the Pronghorn leaped into the fracas. The bartender hurried around the end of the bar carrying a bungstarter, and he slammed the wooden mallet into the back of Jeremiah's head, stunning the blacksmith. Parker's men grabbed Jeremiah's arms, jerking them painfully behind his back. "Hold him, boys!" Parker gasped. Then, setting himself, he began to slug blows into Jeremiah's midsection. When Jeremiah doubled over despite the efforts of Parker's men to hold him up, the saloonkeeper windmilled his fist and brought it down on Jeremiah's temple. Jeremiah collapsed onto the floor at Parker's feet, out cold. Parker drew back his leg, poising himself to kick Jeremiah in the head.

A metallic click sounded from the doorway of the saloon. "Do it and I'll kill you where you stand, you son of a bitch," Cole Tyler said icily as he stared at Parker over the barrel of his drawn and cocked Colt revolver.

Cole's face and hands were blistered from the heat of the fire, and his arms and shoulders ached intolerably from the strain of throwing countless heavy buckets of water onto the blaze. But the gun in his hand didn't waver a fraction of an inch as he pointed it at Hank Parker.

He had left the church while it was still burning, but the fire had been much smaller. The area around the church had been thoroughly wet down by more men with buckets, so there was little danger of the flames spreading. What was left of the church would just have to burn itself out.

So Cole had hurried back down the hill to town, thinking that it was possible he might find Jeremiah at the blacksmith shop. Not likely, he knew that . . . but possible.

Instead, to his great relief, he had found his friend here in the Pronghorn, on the losing end of a battle with

Parker and some of the saloonkeeper's flunkies. The commotion in the saloon had drawn Cole's attention, and from the looks of things, he had gotten there just in time.

"Wait just a damned minute!" Parker protested angrily as he lowered the foot he had been aiming at Jeremiah's head. "Newton's the one you ought to be pointing a gun at, Tyler. He started this fight!"

"It's true, Marshal," spoke up one of Parker's men. "That big galoot came runnin' in here and tried to kill the boss."

"I reckon he had a good reason," Cole said. "You know anything about that fire up at the church, Parker?"

Parker straightened his coat and glowered at Cole. "Only what I heard gents shouting about out in the street," he said. "And I don't appreciate you jumping to conclusions like that. It's bad enough this bastard came in here and tried to tear my head off for something I didn't have anything to do with."

Cole didn't believe Parker for a second. But that issue could be dealt with later, he decided. For now, he had to see to Jeremiah. Motioning with the barrel of his gun, he said, "Step back away from him."

"Gladly," grunted Parker. He moved back to the bar, and the other men cleared out from around Jeremiah's slumped form.

Cole went to Jeremiah and knelt beside him. The big man was breathing, Cole could see that much. Jeremiah looked like he had been beaten badly again; there was blood on his face, and it was already purple and swollen with bruises. In addition, his eyebrows and some of his hair had been singed away, and his hands and face were burned in places. His clothes were nothing but charred rags, and he appeared to have burns scattered all over his body. He was in pitiful condition.

"We've got to get him over to Dr. Kent's," Cole said as he straightened. "Some of you men come over here and pick him up, but be damned careful about it."

The men looked at Parker, who nodded brusquely. "Better do what the marshal says," he told them, then added with a sneer directed at Cole, "otherwise our fine, upstanding lawman is liable to shoot somebody."

Cole ignored the gibe. He stood back while the men gathered around Jeremiah and hefted him with grunts of effort. They carried him out of the saloon and started down the street toward Judson Kent's office.

Pausing in the doorway with his gun still in his hand, Cole looked back at Parker. "Jeremiah had better be all right," he warned. "If he's not, I'll be coming back to see you, Parker."

"He's the one who went crazy and attacked me," Parker snapped. "You can't prove a damned thing against me, Tyler, and as long as you're wearing that badge, you've got to have proof."

A humorless smile touched Cole's lips. "You've forgotten one thing: I put this badge on—and I can damned sure take it off."

With that, he pushed out through the batwings and hurried down the street after the men carrying Jeremiah.

Jeremiah must have stumbled down the hill and in the darkness somehow missed the people rushing up the slope toward the burning church. That was the only thing Cole could figure out after talking to the big blacksmith later that night in Judson Kent's office.

Cole was grateful Jeremiah was still alive, and according to Kent, that was something of a miracle in itself. The punishment Jeremiah had absorbed would have been enough to kill any man with a constitution weaker than Jeremiah's iron one.

"You're a lucky man, my friend," Kent told him as he rested a hand on Jeremiah's shoulder. "And you're going to stay right here in this bed for a few days until you've recovered a bit. We won't be taking any chances with that head of yours this time."

Stubbornly Jeremiah tried to sit up, but he lacked the strength to do so. "Got to . . . see about the church," he complained.

"Don't you worry about that," Cole assured him from the other side of the bed. "I've already heard plenty of folks say that they'll pitch in to clean up the debris. By the time you're able to be up and around, the town will be ready to start building again."

"All that work," Jeremiah sighed as he let his head ease back onto the pillow underneath it. "All that work for nothing." He looked at Cole. "What are you going to do about Parker?"

Cole grimaced. "There's not much I *can* do. Again, you didn't see the faces of the men who jumped you. All Parker has to do is deny knowing anything about it, and unless somebody comes forward to contradict him, we can't disprove his story."

"No one in that lot is going to testify against Parker," Kent said. "They'd be afraid to."

"That's what I figure, too," Cole agreed.

"So he gets away with it," Jeremiah said dispiritedly.

Cole looked at his friend. Jeremiah's body was swathed in bandages where Kent had smeared ointment for the burns on his skin. His left forearm had splints strapped to it to hold it immobile; Kent suspected one of the bones in the arm was cracked but not completely fractured. There were stitches on Jeremiah's forehead where the medico had closed up the worst of the gashes. Jeremiah was a mess, pure and simple, and Cole felt he was letting his friend down by not going after Parker.

"There's nothing I can do about it now," Cole said wearily. "But one of these days, Parker is going to over-play his hand. When he does, he's going to be sorry he ever got off the train in Wind River."

Cole hoped those were more than just empty words.

•   •   •

By the next morning, things were back to what passed for normal in the settlement. Cole and Billy Casebolt rode up to the burned-out church on the knoll and poked around the cooling ashes for anything that might point them toward the men who had done this. Finding any tracks was hopeless; there had been so many people milling around the night before that any sign had been completely obliterated. Unless they got some sort of lucky break—which Cole didn't foresee happening—they weren't going to be able to tie Hank Parker to this atrocity.

When the two lawmen got back to the marshal's office, there was another shock waiting for Cole. Parker himself was waiting there, his face bruised from the battle with Jeremiah. Cole stopped short when he strode into the building and saw Parker. "What the hell do you want?" he demanded.

Parker returned the icy stare Cole was giving him. "Newton attacked me last night for no reason. I want to press charges against him."

Casebolt goggled at the saloonkeeper. "You want to press charges?" he echoed, his voice rising in astonishment and anger. "Why, you low-down, sidewindin'—"

Cole stopped him. "That's enough, Billy," he said. Cole's jaw was so tight that a tiny muscle jerked in it as he faced Parker and went on, "You can swear out a complaint, but it's up to the law to determine whether or not there's enough evidence to proceed with it. And all I saw last night when I got to the Pronghorn was you and three of your men beating up on Jeremiah. I'd say *he's* got a case against *you*."

"That's not the way it was, and you know it, Tyler," snapped Parker. "You're just trying to protect Newton because he's your friend."

Cole shrugged. "If you've got a problem with my decision, Parker, you can go to Cheyenne and see about getting some federal law in here. I'm sure you wouldn't mind having a U.S. deputy marshal come in and start poking around. Dan Boyd might even get the job."

"You and Boyd worked together not that long ago!" Parker protested. "You think I'd get a fair hearing from him or any other federal badge-toter?"

"Maybe your trouble's not with me, it's just with the law in general." Cole brushed roughly past him. "Now, if you don't have anything else to say, stop wasting my time and get out of my office."

Parker pointed a finger at him. "I'm not forgetting this, Tyler."

"I've got a long memory, too," Cole said softly. "I reckon it'll be a while before I forget what Jeremiah looked like last night before Dr. Kent got back from the fire and started patching him up."

Parker glowered at him for a moment longer, then turned on his heel and stalked out of the building.

In a quiet voice, Casebolt said into the silence, "One of these days you're going to have to kill that old boy, Marshal."

"You could be right, Billy." Cole sat down behind the desk and sighed. "You could be right."

The way things had been going, Simone McKay was waiting for another catastrophe. After the brawl at her campaign rally, the attacks on Jeremiah Newton, the destruction of the church . . . well, it was a reasonable assumption that something *else* bad was going to happen.

But it didn't, not the rest of that day, and Simone was pleasantly surprised. She went home from the land office that night, saw no sign of the ghost of her late husband, and slept well.

The next morning, Brenda Durand was waiting when Simone arrived at the land development company.

"I want to see your records," Brenda announced without preamble. "I have a right."

"And good morning to you, too, Miss Durand," Simone said dryly, making an effort to keep her temper in check. Brenda certainly knew how to irritate her. The girl seemed to have a positive genius for it.

Brenda flushed. "Good morning," she said belatedly. "What about those records?"

"Come into my office. I'll gladly open the books for you. As you say, you have a right."

The worst part about it was that Brenda *did* have a right to inspect the company's books. Simone wondered if she had made a mistake by not contesting Brenda's claims in court. It was possible, even probable, that Simone would have lost in any legal action against Brenda. But it would have been a delaying tactic, at the very least. She wouldn't have had to deal with Brenda's annoying attitude while she had so many other, more pressing matters to occupy her attention.

But it was too late for that now. Brenda's involvement in the holdings Simone had considered her own was a fact, and there was little or nothing she could do about it.

"Sit down," Simone said as the two women entered the private office. She gestured at the comfortable chair in front of the desk. "I'll get what you need to see."

"I need to see everything," Brenda said as she sat down. "I want to know everything there is to know about the workings of this company, as well as all the other assets."

"And so you shall," Simone said, still trying to be polite. "Would you like me to have some coffee brought in?"

Brenda considered for a second, then nodded. "That's a good idea. We're likely to need it."

Simone opened the office door again, spoke quietly to one of the clerks in the front room, and then went behind the desk to sit down and open the large bottom drawer to her right. She took out several ledgers and handed them across the desk to Brenda. "Help yourself. If there's anything you don't understand, I'd be glad to explain it."

"I can read a ledger," snapped Brenda. She opened the first one and began poring over the columns of figures written inside. When she was done with the first book, she set it aside and started on the second one.

Simone saw a small frown appear on Brenda's face, and the expression grew more pronounced as the younger woman looked through the ledgers. By the time she was finished, she definitely looked unhappy. Simone didn't bother asking what the problem was. She was sure Brenda would tell her.

"Either your accounting methods are awfully slipshod," Brenda said after a moment, "or there are a great many people who haven't been prompt about paying what they owe. There are a lot of accounts in those books that are overdue!"

"The records are accurate," said Simone. "And as for some of the accounts being overdue . . . it's not that easy to make a living out here, Miss Durand, especially for farmers and ranchers. A bad year can make money awfully tight for several years after that. Everyone I do business with makes an honest effort to pay what they owe, and I accept that on good faith."

"Good faith! Good faith doesn't pay bills, Mrs. McKay. Only cold, hard cash does that."

Simone leaned back in her chair. "You seem to know a great deal about business, especially for a woman."

"No more so than you." Brenda gestured contemptuously at the stack of ledgers on the desk. "Or perhaps I should say I *do* know more than you, judging from those records. I was a clerk for one of the leading attorneys in Baltimore."

"At your age?" Simone frowned in disbelief.

"I have a good head for numbers, and my employer represented many of the city's leading businessmen. It was somewhat unusual, I know, but women are doing more all the time." Brenda smiled, but there was no humor in the expression. "Why, in some places they're even allowed to vote and run for public office."

Simone ignored that last comment and asked, "What would you have me do about the accounts that are overdue?"

"Why, force the people to pay, of course! Either that or foreclose on them and take the land back."

"You wouldn't even give them a chance to get caught up when their farms are more well established?"

"Certainly not. Money is owed when it's owed, not later."

Simone shook her head. "I won't do business that way."

Brenda leaned forward and snapped, "You don't have any choice. I own just as much of this company as you do."

"True, but I'm the managing partner. You agreed to that . . . in the presence of witnesses, I might add." She held up a hand to forestall Brenda's angry retort. "Besides, what you want to do just isn't good business. This isn't a charitable institution. I *have* foreclosed on people when it became obvious that they had no intention of paying off their debt. But every case is different, and I intend to be making money here in Wind River for a long time." Simone came to her feet, her patience gone. "Pay attention, little girl, and you might learn something. But for now, get out of my office. I have work to do."

Brenda gaped at her, astonished and outraged by the tone Simone had taken. Finally she said, "You . . . you can't get away with this!"

"I'm just doing my job. I'm protecting this company and making it as profitable as possible. If you have a problem with that, I'll buy you out."

Simone hadn't really intended to make that offer yet. It was her trump card, the one she was saving for a time when she really needed it. But maybe it was better to play it now, she thought. Maybe she could get Brenda out of her hair once and for all, before Brenda did any real harm.

She wasn't going to be that lucky, Simone saw. Brenda's features were a taut, angry mask as she said, "I've no intention of selling out, to you or anyone else, Mrs. McKay. This is my home now, and I intend to make my fortune here."

"Then stay out of my way," Simone said, and there was something bleak and dangerous about her voice. Brenda must have heard it, because although the younger woman's expression remained defiant, she stood up and flounced out of the office without saying anything else.

Simone let out a sigh and sat down again. She wished that Brenda Durand had never come to Wind River.

Despite being upset by Brenda's visit, Simone was able to force her mind back onto her work, and she spent the rest of the day with it, grateful to have the opportunity to retreat into a world of numbers and documents. That was certainly easier than dealing with real life. She had intended to drop by Judson Kent's house and see how Jeremiah was doing, but by the time she left the office that evening, she was too tired to do so. Instead she started walking toward the big house on Sweetwater Street.

There were quite a few people on Grenville Avenue, and many of them greeted Simone by name, the men tipping their hats respectfully, the women smiling. She was well liked here, but more than that, she was held somewhat in awe. Not only was she the wealthiest, most influential person in town, but she came from a world that many of these people had never known themselves. Philadelphia society might as well have been Mars as far as these frontier folk were concerned.

Sweetwater Street wasn't nearly as crowded. In fact, Simone was by herself on the residential street that was lined with aspens. She could see the mansion bulking at the end of the road. In the houses between here and there, lamplight glowed warmly in the windows as families sat down to dinner.

"Mrs. McKay?"

Simone started a little, surprised by the voice that said her name as she walked past a clump of trees that threw a pool of deep shadow underneath their branches. She turned toward the voice, her heart beating a bit faster as she said, "Yes? Who is it?"

A female figure emerged part of the way from the shadows. Simone couldn't see the woman's face. "Remember me, Mrs. McKay? It's Becky Lewis."

Simone's breath caught in her throat. She wasn't likely to ever forget Becky Lewis. "I remember you," Simone said coldly. "You're the slut who claimed my late husband fathered her child."

"Ah, now, you'd better be careful, Mrs. McKay. You don't want to rile me." The prostitute's voice was mocking.

Simone's chin lifted defiantly. "I gave you money to leave Wind River and make a fresh start elsewhere. What are you doing back here?"

"I came to see you," Becky said. "I thought you might want to know about the baby."

"I have absolutely no interest in you or your brat. You want money again, I suppose."

Becky gave a harsh little laugh. "You've got me pegged, Mrs. McKay. Once a whore, always a whore. Only interested in money."

"Are you denying it?" Simone snapped.

"No, ma'am, I'm not denying it at all."

Simone sighed. "Very well. I don't want you disgracing Andrew's name any more now than when I paid you off the first time. I'll give you a reasonable sum. Just don't say anything more about that . . . that baby."

"You don't have to worry about the baby." Becky's voice caught a little as she went on, "You don't ever have to worry about the baby again." She took a deep breath, and her voice was stronger when she spoke again. "You've got a lot bigger worries than that, Mrs. McKay."

"What are you talking about?"

"I was on the platform at the depot the day the first train rolled in. Remember, Mrs. McKay? I was right there, close by. I saw everything that happened. *Everything*."

Simone's pulse was like a hammer pounding in her head. Carefully she kept her voice from revealing her distress as she said, "What are you talking about?"

"You know, Mrs. McKay. *You* were there, too."

Simone shook her head. "I won't continue this conversation. You and I have nothing more to say to each other, Miss Lewis. Just tell me how much money you want and then go away."

Becky stepped closer, and finally Simone could see her face in the last of the fading daylight. The soiled dove's features were drawn, almost haggard. The fresh, young beauty she had once possessed was now little more than a memory. Her lips drew back from her teeth, giving her a feral look, as she said, "It's not that simple, Mrs. McKay. I'm not going away anytime soon. I want money, sure, but I want more than that." She reached out and jabbed Simone in the chest with a finger, making the older woman gasp and draw back. "You're going to dance to my tune now, lady— or else I'll tell everybody in this precious town of yours about what you did that day on the platform!"

For an instant the most overpowering rage Simone had ever felt gripped her. In her mind's eye she could see herself lunging toward Becky, getting the prostitute's neck between her fingers, and squeezing until the last remains of that pathetic life were gone. She could do it, Simone knew. She was larger than Becky, and the younger woman's wasted look told Simone that her health was not good. She probably didn't have the strength to fight off an unexpected attack.

But then what would she do with the body? Simone asked herself. She could say that Becky had attacked her . . . she could kill the girl, then go screaming back down to Grenville Avenue. Cole would believe whatever story she told him, Simone knew that. It would be easy . . .

"And I ain't the only one who knows about this," Becky said, as if reading Simone's mind, "so you best be real careful. You think about what you're going to do before you do it, Mrs. McKay."

"You . . . you're a hateful bitch!"

"Yes, ma'am," Becky said smugly. "But that's not important. All that matters is what I know about you."

She was right. Simone knew she was right. She wasn't sure just what Becky thought she had seen that day on the platform, but no matter what kind of crazy story she told, some people would believe her. Not Cole, of course, and not many others. But some, and that was enough. Suspicion was the easiest crop in the world to grow once the seeds had been planted. Becky might not be able to ruin her, but she could certainly make life in Wind River miserable.

"All right," Simone said, having to force the words up her throat and out of her mouth. "How much do you want?"

"Five hundred dollars, to start with. And like I said, I'll be around town for a while. There may be some other things I ask you to do."

"Come with me. I'll get you your money."

Becky smirked, the expression barely visible in the dusk. "You sure you want a dirty whore like me setting foot in that fancy house of yours?"

"I don't have much choice in the matter, do I?"

"You sure as hell don't."

Simone started walking toward the house again, her steps much more sure and confident than she felt. Her head was spinning. She had asked herself what else could go wrong, and now she had received her answer.

This was the housekeeper's night off, and that was the only reason Simone was willing to allow Becky into the house. Otherwise she would have made her wait somewhere else. She didn't want anyone to know there was a connection between the two of them. "Stay here," she told Becky when they entered the foyer of the mansion. The lamps had been left lit in the parlor and dining room. "I'll be right down with your money. Don't touch anything."

"Don't worry," Becky said dryly. "Bein' a slut don't rub off."

Simone wasn't sure about that, nor was she certain that she could trust Becky in her house. But with as much as the soiled dove had to gain, it was unlikely she would risk it all to steal a few knickknacks from the parlor.

Without even taking off her coat and hat, Simone went straight upstairs to her bedroom and took a canvas pouch from underneath a stack of clothes in one of the drawers of the walnut chiffonier. It looked strange for the owner of the bank to keep a stash of money hidden amongst her undies, Simone thought, but she liked to have some cash on hand where she could get to it in a hurry. A holdover from her younger days, when she hadn't been quite so well-to-do, she had decided when she put the pouch there. Now she opened it, took out a sheaf of bills, and counted off five hundred dollars.

Becky was still waiting in the foyer when Simone came downstairs with the money. She thrust the cash into Becky's eager hands and said, "Here. That's what you wanted. Now I'll thank you to leave me alone."

"Sure," Becky said. She riffled through the bills, then rolled them up and stuck them down the front of her dress into the cleavage between her small breasts. "I'll leave you alone . . . for now. But I may be back to see you."

"I can wait," Simone said icily.

"And remember, from here on out . . . there's always going to be somebody somewhere who knows what you did."

With that smirk still on her face, Becky turned and left the house. The door closed firmly behind her.

Once Becky was gone, Simone's iron control over her emotions evaporated. She stumbled into the parlor and covered her face with her hands. "Oh, God," she practically wailed. "What am I going to do? What am I going to do?"

She stood there for several long minutes, shuddering but not giving in to the urge to cry. When she was able to think coherently again, she gave a hollow laugh and said aloud, "At least there wasn't a ghost waiting for me here in the parlor tonight."

That was when she heard a footstep behind her and a voice said tentatively, "Simone . . . ?"

10

Dr. Judson Kent stepped out of the general store and turned to lift a hand in farewell to Harvey Raymond, the manager of the emporium. Twilight was settling down over Wind River; it was one of Kent's favorite times of day. He thought he might stroll down to the cafe and have some supper, then take a tray back to Jeremiah. The tray would have to be heavily loaded, Kent knew, because Jeremiah's appetite had come back, and the big blacksmith couldn't get enough of Monty Riordan's cooking.

To Kent's satisfaction, Jeremiah had shown no signs of a lingering head injury during the past couple of days. He had decided that Jeremiah would probably make a full recovery, given time. That was going to be the challenge: keeping Jeremiah in bed where he belonged for a few more days so that he could rest and recuperate from his ordeal.

Kent paused on the boardwalk and glanced down the street at the false front of the Pronghorn Saloon. Already, gaudy light was spilling out through its windows, and

Kent could hear piano music and raucous laughter. The place was a blight on the town, the doctor thought. But like Cole Tyler, Kent knew there was nothing that could legally be done about it.

He was frowning toward the Pronghorn when some impulse made him turn his head the other way. When he did, he saw Simone McKay leaving the offices of the Wind River Land Development Company. Kent lifted a hand and started to call out to her, but something made him stop before he said anything. Simone's back was stiff, and she seemed to be paying little attention to her surroundings. Kent wondered if she was upset about something.

Without quite knowing why he was doing it, he started following her.

At first he fully intended to catch up and speak to her, but he held back, deciding that he wanted to see where she was going. He knew he was spying on her, but he told himself it was for her own good. Simone had been through a great deal lately, and Kent wanted to find out what her mental state was. Perhaps he could be of help to her, he mused.

A few minutes later, still trailing about a block behind her, he saw her turn and enter Sweetwater Street. Now he knew she was going home, and he realized he was being foolish. He felt an unaccustomed flush creeping over his bearded cheeks. He was attracted to Simone, and the past year had been an agony of indecision for him. Once a suitable period of mourning for her husband had passed, Kent had tried to subtly make it known to Simone that he was interested, but he had never been able to fully interpret her reaction. Sometimes it seemed as if she might return his affections, and at others she seemed quite taken with Marshal Tyler instead. And there were other times when Kent was convinced she had no romantic interest in either of them. To be honest about it, he had thought more than once, Simone McKay was as big a mystery to him now as she had been the first time he saw her.

But that didn't mean he should look for things that might be disturbing her just so that he could possibly help and put her in his debt. That wasn't the decent thing to do at all. If he was going to do anything for her, it needed to be out of concern for a fellow citizen, nothing more. When he reached the corner of Sweetwater Street, he told himself, he would turn around and go back to the cafe, just as he had planned.

He paused at the intersection and looked toward the big house at the end of the cross street. Shadows were gathering, and it took him a second to spot Simone. Then he saw her. She had stopped for some reason.

He saw as well the figure that stepped out of the gloom underneath some trees and accosted her.

Kent's frown deepened with uncertainty. If it had been a man who had stopped Simone, he would have gone loping down Sweetwater Street without hesitation to come to her aid. But the person talking to her was female. Kent could tell that much even in the shadows cloaking the street. He drew back against the building on the corner, thrust his hands into the pockets of his coat, and watched curiously.

Simone talked to the unknown woman for several minutes. It was difficult to be sure, but Kent thought her stance stiffened even more. Something was upsetting her, he told himself. Still, he was hesitant to interfere, since Simone seemed to be in no physical danger. Finally Simone turned and moved on toward her house, but the other woman went with her.

"Judson, you've no right to spy on the lady," he muttered to himself. "You're just being an old busybody."

But be that as it may, Kent started down Sweetwater Street, following Simone and her mysterious companion.

Both women went into the house. Kent was *not* going to skulk around the mansion and try to peer in the windows. That would be utterly undignified, and Simone would surely be angry with him if she caught him doing such a thing. Instead he paused half a block away, underneath another aspen tree, and watched the big house.

Minutes ticked by with maddening slowness. Kent was about to give up and leave when the front door of the house opened. One of the women came out and started back up the street, and as she drew closer he was able to tell it was the other woman, not Simone. He moved back, deeper into the shadow, and for some reason found himself holding his breath.

The woman walked past. There was just enough of a faint red glow in the sky to the west to reveal her features to Judson Kent.

His jaw tightened. Time had changed her somewhat, and not for the better, but he knew her immediately. The last time he had seen her, she had been getting on an eastbound train, having been paid by Simone to leave Wind River forever and make a fresh start somewhere else, her and the child she claimed had been fathered by Andrew McKay.

Why in God's name had Becky Lewis returned, Kent wondered, and why, out of all times, *now*?

This was not good, he told himself, not good at all. The young prostitute had threatened once before to ruin Andrew McKay's good name. Had she come back to make the same threat again? Had she wasted the money Simone had given her before and decided to resume her blackmail? And what about the child?

Kent knew he couldn't turn and walk away from this.

Simone was in some sort of trouble, and even if there would never be anything romantic between them, he was still her friend. He made up his mind, squared his shoulders, and walked with long-legged strides toward the house.

He intended to ring the bell, of course, as any proper caller would, but as he went up the walk toward the porch, a glance through a gap in the curtains over the parlor window showed him Simone standing there, her face buried in her hands, obviously quite upset about something. Kent didn't waste time standing on ceremony. He opened the door, moved through the foyer, and stepped into the parlor. The lady of the house was standing there, her back to him. He heard her say something to herself about a ghost, which worried him even more. He said, "Simone . . . ?"

That was when she screamed.

The shriek tore involuntarily from her throat as she whirled around, fully expecting to find the shade of her late husband standing there. But instead her stunned gaze saw the ashen features of Dr. Judson Kent. He took a step back, clearly startled half out of his wits by her reaction.

"Oh, Judson," Simone managed to choke out. "I'm so sorry. . . ."

Then the tears came.

She couldn't hold them back any longer. Although she hated herself for giving in to such weakness, tears flooded her eyes and rolled down her cheeks as once again she buried her face in her hands. She felt Kent's arms around her, felt him pulling her to him. Then she pressed her face against his vest and starched shirtfront and let herself cry.

Long moments passed before Simone could bring herself under control again. Finally she was able to suppress the sobs into a few sniffles. She hiccuped several times as Kent patted her awkwardly on the back. "There, there," he murmured. "It will be all right, Simone. I'm sure it will be."

"Y-You're a doctor," she said. "Can't you be more reassuring than that?"

Kent wore an expression of confusion when she stepped back and looked up at him. Obviously he didn't know what to make of her behavior. Simone wasn't surprised; no one in Wind River had ever seen her act this way. She had never allowed such a thing . . . until now.

"What happened, Simone?" he asked. "Why was Becky Lewis here? Did she threaten you?"

"You . . . you saw her?"

"I, ah, happened to notice the two of you talking on the street outside, and I saw her come in here with you and then leave a few minutes later." A look of guilt passed fleetingly through Kent's eyes, as if he wasn't telling her the entire story, but then he went on, "I was worried about you, Simone, and evidently with good reason. What did that . . . that trollop do to you?"

"She didn't do anything except talk." Simone fumbled a lacy handkerchief from the pocket of her gown and dabbed at her wet eyes. She felt an almost irresistible urge to tell Kent the whole story. But did she dare do that? She asked, "Can I trust you, Judson?"

"Of course you can! Surely you know that by now, my dear. A doctor has to know how to be discreet. I've never told anyone about what the Lewis woman did before, except—" He stopped short.

"Who did you tell, Judson?" asked Simone.

He looked distinctly uncomfortable as he said, "I mentioned the matter to Marshal Tyler. You know that Cole is trustworthy, Simone, and I thought . . . well, it seemed entirely possible to me that Becky Lewis might be the real murderer of your late husband!"

Simone lifted a hand to her mouth in horror. "You mean William Durand didn't . . . "

"I don't know," said Kent. "I just thought it was possible. The Lewis woman was there that day, and she was already holding a grudge against Andrew because of . . . of the baby."

"I know," Simone said, nodding. "I just never thought . . . My God, it *could* be true. But that would mean, when I shot Durand, that he . . . "

"Don't even think about that," Kent said firmly. "William Durand was a criminal. He was an outlaw just like that desperado Deke Strawhorn. They kidnapped you and Delia Hatfield and risked both of your lives. Who knows what other crimes Durand committed? Besides, if you hadn't shot him, Marshal Tyler and Mr. Sawyer would have."

"I know," Simone sighed. "But killing a man . . . that's not something I take lightly."

"Of course not."

Simone took a deep breath and decided to plunge ahead. "That's why I was so upset. Becky Lewis practically accused me to my face of killing Andrew myself!"

Now Kent looked more than surprised. He was absolutely thunderstruck. "You . . . killing Andrew? But . . . but that's insane!"

Simone smiled faintly as she wiped away more of the vestiges of her tears. "I'm glad you think so."

"Of course I think so! You're incapable of harming anyone except in self-defense. Why would she say such a thing?"

"She wanted money," replied Simone. "What else? And I got the feeling that something must have happened to her child, that she didn't have it to hold over my head as a threat any longer. That's why she came up with this crazy story about me killing Andrew."

Kent nodded, frowning in thought. "That makes sense. I suppose the child might have died, or perhaps even been stillborn. Such a horrible experience could make the woman even more bitter and vindictive."

"I suppose so. I've never had children, so I wouldn't know. But that would explain a lot, and so would what you said about Becky being the one who really killed Andrew."

"There's no proof of that, mind," Kent pointed out.

"No, but that would explain why Andrew—" Simone stopped, unsure whether she should go ahead or not. She had risked telling Kent the truth about Becky Lewis's visit, but should she say anything about the other matter that was troubling her? How much had Kent heard when he came into the parlor?

Simone came to the same conclusion she had always reached with every other problem that confronted her in her life: Bold steps were always the best.

"What were you saying, Simone?" Kent asked gently.

She took a deep breath again. "If Becky Lewis really killed my husband, instead of Durand, that would explain why Andrew's ghost has begun appearing to me."

There. She had said it. And once again Kent looked confused and gravely concerned.

"Andrew's . . . ghost?" he repeated.

Simone nodded. "That's right." Her voice grew stronger as she went on, "I've seen him twice now."

"And has this . . . ghost . . . talked to you?"

"He told me that William Durand didn't kill him. He asked me to find out who the real killer was. He said that he couldn't pass on to where . . . to where he was supposed to be until justice had been done."

Kent put his hands on her shoulders. "You're certain about this?" he asked solemnly.

Simone felt a flash of anger and pulled away from him. "You think I've lost my mind!" she accused.

"No, not at all. But I know how much of a strain you've been under—"

"No, Judson, this was real. I know it was. Andrew was right here in this room, and I talked to him. Think about it! If Becky Lewis killed him, it would explain everything!"

"Well . . . I suppose you have a point there. But it's very difficult for me to believe in . . . in spiritual apparitions!"

"I won't argue with you about that. You can believe whatever you want to about that part of it. The important thing is that I think you're right about that whore, Judson. She killed my husband!"

Kent winced a little, and Simone supposed it was because he wasn't accustomed to hearing such coarse language from her. He wouldn't think anything of it, though, knowing how upset she was at the moment.

"There's something else to consider," Kent said after a few seconds of silence. "If Miss Lewis's accusations against you became public knowledge right now, they could damage your bid for election a great deal."

Simone nodded slowly. "You're right. I wonder if that's why she showed up now. Maybe she thought it would be easier to blackmail me because I have more to lose." She began to pace back and forth agitatedly. "What am I going to do, Judson? I can keep paying her off, but she said she was going to want more than money. What could she have meant by that?"

"I'm sure I don't know," Kent said. "But I'm going to try to figure it out, and I'm going to find a way out of this mess for you, Simone."

She stopped pacing and smiled up at him. "You'd do that for me? You'd help me again?"

"Of course. It's the very least I can do."

"You are the sweetest man, Doctor." Acting on impulse, Simone stepped closer to him. She put a hand on his arm and came up on her toes. Kent didn't pull back. Simone closed her eyes and parted her lips a little.

His mouth came down on hers, just as she expected.

Night had settled down completely over Wind River, and a light evening breeze had sprung up, tugging at Cole Tyler's long brown hair as he walked down Sweetwater Street. The land office had been closed when he went by there, and a quick stop at the Territorial House had told him that Simone wasn't there, either. Michael Hatfield at the *Sentinel* had said that he hadn't seen Simone all day. That pretty much left just the big house at the end of Sweetwater Street.

Cole had stopped by Judson Kent's a little earlier to check on Jeremiah. The doctor hadn't been there, but Jeremiah had answered Cole's hail and told him to come on back to the bedroom. The big blacksmith was propped up on some pillows, his Bible open on his lap in front of him. He had grinned at Cole, assured the marshal he was feeling better with every passing hour, and asked if Cole knew when Dr. Kent would be bringing him some supper. Cole had pleaded ignorance of that with a grin, adding, "If I see Judson, I'll tell him you're hungry enough to eat a bear."

"Not a bear," Jeremiah said, "but maybe a side of beef."

Cole hadn't run into the British physician on his way around town, either, but he didn't think anything of that. Kent could be most anywhere around Wind River, even though it was getting on toward suppertime. Sick folks didn't keep a regular schedule.

He wanted to see Simone for a couple of reasons. For one thing, he wanted to let her know that Jeremiah was doing all right; Cole knew she had been worried about the big man. For another, he wanted to find out if she had

had any more trouble with Hank Parker, or anybody she suspected of working for Parker. Cole planned to keep a close eye on that situation, still convinced that Parker would make a mistake sooner or later that would allow the law to move against him. Cole hated the feeling of futility that had begun to settle on him lately.

So Cole allowed his steps to take him toward Simone's house. He could come up with all the excuses he wanted, but deep down he knew he was looking for Simone simply because he wanted to see her. He wanted to make one more attempt at figuring out whether the future held any possibilities for the two of them or not. The way he had been feeling about Rose Foster lately, he wasn't sure of anything anymore.

He opened the gate in the picket fence that ran around the big yard in front of the mansion. It moved silently on its hinges. The handyman who worked part of the time for Simone did a good job of keeping the gate oiled. Cole went up the walk and stepped onto the porch, moving with the habitual quiet grace of a seasoned frontiersman.

A lamp was lit in the parlor, and the curtains over the window stood partially open. Movement through that gap caught Cole's eye. Without meaning to be sneaky about it, Cole glanced in that direction, as anybody would have under the circumstances.

He saw Simone—in the arms of Judson Kent.

He saw Kent kissing her, saw the way the doctor's arms went around her, saw the way Simone embraced him in turn. Cole stood there for a long moment, his feet seemingly rooted to the planks of the porch.

Then, with a sigh too soft to be heard, he turned and walked away, as quietly as he had come.

The evening's festivities hadn't really gotten started yet
when Hank Parker heard the faint tapping sound on the
glass of the window behind him. He was in his office at the
Pronghorn, but the door into the main room of the saloon
was open. Parker could see a lot of the room and hear the
music and laughter. It would be a lot louder in an hour or
so, once the patrons had had time to do some serious
drinking. This was just the prelude, he had been thinking,
remembering the word that had been used by a whore he
had known back in Council Bluffs who had been convinced that one day she would be a famous opera singer.
She had died not long after Parker met her, a knife stuck
between her ribs by a customer who didn't want to pay.

He put all of that out of his mind as soon as he heard
the insistent little noise and turned around to see Becky
Lewis peering through the glass at him. He made a gesture at her to wait, then stood up and closed the office
door. Once he had shot the bolt so that they wouldn't be
disturbed, he went to the window and slid the pane up.

"Come on," he said, extending his hand toward Becky.

"What do you expect me to do, climb in through the window?" she asked irritably. "It's bad enough you've got me sneakin' around this alley back here. I might've stepped on something sharp in the dark. I already stepped on *something*, but I ain't sure what it is. Sure smells bad, though."

Once a low-class whore, always a low-class whore, Parker thought, but he kept the reaction to himself. He said firmly, "Take hold of my hand. It won't be hard to climb in."

"Oh, all right," Becky groused. She grasped his hand, his big fingers practically swallowing up her smaller ones, then took hold of his wrist with her other hand. He hauled her up and through the window like she didn't weigh much of anything. When she was inside the office, she looked at the sole of one of her high-buttoned shoes and made a face.

Parker said, "I told you why we have to be careful. I don't want folks connecting up the two of us just yet. Bud's the only one who really noticed you coming here the other night, and he's not going to say anything if he knows what's good for him—and take my word for it, he does."

"You're ashamed of me, that's what it is," sniffed Becky.

"You know damned well that's *not* it. But that son of a bitch lawman Tyler is just biding his time, watching me and waiting for a chance to nail me on something. I don't intend to give him that chance."

"The McKay woman can't accuse me of blackmailin' her without sayin' what I'm blackmailin' her about."

"Maybe not, but I don't trust her, nor Tyler either. Just do what I tell you, Becky, and everything will be all right."

"Yeah, I guess." She sat down in the chair in front of the desk, flouncing her long skirt around her ankles.

Parker leaned forward, his knuckles on the desk. "You went to see Mrs. McKay this evening, like I told you?"

"Of course. Did you think I couldn't handle it?"

"What did you tell her?" Parker asked sharply.

"Just what we agreed on. I hinted around that I knew what she had done, killin' her husband and all on that railroad station platform. She gave me this." Becky's hand delved into the bosom of her dress and came out with a roll of greenbacks. She started to toss the money onto Parker's desk, then hesitated. "I reckon you want this?"

Parker surprised her by shaking his head. "You can keep it. There's a lot more than that just waiting out there for the taking."

"I suppose so." Becky tucked the money away in her dress again.

"How did Mrs. McKay react when you started hinting?"

"Well, she didn't break down and admit that she done it, if that's what you mean." Becky grinned. "But I could tell she was worried. She's guilty, sure enough."

Parker grunted. He wasn't convinced of that, but he didn't much care one way or the other. It didn't matter to him who had killed Andrew McKay. All that was important was that Simone had been willing to pay hush money to a whore. *That* was what he would use against her.

That and one other thing . . .

"What do I do now?" asked Becky, breaking into the pleasant fantasy that had filled Parker's head. "You want me to keep lyin' low?"

He nodded. "That's right. You can wait in here until later, then when nobody's paying any attention I'll sneak you upstairs to my room. I've got some more work for you to do, but not until tomorrow."

Becky stood up and sidled over to him, trying to look seductive. It was a pretty pathetic attempt, but Parker didn't tell her that. "We goin' to have some fun again tonight?" she asked.

He put his arm around her waist and pulled her against him. "What do you think?"

"I think I'm mighty glad I came back to Wind River, Mr. Parker. Mighty glad."

So was he. Not because he got any great pleasure out of bedding a worn-out soiled dove like as Becky. Being the thousandth man to do that didn't mean much of anything.

Hank Parker was more interested in being first, and in only a few days now, he was going to achieve that goal.

He was going to be the first mayor of Wind River, and Simone McKay was going to be damned sorry she had ever decided to run for the office.

Michael Hatfield was whistling as he set type. He wasn't much of a whistler, but he tried to carry a tune as best he could. For some reason, it helped him concentrate on the delicate task he was carrying out. And it made him seem more Western, too, he thought. Back in Cincinnati he had never whistled much, but out here it seemed as though everybody did. Besides, he was in a good mood. The election was less than a week off . . . the election that might never have taken place if it hadn't been for him and his editorials in the *Sentinel*. He liked to think that he had done his part to nudge Wind River down the path that led to civilization.

But then his good mood disappeared completely when the little bell over the front door of the newspaper office jingled and he looked up to see Hank Parker coming in.

Parker wasn't whistling, but he looked mighty pleased with himself. There was a smirk on his heavy features. He said, "Good morning, Hatfield. Beautiful day, isn't it?"

Michael's suspicions deepened. If Parker was this cheerful, something had to be really wrong. "What do you want, Parker?" Michael asked, not bothering to conceal his dislike for the man.

If Parker noticed the hostile tone in Michael's voice, he gave no indication of it. He said, "You've been pretty outspoken in your support of Mrs. McKay for mayor." Parker held up a hand as Michael started to say something. "No, let me finish. You've got every right to support Mrs. McKay and to say so in your newspaper. Or should I say, *her* newspaper. She does own the *Sentinel*, after all."

"Mrs. McKay gives me a free hand," Michael said stiffly. "She's never told me what to write or which causes to support."

"Well, that's mighty admirable. You pride yourself on being fair, don't you?"

"A journalist has to be objective," Michael said.

"That's why I'm bringing you this story." Parker took a cigar out of his vest pocket and rolled it between his fingers as he went on, "I figure you'll print the truth. And the truth is that Simone McKay killed her husband, Andrew, murdered him in cold blood."

Following that pronouncement, Parker calmly put the cigar in his mouth while Michael stared at him, thunderstruck. For a long moment Michael was unable to say anything. When he could finally speak again, he came to his feet and said, "That . . . that's insane! You'd better get out of here, Parker, before I go find Marshal Tyler and tell him you're spreading scurrilous lies about Mrs. McKay!"

"You mean you're not even willing to listen? What kind of newspaperman are you, Hatfield?"

"The kind who knows a lunatic when I see one!" Michael knew he was treading on dangerous ground. Parker was well known for his short temper and violent tendencies. But Michael didn't care about that right now. He was too outraged by what Parker had said to be scared.

Parker just grinned and said around the cigar, "I can prove it."

The saloonkeeper's calm, confident demeanor took Michael by surprise. This wasn't the same blustery blowhard he had known for more than a year. He had never seen Parker quite so sure of himself.

Parker must have seen that reaction on Michael's face, because he asked, still grinning, "Want to hear about it?"

"Go ahead," Michael said cautiously, hoping he wasn't making a mistake.

Without being asked, Parker pulled a straight chair over in front of Michael's desk and sat down. Michael resumed his own seat behind the desk. Parker leaned back and said, "You were there that day at the railroad station. You know how much confusion there was on the platform when that fight broke out. What would you say if I told you there was a witness who saw Simone McKay slip a gun out of her bag, shoot her husband, put the gun away, and then start faking hysterics?"

"I'd say whoever claims to have seen that is lying," Michael said flatly. "And this so-called witness can't be you, Parker. You were still on the train that had just pulled in."

"Never said it was me who saw it."

"And the unsupported word of one witness doesn't mean anything, either."

"Maybe not." Parker was still unruffled. "But it would mean something if Simone McKay was paying this witness to keep quiet about the whole thing."

Michael felt a tingle of foreboding, but he tried not to let Parker see it. "You're saying that Mrs. McKay is being blackmailed?"

"That's what I hear," Parker replied smugly.

"You're admitting to blackmailing her?"

"How could I blackmail anybody?" Parker asked, his voice bland. "Like you said, I was still on the train. I didn't see a thing. But if you were to go up to that burned-out church tonight, *you* might see something, Hatfield."

Michael blinked in confusion. "What's the church got to do with anything?"

"Mrs. McKay and the blackmailer will be getting together there. If you're lucky, you'll hear the whole thing for yourself."

"How can you be so sure of that?" Michael asked quickly. "What's your part in all this, Parker?"

The visitor shrugged. "I'm a saloonkeeper. I hear things. And I figure it's my duty as a citizen of Wind River, as well as a candidate for mayor, to bring out the truth. That's why I'm here talking to you. Hell, maybe there's nothing to it. Maybe it's all a pack of lies. Either way, it's your job to find out the truth and print it, right?"

Reluctantly, Michael nodded. What Parker said had some validity. If there was a rumor going around that the settlement's leading citizen was guilty of a crime, that had to be investigated, whether Michael believed the story could be true or not. The rumor itself was newsworthy.

Besides, Michael thought, if the rumor was false—which he had no doubt it was—then he could make sure in his reporting of the story that Hank Parker looked bad for spreading it. Parker wanted to ruin Simone's campaign; that was the only reason he was here, despite any high-flown statements about finding out the truth. His little plan was liable to backfire on him, though, Michael decided.

"What time is this meeting at the church?" he asked.

"An hour after dark is what I've heard."

"I'll be there," Michael said.

"You'd better be quiet and stay in the shadows," cautioned Parker. "If they know you're there, you'll scare them off."

"I'll be careful."

Parker stood up, still looking pleased with himself. He pointed the cigar at Michael and said, "You'll be thanking me when this is all over, Hatfield. You'll be the best-known newspaperman in the whole territory."

"We'll see," Michael said. He couldn't imagine ever thanking Hank Parker for anything.

"Just print the truth. That's all I ask." Parker turned and left the newspaper office.

He'd print the truth, all right, Michael told himself. But Parker might not like that truth. This was one time the man's schemes weren't going to work. . . .

Simone was still so shaken by Becky Lewis's visit to her the night before that she stayed home all day, not even going to the land office. That must have taken the housekeeper by surprise, but the woman knew better than to say anything. She had seen Simone take spells like this before. Simone didn't come out of her bedroom until the middle of the day, showed little appetite, and spent most of the afternoon in the parlor, sipping brandy. Her mood was decidedly gloomy, and she brightened up only when, late that afternoon, the housekeeper stepped into the arched entrance between the foyer and the parlor and said, "There's a visitor to see you, ma'am."

A smile appeared on Simone's face as she looked up from where she sat in an overstuffed armchair. Perhaps Judson Kent had thought of some way to deal with the problems plaguing her. She said, "If it's Dr. Kent, show him right in."

"That's just it, ma'am. The caller isn't Dr. Kent."

"Marshal Tyler?"

"No, ma'am. It's . . . well . . . "

"For God's sake," Becky Lewis said as she brushed past the older woman, "just let me in. Mrs. McKay knows who I am."

Simone came to her feet, anger flooding through her. "What are you doing here?" she demanded coldly.

"We have to talk," Becky said. She looked at the housekeeper. "Alone."

Simone hesitated, then nodded curtly to the woman. "It's all right. I'll speak with this . . . lady."

"You're sure, Mrs. McKay?" asked the housekeeper.

"I'm certain. Leave us alone."

The housekeeper withdrew, and Simone waited until she heard the door into the kitchen being closed before she said to Becky, "How dare you come here in the open like this?"

Becky shrugged carelessly. "Things have changed. You and I have got to have another meeting."

"Well, you're here now," Simone said with an exasperated sigh. "Whatever you've got to say, you might as well go ahead and say it."

To Simone's surprise, Becky shook her head. "Not here. I don't trust that old bat. She could be eavesdropping."

"I'm sure she's not."

"I don't care. We're going to meet somewhere else tonight, where nobody can horn in on what we've got to say."

"I don't have anything to say to you," Simone replied coldly.

"That's where you're wrong. We're going to talk about what you did."

"I suppose you want more money. You went through that last payment awfully quickly, didn't you?"

Becky shook her head again. "It's not about money this time, Mrs. McKay. I told you I might want something else besides cash."

"Well, what is it?" snapped Simone.

"Not yet. Tonight, an hour after dark. Up there on the knoll, at what's left of that church that burned up."

Once again Simone was surprised. "Why there?"

"Because I say so, that's why!" Becky's voice crackled with spitefulness.

With an effort, Simone controlled her own temper and managed to nod calmly. Becky's mind was obviously none too stable, and it would probably be best to humor her, at least for the time being. But for her own sake, Becky would do well not to push this thing too far . . .

"All right, I'll be there," Simone said. "An hour after dark. And you don't want money?"

"Oh, if you want to bring along some greenbacks, I reckon it would be all right. But that's not the main thing. I'll tell you what to do when you get there."

Although every fiber of her being resented being ordered around this way, especially by a whore such as Becky Lewis, Simone nodded again. She wondered if she ought to tell Judson Kent about this, so that he could follow Becky when she left the rendezvous and see where she went. Simone suspected that someone had put Becky up to the blackmail, and the logical suspect to have done that was Hank Parker.

"One more thing," Becky said, as if reading the other woman's mind. "Don't tell anybody about this. Not a soul. If you do, the whole deal's off and I start yelling at the top of my lungs about everything I know."

Simone nodded again. She supposed it wouldn't hurt anything to go to the meeting alone. She wasn't afraid of Becky. If there was trouble, Simone was confident she could handle the younger woman. In fact, that might be the best way out of this mess. . . .

"An hour after dark," Becky said again, then turned to leave.

"I'll be there," Simone said as she followed Becky through the foyer and then shut the door behind her. She added softly to herself, "Oh, yes, I can promise you I'll be there."

Michael was distracted at dinner that evening, and his wife noticed his mood. "What's wrong, Michael?" Delia asked.

He shook his head and replied, "Nothing. I've just got some newspaper business on my mind."

"When *aren't* you thinking about that newspaper?" Delia's voice was touched lightly with resentment. She was feeding the baby some mashed-up sweet potatoes, and Lincoln was swallowing them hungrily. The boy had a good appetite, Michael thought, and he was growing awfully fast. He was going to be walking soon.

Michael looked across the table at his daughter. Gretchen had a mischievous look in her eyes as she ate, which was nothing unusual. She was probably thinking about what sort of trouble she could get into next. Michael felt a tightness in his chest as he looked at his family. It was a warm sensation, if a bit frightening. He loved them all so much. His children were the light of his life, and even though Delia still missed Cincinnati and halfway wished they could return there, she and Michael had grown closer in recent months . . . since he had come all too close to betraying her with another woman. He had learned his lesson, and he would never let anything come between him and his family again.

But he had a responsibility to the newspaper, and to Simone McKay, too. He wasn't going to let her or the *Sentinel* down. That was why he had to go out tonight, whether Delia understood or not.

Finished with his meal, he pushed his plate back. "I have to go back down to the office for a while," he said.

"Why?" Delia asked with a frown. "It's three days until the next edition."

"I know. There's just some work I have to catch up on." He couldn't bring himself to tell her that he was going to go skulking around up there at the burned-out church so that he could spy on a meeting between Simone and some mysterious blackmailer.

"Can't it wait?"

Michael shook his head. "I'm afraid not."

"All right, then." Delia managed to smile, although he could tell the expression was a reluctant one. "Will you be back in time to read a bedtime story to Gretchen?"

"I don't know," he replied honestly.

"Read now!" Gretchen suggested enthusiastically.

Michael glanced out the kitchen window and saw that the light of dusk was still fading outside. It would be a while yet until the meeting took place—if indeed there even *was* a meeting, which he still doubted. He smiled at his daughter and nodded. "We'll read now," he told Gretchen. She was finished with her food, too, so she got up from the table and ran off to find the storybook.

All those stories had happy endings, Michael thought as he stood up and followed her.

He hoped the one he was living did, too.

• • •

Simone adjusted her hat and studied her reflection in the mirror above her dressing table. It was purely an automatic gesture on her part, because she didn't really care how she looked tonight. Why should she take any great pains with her appearance? she asked herself. All she was doing was going to the ruins of a burned-out church to talk to a blackmailing slut.

Suddenly she felt another presence. She stiffened in the chair and looked in the mirror, expecting to see someone standing behind her. There was no one there. Simone closed her eyes and breathed deeply a couple of times. She had to get hold of herself. She had to be thinking clearly, tonight of all nights.

She stood up and turned around.

Andrew gazed mournfully at her.

Simone gasped and took an involuntary step back, knocking over the chair in front of the dressing table as she did so. She pressed a hand against the bosom of her dress and said, "Andrew! You . . . you startled me."

Unlike the other times he had appeared to her, he didn't say anything. He just stood there a few feet away, a solemn look on his face, and stared at her.

"What . . . what do you want?" she asked, expecting him to say something again about finding his killer. Instead there was no reply. Silence hung over the room.

Simone's heart began to pound in her chest, and she could hear the beat hammering inside her head. "Why are you doing this?" she demanded. An unreasonable anger welled up inside her. "Why don't you just go away? You're dead. You ought to just go away!"

She caught herself, aware that her voice was rising hysterically. Forcing herself to be calm, she said, "I think I'm imagining you, Andrew. I think Judson Kent was right. I've been under such a strain that I've started seeing things." She drew herself up and squared her shoulders. "So maybe I'm crazy for even talking to you, but you might as well get out of my way. I have places to go and things to do."

With that, she strode forward, straight toward him. He shredded before her, like fog blowing away in a high wind, and she felt only a touch of lingering coldness as she passed through the place where he had been. She opened the door and strode out of the room.

If she could deal with a ghost, she could certainly deal with a dim-witted trollop such as Becky Lewis, Simone told herself. Before this night was over, Becky was going to be very sorry she had ever come back to Wind River.

Cole Tyler and Billy Casebolt walked along Grenville Avenue. It was too early to make the evening rounds; the first stars were just coming out in the sky overhead. So for the time being, the two lawmen were just enjoying the early evening as the heat of the day faded and a breeze sprang up.

"Goin' to be a nice night," Casebolt said.

"I hope so, but I'm not so sure," replied Cole. He nodded toward the west. "There are some clouds moving in. Might get a little shower before morning."

"Wouldn't hurt nothin' if we did. We could use a little rain. Been a pretty dry summer so far."

Cole nodded. In this part of the country, not far from the arid Great Basin, rain was a precious commodity. Many of the streams in the area relied almost as much on the annual snowmelt as they did on rainfall.

A flicker of lightning, far off in the distance, caught

Cole's eye. Might be just heat lightning, he thought. Might not mean a thing.

Just like it didn't have to mean anything that he had seen Simone and Judson Kent in each other's arms the night before, embracing like they were the only two people in the world. Cole had carried that image around in his head all day. But it didn't have to mean anything. Sure, it might be just as insubstantial as that distant lightning.

Only time would tell.

Jeremiah Newton said impatiently, "When can I get up out of this bed and get out of here? I've got things to do, a church to rebuild."

"Not just yet," Judson Kent replied as he placed the tray of food in front of the big blacksmith. "I think you'll probably be recovered enough from your injuries to go home tomorrow, but I don't want you doing any work yet. That means no hammering in that shop of yours, and no work on the church."

"The blacksmithing work will wait, but the Lord's won't," Jeremiah said with a scowl.

"I won't presume to speak for the Creator, but I doubt that He wants you to collapse from your head injuries or rebreak that arm before it mends properly." Kent smiled. "Be patient, Jeremiah. I know it's difficult, but I assure you, it's for the best. You'll be back on your feet and working to rebuild the church before you know it."

"Well, all right," Jeremiah said with a sigh. He turned his attention to the food on the tray and perked up visibly as he saw the pile of pork chops, the bowl of beans, and the biscuits that Rose Foster and Monty Riordan had sent over from the cafe.

Kent left Jeremiah to the meal and went back to his office. He sat down behind his desk and sighed. He had already eaten at the cafe before bringing the tray back here to his house, but he hadn't really tasted the food. He was as distracted as he had been all day, his mind full of the problem that Simone McKay faced.

Was it possible that Simone was losing her mind? All that talk of ghosts seemed to indicate as much. But Kent knew all too well how the mind could play tricks on a person, especially in times of great worry. Whether the ghost of Andrew McKay had really appeared to his wife—and Kent, rational physician that he was, had a difficult time believing that—Simone had a real problem that was even more pressing. Becky Lewis, and the ridiculous but still vicious blackmail threat she represented.

Kent wondered if he should tell Cole Tyler that Becky was back in town and causing trouble for Simone. Cole was the only one with whom Kent had shared his suspicions about Becky being responsible for Andrew McKay's death. Perhaps he and Cole ought to pay a call on Miss Lewis and warn her that if she persisted in her efforts to embarrass Simone, she herself would be investigated as a possible murderess. That might be enough to scare her off, Kent mused.

But it might not be. Kent remembered Becky as not very bright but possessed of an animal-like cunning, a survival instinct that meant she would react ruthlessly if anyone crossed her. If she was pushed, she might do her best to ruin Simone and take her chances with anyone who came after her.

It was a dilemma, and so far Kent had not been able to see a good way out of it. Perhaps he ought to go visit Simone anyway, he thought, just to make sure that she was bearing up all right under the strain. He looked up at the human skeleton that hung from a rack behind the desk and asked, "What do you think I should do, Reginald?"

There was no answer, of course, just a mocking grin from the skull. Kent sighed, stood up, and took his hat and coat off the pegs beside the door. He called out to Jeremiah that he would be back in a little while, then went out into the evening and turned his steps toward Sweetwater Street.

The usual evening breeze had turned into a wind by the time Michael began walking up the knoll toward the shell of the destroyed church. Full darkness had fallen some time earlier, and the night promised to be even blacker than usual because clouds had moved in from the west and obscured some of the stars. As Michael glanced overhead he saw even more of the pinpoints of light being gobbled up by the quickly moving clouds. He had to use one hand to hold his hat on his head.

He was probably wasting his time, he told himself. Hank Parker had just been blowing smoke about Simone paying off some blackmailer to keep quiet about her murdering her husband. The very idea of a lady such as Simone being a killer was laughable. Or at least it would have been, Michael thought, if it hadn't been so outrageous. He was angry that Parker would even attempt to spread such a scandalous rumor.

As he drew near the top of the slope, Michael's eyes searched around the skeletal framework of the burned-out church. Suddenly he spotted something that looked out of place. Stopping in his tracks, he narrowed his eyes and peered intently through the gloom.

The shape he had seen near the ruins of the building was a buggy, he realized. A small buggy with a single horse hitched to it.

The kind of buggy that Simone McKay drove.

Michael gave a little shake of his head. Just because somebody was up here didn't mean it was Simone. Maybe Parker had brought the buggy up here. Maybe this was all part of the saloonkeeper's scheme to make Simone look bad so that he could win the election.

That was what Michael was telling himself when he heard the scream.

The frightened cry came from inside the ruins of the church. It was a woman's scream, Michael realized as he broke into a run, but it hadn't sounded like Simone's voice. Of course, it was hard to tell about a scream. Without really thinking about what he was doing, he rushed forward and vaulted over a pile of rubble and ashes. He wished there were more light so he could see where he was going. Frantic motion caught his eye. A vague shape was moving around in the center of the church—no, it was two shapes, Michael realized. And they were struggling . . .

Michael saw the figures only for an instant, just long enough for something strange about them to register vaguely on his brain, then his foot slipped on something and he fell, landing hard on the charred planks of the floor. Splinters gouged painfully into the palms of his hands. Michael tried to scramble to his feet, slipped again, and fell once more. Several seconds passed while he clambered upright again, searching for more secure footing in the ruins.

"Oh, God!" a woman said.

And this time Michael was sure that the voice did belong to Simone McKay.

"Mrs. McKay!" he shouted as he hurried forward. "Mrs. McKay, are you all right?"

"Michael?" Simone's voice sounded strange, all stretched and out of shape, but definitely hers. "My God, Michael, is that you?"

Panting from the exertion, Michael came closer to her. He could barely see her in the gloom, but he could tell now that she was alone. That didn't make sense. He was sure he had seen two people. He fumbled a match out of his pocket as he came up to Simone and said, "It's just me, Mrs. McKay. What's going on h—"

He was scratching the lucifer into life as he asked the question. The words froze in his throat as the match flared and spread its glow in a rough circle. By the light of the match, he saw Simone standing there, a small hand-bag clutched tightly in her hands, a horrified look on her face. There were sooty smudges on her dress and shoes from climbing through the rubble of the church. She was staring down at the ground in front of her, and Michael followed her gaze with his own eyes.

A young woman lay there on her back in the ruins, staring sightlessly into the night. The fingers of one hand were wrapped loosely around the hilt of the knife that protruded from her breast. A crimson stain spread slowly on the cheap dress around the blade of the knife.

She was dead. Michael knew that without even checking.

And from the looks of things, Simone McKay had killed her.

Simone suddenly reached toward Michael, her fingers digging painfully into his arm as her hand gripped him. She said, "Is . . . is she . . . "

"I'm pretty sure she's dead," Michael replied, his own voice wavering. "I . . . I guess I'd better make certain."

Reluctantly he sank to one knee beside the body and

reached out with his free hand, checking for a pulse in the young woman's neck. He didn't find one, just as he had expected. When he held his hand in front of her open mouth, there was no warm breath to be felt. She was gone, all right.

Michael looked up at Simone and shook his head. "I'm sorry. Who . . . who was she? Did you know her?"

He was afraid he already knew the answer to at least one of those questions. This young woman had to be the blackmailer, the person Simone had come here to meet.

Before Simone could answer, the forgotten match burned down to Michael's fingers and made him yelp in pain. He dropped the match, which flared out and allowed darkness to plunge down again. He was reaching for another one when both he and Simone heard the rapid hoofbeats of an approaching horse. Michael had no idea who could be galloping up the knoll, but after what he had already seen this evening, he didn't think anything would surprise him now.

Michael came to his feet, and both he and Simone swung away from the body and toward the sound of the horse. A moment later Michael saw the animal, its light-colored hide making it more visible in the darkness. The rider swung down from the saddle and called out, "Who's in there?"

Simone gasped, "Cole!"

Michael knew the lawman probably had his gun drawn and was ready for trouble, so he said loudly, "It's Michael Hatfield, Marshal! I'm going to strike a match!"

"Go ahead," Cole said as he began to make his way through the ruins of the church toward them. Ulysses, his big golden sorrel, would stay where Cole had dropped the reins.

Michael struck a second match. Cole was squinting

against the light as he came up to them, but that didn't prevent him from noticing the body right away. He nodded grimly toward the young woman and asked, "Is she dead?"

Michael nodded. "I checked for a pulse or breathing. I didn't find either one."

Just as Michael had thought, Cole's heavy .44 revolver was in his right fist. He holstered the weapon and turned to Simone. "Are you all right?"

She nodded shakily. "I'm fine."

"Billy and I heard somebody scream up here. Since Ulysses was already saddled and at the hitch rack, I thought I'd ride up and see what was wrong. I sent Billy for Dr. Kent in case somebody was hurt." Cole glanced at the body again. "Looks like Judson's going to be too late to help her. Do you know who— Wait a minute! That's Becky Lewis, isn't it?"

Michael was getting lost. He didn't know any Becky Lewis, although he had to admit that the dead woman looked a little familiar, as if she was someone he had seen before but didn't really know. Cole obviously knew her, though, and so did Simone.

"Yes," Simone said, her voice as bleak as her expression, "that's Becky Lewis."

"I didn't know she was back in town. What happened?" Cole's voice was sharp as he asked the question, and he was clearly upset.

"I don't know," Simone began, but then the sound of more people approaching the church made her fall silent.

Judson Kent's buggy rolled to a stop near the burned-out shell of the building, followed closely by Billy Casebolt on horseback. The deputy dismounted and joined the physician as they both hurried through the rubble. Casebolt was carrying an unlit lantern, Michael saw as the two men came up to join the group. He was grateful for that, because he didn't want to have to keep striking matches.

Casebolt took the match from Michael as it was about to burn down and lit the lantern with it. The circle of light widened, and Kent got his first good look at the woman on the ground. "My God, Simone!" he exclaimed. "You didn't have to—"

"What?" asked Cole as Kent stopped short. "Didn't have to what, Judson?"

"I didn't kill her, Judson," Simone said raggedly. "You've got to believe me, I didn't kill her!"

"Was this Becky Lewis the person who was trying to blackmail you, Mrs. McKay?" Michael asked.

Cole looked at him in surprise while Kent exclaimed, "Good Lord, how did you know about *that*?"

Cole's eyes turned back toward Kent. "*You* knew about this so-called blackmail?"

Billy Casebolt scratched his jaw and said, "I ain't understandin' a durned bit of this."

"Neither am I," Cole said, "but I'm damned well going to. Billy, get a blanket from Dr. Kent's buggy and cover up that woman. Then you can go back down to town and tell the undertaker to bring a wagon up here." His hard gaze swept over Simone, Kent, and Michael. "The rest of you come with me. We're going to my office and sort this out."

Simone held a hand out toward him. "You've got to believe me, Cole. I . . . I didn't have anything to do with this woman's death."

"Right now I don't know enough to believe or disbelieve anybody. Come on, all three of you."

He stepped back and motioned for them to precede him. Kent sighed and went first, then Michael, and finally Simone. Cole brought up the rear of the procession.

He had come up here to get a story, Michael thought. From the looks of things, he had gotten one, all right.

He had gotten a hell of a lot more than he had expected, more than he had ever wanted.

13

"All right, start from the beginning," Cole said as he sat down behind his desk and looked at the other three people in the marshal's office. All of them wore expressions that seemed at least a little guilty to him.

"You can't blame Simone for this, Cole," Kent said. "She's been under a great deal of pressure—"

"I can speak for myself, Judson," Simone broke in.

"Yes, of course you can, but I was simply trying—"

Once again she didn't allow him to finish. "You're trying to protect me. I know that, and I appreciate it. But it's not necessary. I haven't done anything wrong."

Cole tried to rein in the impatience he felt. They weren't getting anywhere this way. Maybe he ought to ask some specific questions, he decided.

"What about the blackmail?" he said as he looked intently at Simone. "Was Becky Lewis holding something over your head?"

"She thought she was," replied Simone. Her chin lifted defiantly. "She claimed that she saw me murder Andrew."

Cole's eyes widened in shock. That was an answer he certainly hadn't expected. His mind went back to the day he had first arrived in Wind River. He remembered the brawl that had broken out on the platform of the Union Pacific station and how the fight had been abruptly ended by the crack of a gunshot and a woman's scream . . . Simone's scream when she saw that her husband had been wounded. He recalled as well how she had come to his hotel room that night to plead with him to accept the job he had already been offered by a committee of the town's leading citizens, including Judson Kent and Michael Hatfield. Cole had turned down that proposal, but he had been unable to refuse when the grieving widow had asked him to pin on the marshal's badge and track down the person who had killed her husband.

After the showdown with William Durand, Cole had been convinced that the man was responsible for Andrew McKay's murder, but then Kent had told him about Becky Lewis's pregnancy. It was possible that Becky had killed McKay in a fit of anger when he refused to acknowledge that he was the father of her child. But by that time, Becky had left town, Durand was dead, and it had seemed best to just let the whole matter drop.

Now Becky Lewis had come back to Wind River, only to be murdered herself.

Those thoughts flashed though Cole's mind in a matter of instants, but his silence was long enough to make Simone ask worriedly, "You don't think I had anything to do with Andrew's death, do you, Cole?"

"I never did before," he replied honestly. "But if you were innocent, why were you up there meeting with the Lewis woman tonight?"

Kent didn't let Simone answer. Instead he said hotly, "Because the sheer fact that Simone was being accused of such a heinous crime would have damaged her chances in the election—which is assuredly what Hank Parker intended to do when he sent that trollop to bedevil her!"

Cole held up his hands. "Hold on there. *Parker's* mixed up in this now?"

"He came to see me this morning," Michael said. "He told me somebody was blackmailing Simone and that if I wanted to find out about it, I should be up at the church an hour after dark."

"And you believed him?" Simone asked the young newspaperman.

Michael looked extremely embarrassed, and Cole didn't blame him. Simone was his boss, after all. "I thought the whole thing was ridiculous," he said. "But I wouldn't have been doing my job if I didn't check it out."

"You could have asked me," Simone said coldly.

"I didn't want to bother you. Like I said, I never thought it would amount to anything. I was as surprised as I could be when I saw your buggy parked up there."

"What else did you see, Michael?" Cole asked quietly.

Michael glanced at Simone again, obviously reluctant to go on. Then he said, "I heard a woman scream, and I thought Mrs. McKay might be in some sort of trouble. So I started into what's left of the church, and I caught a glimpse of somebody. Two people, really."

"What were they doing?"

Michael's reply was little more than a husky whisper. "They were fighting." He hesitated, then went on, "I fell down in the ruins and had trouble getting back up, and when I did, there was only one figure still on its feet. I went over to it and struck a match and found Mrs. McKay standing there over the body."

"I . . . didn't . . . kill . . . her," Simone grated. "I found the slut there, just like Michael did."

Cole's brain was still whirling, but everything he had heard was beginning to form a pattern. He didn't like the picture, but it was undeniable. To make sure everything was straight in his mind, he looked at Simone and said, "You went up there to meet Becky Lewis because she was blackmailing you."

Simone started to say something, stopped, then nodded curtly and said, "Yes. I did."

"Had you already given her any money?"

"I paid her five hundred dollars."

"Why?"

Kent said in exasperation, "Surely you can see why, Marshal! Simone couldn't afford to have such rumors spread around town only a few days before the election!"

"Is that the only reason you paid her, Simone?"

She nodded. "Yes. I thought if I could stall her until after the election, I could deal with the problem then, perhaps offer her enough to get her to leave town again."

Cole looked at the doctor. "You knew about all this, Judson?"

"I was aware of what a strain Simone has been under, and when I saw that she needed my help, I offered it gladly." Kent's back was stiff as he replied, and his tone was none too friendly.

Cole didn't feel very friendly himself. *I'll just bet you offered to help, Judson, old boy,* he thought. *Was that before or after she kissed you?*

He shoved that unwanted image out of his mind and went on, "Did you know about this meeting tonight?"

"No," Kent answered after a second's hesitation. "I didn't."

"The Lewis woman came to see me again today," Simone said. "I hadn't seen Judson since then, so I didn't have a chance to tell him about her demand for a meeting at the church. I might not have told him anyway, even if I had seen him. This was my problem, not his."

Cole leaned back in his chair. "This looks bad for you, Simone, mighty bad. Most lawmen would have had you locked up by now."

"My God!" Kent burst out. "You can't really believe that Simone—"

"I believe what the evidence tells me," Cole said, letting some of his own anger come through at last. He looked at Simone and said, "You went to meet Becky Lewis in a deserted place. She was a threat to your election campaign. You knew about her and your husband and the baby. For all I know, you may have thought *she* killed Andrew. She winds up dead with a knife in her chest and you standing over her. What do *you* think it looks like, Simone?"

"I didn't kill her," Simone repeated. "I had just gotten there myself. I heard the scream, just like Michael. I went out into what's left of the church, and I . . . I practically tripped over her body. Then Michael came up and struck a match and I . . . I . . ." A great shudder went through her, and she lifted her hands to her face. "I shouldn't have gone up there," she said hollowly. "That's what he was trying to warn me about."

"Who?" asked Cole.

Kent leaned forward suddenly and said, "No, Simone."

She ignored the doctor. "Andrew," she said. "Andrew came to me again tonight, but he didn't say anything this time. He just looked at me so solemnly." She started up out of her chair. "He was warning me not to go to the church!"

Kent was on his feet by now, as were Cole and Michael. The physician took hold of Simone's shoulders and pulled her against him. She began to sob. Kent looked past her at Cole and said fervently, "You can see how upset she is! You've no right to treat her this way, no right at all. You can't pay attention to anything she says while she's in such a state."

Cole felt a little dizzy from everything that had happened. He had never run into anything like this when he was hunting buffalo for the Union Pacific or scouting for the army or guiding wagon trains, that was for sure. But he could see it all clearly enough to know what he had to do, whether he liked it or not.

"Simone," he said. "Simone!"

She turned her tear-streaked face toward him, even as Kent tightened his grip on her.

"You're under arrest," Cole said, "for the murder of Becky Lewis."

"No!" Kent shouted. "That's insane! You can't—"

Simone shook her head. "No, Judson. It's all right. Cole's just doing his job." She pulled away from Kent and stepped toward the desk. "Go ahead, Cole. Do what you have to do. But then do the *rest* of your job . . . find out who really killed Becky Lewis."

Once again she was pleading with him to solve a murder, Cole thought. Once again he was feeling the power of those dark eyes. But there was one vital difference.

This time he was afraid that the real killer was already under arrest.

The rainstorm Cole had halfway expected the night before had never materialized, but a storm of another sort certainly had. He was still feeling the effects of the emotional tempest that had resulted from his arrest of Simone when he stopped at the Wind River Cafe the next morning for breakfast.

"Good morning, Marshal," Rose Foster greeted him from the other side of the counter. There was an expression of concern on her pretty face. "I hope you don't mind me saying so, but you look like you had a hard night, Cole."

"Hard enough," Cole said with a nod.

"I . . . heard about Mrs. McKay," Rose said as she reached for the coffeepot and a cup. "I guess the whole town has heard about it already. That must have been difficult, having to arrest her like that."

"Yes. It was."

"I'm sorry," Rose said quickly. "You don't want to talk about it. I understand. Let me get you a stack of Monty's flapjacks—"

"It's all right, Rose," Cole told her, breaking into her apology. He smiled a little. "I reckon you're right about the whole town knowing about it, so there's no point in pretending it didn't happen."

"Maybe not, but there's no point in rehashing it, either." Rose poured the coffee.

Cole was grateful that she understood. It would have been easier to discuss the case if he knew what to think about it. But even after pondering the facts all through a long, mostly sleepless night, he still wasn't sure what to believe. It was hard to accept the idea that Simone McKay could be a killer. She had been a friend to Cole during his time in Wind River, even if things between them had never really developed the way he thought they might.

When he came right down to it, though, all he really knew about Simone was the face she had presented to the public in the past year and a half. He knew little of her background, little about the real woman behind the public figure. What was she really capable of? Cole couldn't answer that question.

The door of the cafe opened behind him, and quick footsteps approached. "Marshal Tyler!" the voice of Brenda Durand said. "I've been looking all over for you."

Cole sipped his coffee before swinging around slowly to face the young woman. As usual, Brenda didn't look happy. "Is something wrong, Miss Durand?" Cole asked.

"Is something wrong?" she repeated in an astonished tone. "My God, Marshal, I've heard all about how you arrested Simone McKay for murder last night! The woman's my business partner. I'd say something's wrong!"

Cole shook his head. "I don't see what this case has to do with your business holdings, Miss Durand."

"Simone McKay can't run the land development company and oversee the rest of our holdings from a jail cell!"

"Are you suggesting that I let her out?" Cole asked dryly, well aware that everyone else in the cafe was listening to this exchange.

"Of course not. If she killed that woman, she belongs behind bars." Brenda folded her arms across her bosom and looked intently at him. "I think I ought to be officially put in charge of the business."

Margaret Palmer came into the cafe then, breathing a bit heavily. "My goodness, Brenda, I can't keep up with you when you start rushing around like that," she complained. "What are you bothering the marshal about?"

"Your granddaughter's not bothering me, ma'am," Cole said with a polite nod to Margaret, "but she's asking me to do something that I can't do. I'm just a local lawman. I don't have any say over who runs a business or anything like that."

"Then you can't *stop* me from taking charge," Brenda pointed out. "Mrs. McKay can't do it anymore, so as an equal partner, I have every right to assume control."

"Now, I don't know—" Cole began.

"You said yourself this matter doesn't fall within your jurisdiction," Brenda said, a touch of glee creeping into her voice. He had fallen neatly into her trap, Cole realized. By declaring himself powerless to force Simone to relinquish control of the business, he had also made it impossible for him to prevent Brenda from carrying out her plans. She was smart, he had to give her that. Too damned smart.

"I think I'll go over to the jail right now and tell her not to worry, that I'll take care of everything," Brenda went on, her smile widening.

"I don't think so," Cole said. "I might not be able to interfere in business matters, but I still make the rules when it comes to the jail. And all visitors have to be cleared with me or Deputy Casebolt."

Brenda's look of self-satisfaction disappeared instantly and was replaced with an angry pout. "You can't do that."

"Yes," Cole said. "I can."

"It's all right, Marshal," Margaret said. "We'll go through the proper channels, and we won't bother poor Mrs. McKay right now."

"But Grandmother—" Brenda exclaimed.

"No, dear, Marshal Tyler is right. We'll speak to Mrs. McKay another time."

"I reckon that's a good idea," Cole said. He regarded Brenda for a moment, then continued. "Besides, I'd be a mite careful if I was you, Miss Durand. You don't want to get Mrs. McKay's hackles up any more than they already are when it hasn't even been proven that she's guilty."

"But you arrested her!"

"I didn't have any choice. The evidence indicates she might have killed Becky Lewis. But determining the actual truth is a job for a court of law—and the circuit judge won't be around for nearly two weeks yet."

Brenda looked as though she wanted to throw her hands up in exasperation. "You don't honestly think there's a chance she's innocent, do you? The way I heard it, she was found with the bloody knife practically in her hand."

Cole reined in his temper, and in a tightly controlled voice said, "I'm not going to talk about the details of the case with you, Miss Durand, but I reckon there's always a chance somebody is innocent. And I intend to give Mrs. McKay every chance to prove that she is."

"You're wasting your time," Brenda sniffed.

Margaret put a hand on her granddaughter's arm. "Come along, dear. Let's give Marshal Tyler a chance to eat his breakfast. I think we've disturbed him enough for one morning, don't you?"

"I don't think anybody in this town knows what it is to be disturbed," snapped Brenda. "But they will once *I'm* in charge. There are going to be some changes made around here."

Determinedly Margaret steered Brenda toward the door. When they were gone, Rose Foster sighed behind Cole and said, "God help us all if that little brat *does* wind up running things."

"It won't come to that," Cole said as he turned back around to face the counter.

"Are you sure?"

It was Cole's turn to sigh. "I'll tell you the truth, Rose. I'm not sure of anything except that life can get a lot more complicated than a fella ever thought it could."

Cole didn't care much for the idea of visiting the undertaking parlor right after breakfast, but he wanted to make certain Becky Lewis's body was being tended to properly.

He also wanted to pick up the knife that had been taken from her body.

Dr. Judson Kent was at the undertaker's when Cole got there. The physician was just emerging from the building, in fact. He gave Cole a chilly stare as the marshal approached, then nodded curtly. "Marshal Tyler," he said.

"Morning, Judson," Cole responded. "I hope you're not holding it against me that I had to do my job last night." He felt a little like a hypocrite as he made the statement. He had sure as blazes held it against Kent when he had spied the doctor kissing Simone a couple of nights earlier.

"If you were doing your job, Marshal," Kent said, "you'd be out trying to discover who really killed Becky Lewis. You and I both know that Simone McKay is incapable of such a violent action."

"How do we know that?" Cole asked, playing devil's advocate. "How much do we really know about her?"

"Enough," snapped Kent. "Enough to know that it's ludicrous to consider her a murder suspect."

"Don't worry, I intend to do some poking around. Just because Simone is in jail doesn't mean I'm going to stop investigating. In fact, I came over here this morning to get the knife that was stuck in the Lewis girl. Maybe it can tell us something."

Kent looked a bit uncomfortable. He stood there stiffly for a moment, pushing his lips in and out, then snorted and said, "I have the knife. I was going to bring it over to your office."

Cole had to wonder if Kent was telling the truth. Maybe what he had really intended was to switch the knife with another one, especially if there was something about the weapon to connect it to Simone. Cole was glad he had gotten there when he did. He held out his hand and said, "You can go ahead and give it to me now."

Kent hesitated, obviously reluctant to turn over the knife. Then he reached inside his coat and took out a small object wrapped in a handkerchief. Cole took it from him and unwrapped it.

This was the first good look he had gotten at the murder weapon. It was a perfectly ordinary kitchen knife with a blade about six inches long and a wooden handle with a decorative design carved into it. There was something familiar about it, Cole realized as he studied it. He frowned and said, "This reminds me of something . . . like I've seen one just like it before."

"You have," Kent said heavily. "You'll recognize it sooner or later, I expect, so there's no point in concealing its origin from you."

Cole snapped the fingers of his free hand. "The hotel," he said. "This is just like the knives they use in the kitchen and dining room of the Territorial House. Hell, it *is* one of those knives."

Kent nodded. "Yes, it is indeed. I recognized it, too."

"And Simone owns the hotel. She's in and out of there all the time."

"Yes, and it would have been quite easy for her to take one of the knives from the dining room," Kent said angrily. "But there are scores of other people who pass through that establishment. There are travelers, and there are people from here in Wind River who eat regularly in the dining room. Any one of them could have taken that knife just as easily."

"Maybe so, but you've got to admit this is one more thing that points at Simone."

"I don't admit any such thing—" Kent began, then stopped and looked past Cole along the boardwalk.

Cole turned and followed the doctor's gaze. He saw Michael Hatfield coming toward them, carrying a stack of newspapers. The young journalist wore a glum expression.

"What's wrong, Michael?" Cole asked. "I thought the next edition of the paper didn't come out until after the election."

"I had to print an extra," Michael replied. "Wind River's first one. I thought it would be exciting, but . . . it wasn't." He held up one of the papers so that Cole and Kent could see the headlines.

MRS. MCKAY ARRESTED, the largest one read. MAYORAL CANDIDATE WITHDRAWS FROM ELECTION was underneath in smaller type.

Cole reached out to take the paper. "What the hell—?"

Kent took one of the newspapers from Michael as well. "She can't do that!" he exclaimed. "The election is day after tomorrow!"

"She's done it," Michael said. "I got a message from the jail that she wanted to talk to me early this morning, before sunup. I went over there, and Deputy Casebolt let me talk to Mrs. McKay. She said she was quitting the race for mayor and told me to print a single-sheet extra to cover the story."

"She's given up," Kent said hollowly. "By God, I never thought Simone McKay had any quit in her!"

"I guess she figured that it was better for the town this way," Cole said, his voice quiet.

"Better?" repeated Kent. "How? Without Simone in the race, Hank Parker will be running unopposed. He'll win!"

"Yep, I reckon so. But if Simone had stayed in and won, Wind River's mayor would be in jail facing murder charges. It'll be at least two weeks before Judge Sharp comes through here to hold court, maybe longer."

"The town could have survived two weeks with its mayor in jail," Kent said in disgust. "This . . . this is outrageous! I'm going to go over to that jail and have a talk with her!"

"You're welcome to try," Michael said. "I already did my best to change Mrs. McKay's mind, and it didn't get me anywhere. Maybe you'll have better luck, Dr. Kent."

Kent crumpled the single sheet of newsprint in his hand, not even seeing the pained look that crossed Michael's face as he did so. "For the sake of this town, I had better convince her," he said, then turned on his heel and strode off toward the marshal's office and jail.

"What do you think, Marshal?" Michael asked Cole. "Did Mrs. McKay do the right thing?"

"I don't know. I wish I did."

Cole looked down at the newspaper in his hand, but he wasn't really seeing the words any longer. He was thinking about what Wind River would be like with Hank Parker as the mayor and Brenda Durand running just about everything else. He had faced a lot of dangerous situations in his time, but that prospect was downright scary.

It was time for him to get busy. If Simone was innocent—and now he hoped more than ever that she was—then Cole still had himself a killer to catch.

14

It was early afternoon when Cole ambled into the Pronghorn Saloon. Hank Parker wasn't there, which was exactly the way Cole wanted it. He had been keeping an eye on the place for the past couple of hours, waiting for Parker to leave. Finally the burly saloonkeeper had emerged from the building and headed toward the general store. Cole waited until Parker went inside the emporium before starting down the street to the Pronghorn.

The saloon was fairly busy, considering the time of day. Some railroad workers were clustered around one of the poker tables. Four cowboys from one of the outlying ranches were at one end of the bar, laughing and talking and buying watered-down drinks for a couple of tired-eyed percentage girls. Two more men, prospectors from the looks of them, nursed beers at the other end of the bar. Only one bartender was on duty at the moment, a man Cole vaguely recognized. After a moment of thought, he recalled that the bartender's name was Bud.

The talk in the room died down a little at Cole's

entrance, but it resumed its normal level by the time the marshal reached the bar. Evidently nobody in here had any reason to worry about the presence of the law.

At least, none of the customers did. Bud was frowning as Cole came up and put his left hand on the hardwood. Cole nodded to the bartender and said, "Howdy."

"Mr. Parker ain't here," Bud answered without being asked. "He'll be back in a little while."

Cole shrugged and shook his head. "Don't make any never-mind to me if Parker's here or not. I didn't come to talk to him. I just want to buy a beer. Hot and dry out there today."

Bud's frown deepened. "I always thought you did your drinking somewheres else, Marshal."

"Your boss is always bragging about how the Pronghorn has the coldest beer in Wind River," Cole said with a grin. "Thought I'd give it a try and see if he's lying."

Bud picked up a glass from a tray on the backbar and began drawing the beer. "Mr. Parker don't lie about nothing," he said.

"Is that a fact?" Cole picked up the glass the bartender placed in front of him, took a healthy swallow of the beer, and nodded in satisfaction. "That's good, and as cold as Parker claims it is. I reckon he's a truthful man after all. How about you, Bud?"

The bartender looked surprised. "What do you mean, Marshal?"

Cole took another sip of the beer. "You always tell the truth, Bud?"

"Well . . . about as much as the next fella, I reckon."

"Good. Then you can tell me if Parker was in here last night."

Cole thought he saw a faint flicker of apprehension in the man's eyes. Bud hesitated, then said, "Why, sure he was in here. He's always in here. This is his place."

"Lives upstairs and everything, doesn't he?"

Bud nodded. "That's right."

"So he was here all night?"

Again the slight hesitation. "I didn't see him leave."

Cole didn't give any sign that he didn't believe the answer. Instead he nodded and said, "That's good. You know Becky Lewis, Bud?"

The bartender's jaw tightened, and his narrow features flushed a little. "I know what you're trying to do," he said angrily. "You're trying to get me in some sort of trouble. Hell, yes, I know who Becky Lewis is . . . I mean, was. Everybody in town does that can read, and most of them that can't."

Cole shook his head. "I didn't ask if you knew who she was, Bud. I asked if you knew *her*."

"Why would I?" Bud asked, his voice even more surly now.

"She used to work the saloons in Wind River," Cole said with a shrug. "Parker had his tent then, and I reckon she was in there quite a bit."

"I wouldn't know about that," Bud said. "I never went to work for Mr. Parker until after he built this place."

"Is that so? But you were around town before that, I recollect. You'd know Becky Lewis if you saw her, wouldn't you?"

Bud took a deep breath. "I don't know. Maybe."

Cole leaned closer to him. "Seen her around here lately, Bud? Right here in the Pronghorn, maybe?"

"No," Bud snapped with absolutely no hesitation. "No, I ain't seen her—and now I reckon I never will."

"Oh? I thought you might have." Cole's tone was mild, not threatening or accusing at all. He had already learned what he wanted to know. Bud's initial hesitation and then his certainty as he denied ever seeing Becky Lewis in the

Pronghorn were more than enough to convince Cole that he had been right. There *was* a connection between Becky and Parker, and Bud had orders not to say anything about it.

Parker had tipped his hand by paying that visit to Michael Hatfield, though. No one else stood to gain by pointing Becky Lewis and her blackmail at Simone McKay like a loaded gun. That had been obvious from the first.

But if Parker and the Lewis woman had been working together to make life miserable for Simone, then Cole couldn't see any reason why Parker would have wanted his accomplice dead. Without Becky, there was no way for Parker to continue indirectly blackmailing Simone. Parker wasn't the kind of man to kill a cash cow.

Cole picked up his beer, drained the glass, and dropped a coin on the bar beside the empty. "Thanks for the beer and the conversation, Bud," he said. He turned and walked out of the Pronghorn as deliberately as he had entered.

Parker was nowhere to be seen on the street. Probably still inside the general store, Cole decided as he headed toward the marshal's office.

Hank Parker didn't like to be pushed; Cole knew that about him quite well. Whenever he thought somebody was prodding him, he prodded in return.

That was why Cole had gone to the Pronghorn. He knew Bud would report the conversation to Parker. He had given Parker the first push.

Now he would wait and see what happened when Parker pushed back.

Judson Kent entered his office to find Jeremiah Newton fully dressed and waiting for him. The doctor frowned and said, "What are you doing out of bed, Jeremiah?"

"You said I could go home today, Brother Judson," replied the big blacksmith. "That's what I intend to do."

"I said you *might* be able to go home," Kent corrected as he hung up his hat and coat. He went behind the desk and sat down, Reginald's skull grinning over his shoulder. "I can't make that determination until I've examined you again," Kent went on.

"Then go ahead and examine me," urged Jeremiah. "I have things to do, Doctor. Important things."

"I'm sure that you do. Very well." Kent stood up and came around the desk again. He bent over and studied Jeremiah's eyes for a moment, then took the blacksmith's wrist and searched out a pulse among the thickly corded muscles. When he was satisfied with that, he took a stethoscope from a drawer in the desk and listened to Jeremiah's breathing.

"Well, you certainly seem to be hale and hearty," Kent announced a moment later. "How's that arm? Much pain in it this morning?"

"It's still a little stiff and sore," Jeremiah admitted, "but I'll be careful about not using it too much. There's no real reason to keep me here any longer, is there?"

"Not really." Kent smiled thinly. "All right, Jeremiah, you can go home. But try to take things a bit easier for a while, and if you experience any dizziness or headache or stomach upset, you come back to see me right away, do you understand?"

"Sure, Brother Judson," Jeremiah said with a grin. He stood up. "How much do I owe you?"

Kent waved a hand. "Don't worry about that. Consider your treatment a charitable contribution on my part."

"That's not right," Jeremiah said. "You'll never get rich doing things like that."

Kent put a hand on the shoulder of Jeremiah's uninjured

arm. "My friend, I didn't come to Wind River to get rich. Far from it, in fact. I simply wanted a place where I could practice medicine, do some good for people, and make some friends. I've been able to do all of those things in abundance in our fair community."

Jeremiah nodded slowly and said, "Reckon I know what you mean. I feel the same way. About preaching and blacksmithing, I mean, not doctoring."

"I know what you mean," Kent assured him.

Jeremiah thanked him again and left. Kent went to the window of the office and watched the big man stride away on the boardwalk outside. Jeremiah had gone less than a block when he was intercepted by a group of men coming from the other direction. Kent frowned slightly. He saw Michael Hatfield in that group, as well as Harvey Raymond, the manager of the general store, Lawton Paine, who owned the boarding house where Cole Tyler lived, and Nathan Smollett, the manager of the bank. There were several other men with them, all of whom Kent recognized as merchants and leading citizens of Wind River. Jeremiah was talking animatedly with the men, and suddenly he turned and pointed in the direction of the doctor's office. Kent took a step back, feeling as if Jeremiah was pointing straight at him.

A moment later he saw that that might have been true. Jeremiah started back toward the office, accompanied now by the men who had been talking to him.

"Odd," Kent muttered to himself. "I wonder what that was all about."

There was a good chance he was going to find out, he realized. The group led by Jeremiah turned in at the entrance to the doctor's office.

Jeremiah was grinning as he and his companions trooped into the office to face Kent. "There's your man, right there," he said as he pointed again at Kent. "They asked me, Brother Judson, but I told them they needed to come and see you."

"What about?" Kent demanded, confused by this turn of events.

Harvey Raymond spoke up. "We want you to run for mayor, of course," the store manager said.

"Run for mayor!" exclaimed Kent. "Me? You must be joking."

"No, we're not, Doctor," Michael said excitedly. "Like Jeremiah said, we asked him first, but he pointed out that you'd be much better for the job."

"I'm a preacher, not a politician," Jeremiah said, still grinning.

"And I'm a doctor," Kent snapped. "I know nothing about running a town."

"You're an honest man," Lawton Paine said. "I can't think of a better qualification than that. You're educated, and you care about Wind River. Nobody can argue with that. Jeremiah was right when he told us that if he ran, folks would be liable to think he was doing it just because he's been squabbling with Parker over that land. Nobody can say that about you. You don't have any ax to grind with Parker—other than that he's a low-down skunk and probably a crook."

That speech was longer than any Kent had ever heard the normally dour and taciturn Lawton Paine make. And everything Paine said made sense, too, Kent had to admit. But . . . *mayor*? Him? Such a possibility had never even entered his mind.

"Look, Dr. Kent," Michael said, "if you don't run, Parker's going to win. You said so yourself when we were talking with Marshal Tyler a while ago. In fact, that's what gave me the idea of trying to find another candidate to replace Mrs. McKay. There's no one better qualified than you."

"But . . . but what about Marshal Tyler?" Kent suggested. "He could run."

"A good lawman has too many enemies to make a successful politician, and there's not a better lawman in the territory than Marshal Tyler. He's just stepped on too many toes in the course of his job. But a man like you, Doctor, who's admired by practically everybody in town, you could win, even getting into the race now."

Kent rubbed a hand over his bearded jaw and frowned deeply as he thought about what Michael and the others were saying. It was true that with Simone out of the election, Parker would win easily . . . unless someone else opposed him. And it was also true that Kent had no real enemies in Wind River. He had never believed in false modesty; he knew he was looked up to by most of the citizens in the settlement. Yes, he thought, he could indeed win. But did he want to?

Even if the alternative was Hank Parker?

"Yes." Kent heard the word come out of his mouth, and it surprised him a little, as did the ones that followed it. "Yes, I'll do it. I suppose I have little choice. *Someone* has to prevent Hank Parker from being elected."

His visitors clustered around him, congratulating him and slapping him on the back. "It's about time somebody decent threw his hat in the ring," one of the men said.

"We'll start spreading the word right away. Michael, you can print up some flyers, can't you?"

Michael grinned and said, "Sure. What I'm wondering is, after the election, do we call you Dr. Kent or Mayor Kent?"

"I suppose that would depend on whether I was drafting an ordinance or setting a broken leg," Kent replied dryly.

He just hoped that after the election they wouldn't be calling him the biggest damned fool in all of Wyoming Territory.

Cole was standing on the boardwalk in front of the marshal's office that evening when Billy Casebolt came up to him. The deputy was just getting back from supper, and Cole was trying not to think about Simone McKay sitting in the cell block, eating her own meal from a tray Cole had brought over from the cafe. Brooding over the situation wasn't going to help it any.

"Well, the whole town's sure a-buzzin'," Casebolt commented as he leaned on the railing along the edge of the boardwalk. "From what I've heard, Doc Kent ain't goin' to have no trouble whippin' Parker day after tomorrow."

"I wouldn't count on it being that easy," Cole said. "Nothing ever is. Still, I'm glad Judson is running. He's got a good chance of beating Parker."

Casebolt studied the marshal shrewdly. "I got the feelin' you and the doc ain't gettin' along so good these days."

Cole shrugged. He wasn't even going to attempt to explain all his contradictory feelings about Simone and Kent to Billy. Cole didn't know himself what they all meant. "I think Judson will do a fine job as mayor," he said. "I intend to vote for him."

"Oh, I reckon I do, too. Sure ain't votin' for no skunk like Parker, even though I reckon he's got a head start on most politicians."

Cole looked over at the deputy. "A head start? How do you figure that?"

"He's already a low-down crook. He don't have to waste time gettin' that way whilst he's holdin' office."

"I guess you've got a point," Cole chuckled. He stepped

down off the boardwalk. "Think I'll take a turn around the town, even if it is a little early. Mrs. McKay ought to be finishing her supper soon."

"I'll tend to it," Casebolt said with a nod. When Simone was finished eating, he would retrieve the tray from the cell and take her to the outhouse behind the jail. It was a far cry from the fancier facilities of the Territorial House or Simone's own mansion, but she had been arrested for murder, after all. A few hardships were to be expected.

That didn't mean Cole had to like what Simone was going through. He felt a touch of impatience as he wondered if Bud had had that discussion with Hank Parker yet, telling Parker that Marshal Tyler had come poking around and asking questions.

He crossed the street and then ambled along the opposite boardwalk toward the Pronghorn, not really thinking about where his steps were taking him. It was almost full dark, with only a faint red glow left in the western sky from the sunset. The saloon was on the eastern end of Grenville Avenue, along with most of the other drinking establishments, dance halls, bordellos, and the like. Lights, music, and laughter began to fill the oncoming night.

Cole was passing the mouth of an alley when he heard a man's voice call softly, "Hey, Marshal!"

He had swung halfway toward the sound of the voice before instinct took over and pitched him forward, off his feet. The Colt was in his hand before he landed on the dirt in the alley mouth. A roaring blast of exploding gunpowder slapped against his ears as twin tongues of flame leaped from the muzzle of a shotgun. Cole felt a stinging sensation in his shoulder and another in his side as buckshot lanced into him. But there was no time to worry about that because the .44 was bucking in his hand as he triggered three shots toward the spot where the shotgun blast had come from.

His ears were ringing from the gunshots, but he still heard a loud clatter, as if somebody had knocked over some barrels or crates. Cole rolled to the side of the alley, trying to be as quiet about it as possible, and pressed himself against the foundation of the building there. He had his thumb on the hammer of the Colt, ready to drop it again if he saw anything to shoot at. The ringing in his ears began to die away.

That let him hear the shouts of alarm coming from Grenville Avenue, as well as the sound of running footsteps from farther along the alley. The bushwhacker might be trying to lure him into a trap, but Cole didn't think so. The steps had an erratic, frantic quality to them, like the gunman was wounded and trying desperately to get away while he still had the chance. Cole came silently to his feet and moved down the alley, the heavy revolver held steady in his fist in front of him.

A moment later he came to a jumble of knocked-over crates, just as he had suspected. His foot struck something else on the ground, and as he leaned over to pick up the object with his free hand, his fingers encountered something wet and sticky on it. Blood, from the feel of it, Cole thought. And the thing he picked up off the floor of the alley was a greener, all right. At least one of his slugs had found its target.

He dropped the shotgun and broke into a run, unwilling to let the ambusher get away. The running footsteps still sounded faintly. Cole dashed along the narrow alley and came out into a wider lane at the rear of the buildings. The steps came from his left. He swung in that direction and caught a glimpse of a running figure, silhouetted against a lighted rear window in a building down the street.

"Hold it!" Cole shouted.

The figure stopped and turned, and orange muzzle flame licked into the darkness once again. Cole could tell from the sound of it that this shot came from a pistol. The slug went wild, though, whining far over Cole's head. The man was hurt too badly to aim very well.

"Drop the gun!" Cole ordered. He wanted to take the bushwhacker alive if possible.

But the man fired again and again, and the second shot kicked up dust from the ground not six feet to Cole's left. He grated a curse and squeezed the trigger of his own revolver.

The gun cracked, and Cole heard a grunt of pain. The shadowy figure flew backward, flopping onto the ground. Cole ran toward him, one chamber in the Colt's cylinder still loaded and ready to fire. Didn't look like he was going to need it, though, he thought as he came closer. The fallen bushwhacker sprawled motionless. Cole kept the gun trained on him anyway.

A lanky form pounded out of an alley down the street, and Billy Casebolt's voice yelled, "Hey! What's goin' on back here?"

"Down here, Billy," Cole called to the deputy. "It's all right now. Looks like the shooting's over."

Casebolt came up to him and asked anxiously, "You all right, Marshal?"

"I picked up a couple of pellets of buckshot, but other than that I'm fine. Got a match, Billy?"

Casebolt lowered the shotgun he was holding and fumbled in his shirt pocket. "Yeah, just a minute . . . there."

He struck the match on the breech of the greener and held it low enough so that Cole could see the face of the ambusher. The features were coarse, the jaw covered with several days' worth of beard stubble. The rough range clothes and the worn but well-cared-for six-gun lying next to the man's body confirmed Cole's first impression.

"Looks like one of those hard cases who drift through here," Cole said. He hunkered on his heels next to the dead man and quickly checked the man's pockets. He didn't find anything except the makin's—and a roll of greenbacks.

"Hired gun," Casebolt said contemptuously.

"I reckon you're right. I wish I hadn't killed him, though, so I could ask who hired him. I tried to shoot low, but he must have crouched or stumbled just as I squeezed the trigger. Bullet took him right under the heart."

Casebolt spat into the dirt. "I can make a pretty good guess who paid this lobo to come after you, Marshal. I got a feelin' you can, too."

Cole nodded. Casebolt didn't know the half of it, he thought.

This ambush attempt had to be Hank Parker's way of pushing back.

15

The buckshot wounds in Cole's shoulder and side were minor, just as he had thought. Judson Kent cleaned them and bandaged them, then gave Cole a perfunctory warning about taking it easy for a couple of days. His tone made it clear that he knew the marshal would disregard the caution.

Cole wasn't just about to take it easy. His instincts told him that he was making progress, and he had no intention of letting up on Parker. At first he had been convinced that Simone was guilty of killing Becky Lewis, probably in a fit of anger, but now he wasn't so sure. Parker wouldn't have sent somebody to ambush him unless Cole was getting closer to something Parker didn't want uncovered.

Unfortunately, there was no way to prove that Parker had sent the bushwhacker after him, Cole realized by the middle of the next day. The dead man's body was at the undertaker's, but no one had claimed it or even identified him yet. Billy Casebolt recalled seeing the man around town over the past few days, as did Cole himself, but neither of them had noticed him hanging around the Pronghorn. Nor had anyone else who was willing to admit to having seen him. The consensus seemed to be that he had done his drinking in some of the smaller, more squalid dives on the eastern edge of town. That didn't mean much, however. Parker wouldn't have been likely to hire someone who could be tied to him too easily.

Cole hadn't told Simone about the ambush attempt, not wanting her to leap to the same conclusions he had and get her hopes up when they might not pan out. But as he brought the tray containing her noon meal into the cell block, she came to the door of her cell and asked worriedly, "Are you all right, Cole? I heard that there was some trouble last night."

He bit back a curse and asked, "Where'd you hear about that? I told Billy to keep quiet—"

"It wasn't Deputy Casebolt who told me. Judson mentioned it when he came by to visit me a little while ago. He said that someone tried to kill you, that you were wounded twice."

Cole grimaced. "I've had mosquito bites that were worse," he said. "It's nothing you need to worry about."

"I see." She didn't sound convinced, but she changed the subject by saying, "I'm glad that Judson has taken my place in the election, aren't you? I think he's going to be a fine mayor."

"He's got to get elected first." Cole put the tray down on a three-legged stool and unlocked the cell door. He swung it open, picked up the food, and carried it into the steel-barred enclosure.

"Just set it on the end of the bunk," Simone told him. "I'm not very hungry right now, but I'll eat it later."

"All right." Cole did as she had told him, then straightened and said, "I'm sorry about all this. I know how uncomfortable it must be for you to stay in here."

"It's not very pleasant," she admitted. "In fact, I was wondering if you might consider taking me over to my suite in the hotel instead."

Cole frowned. "Couldn't very well do that. You're a prisoner, after all—"

"And I'd be under house arrest. You've heard of that, surely."

"Well, yeah, but that's usually done in the army. I don't have a bunch of troopers to stand guard over you day and night."

"You could lock me into my suite," she said. "If I didn't have a key, I'd be just as secure there as I am here. There's no balcony outside the windows, so I hardly think I'd attempt to clamber out of them and jump two stories to the ground, do you?"

"I reckon not," Cole allowed. "I don't know how it'd look, though. Folks might think I was giving you special treatment because of who you are. And that's what I'd be doing, when you get right down to it."

"That's true. You do whatever you think is best, Cole. I'll abide by your decision."

Her attitude just made it more difficult, he thought with a scowl. He said, "I'll think on it and let you know later."

"Of course." Simone smiled.

Her request was a reasonable one, Cole told himself as he left the cell block. She had spent two nights in jail already, which was enough to prove to anybody that he was serious about his job, and she would be a lot more comfortable in the hotel. If anybody didn't like it, well, he was the marshal and it wasn't really anybody else's business, was it? He almost had himself talked into it. Later, when

Billy Casebolt got back, he would have the deputy transfer Simone over to the hotel and take care of locking her into her suite. That would be better than if he handled the chore personally, he decided. Hell, it was just a matter of common sense. A lady like Simone couldn't stay in a drafty, uncomfortable jail cell for two weeks or more waiting for the circuit court judge to arrive and hold a trial.

With that issue resolved, Cole felt a little better, but not much.

It was less than twenty-four hours until the voting began, and Cole had a feeling that in Wind River, Election Day might turn out to be more like judgment day.

One of the advantages of throwing one's hat into the ring so late in the game was that a great deal of campaigning wasn't required, Judson Kent reflected that evening in his office. There simply wasn't time for a lot of speech-making. He had agreed to run the day before, and the election was tomorrow. If one had to become involved in politics, that was the way to do it.

Still, he was tired. The fact that he was running for office didn't mean that he could ignore his medical practice, and he had seen quite a few patients today. Now, the last one had left, and Kent was ready to get some supper, perhaps do some reading in his medical journals, then retire early. Tomorrow would be a long day.

He was sitting at his desk, his sleeves rolled up, his boots propped on a footstool. It felt good to simply sit there and relax. Kent looked up at Reginald and grinned. "A quiet moment, eh, old boy? Not many of those these days, are there?"

The skeleton didn't answer.

The sound of quick footsteps on the boardwalk outside made Kent look toward the front window. The curtain was drawn tightly over the glass, so he couldn't see whoever was out there. He hoped the steps didn't belong to a late patient, and he said aloud, "Keep going, keep going . . . "

He let out a little groan as he heard the footsteps slow, then stop. Then the front door of the building opened. Two men appeared in the foyer. They peered into the office, and one of them said anxiously, "Are you Doc Kent?"

The Englishman got to his feet and nodded. "I am indeed Dr. Judson Kent. What can I do for you gentlemen?"

"You got to help us, Doc," the second man said. "Our pard Red got hisself kicked in the belly by a horse. I'm afraid he's hurt bad."

Kent frowned. "Where is he?"

"Down the street," said the first man, "behind the hardware store. He's holdin' himself and moanin' awful bad, and we were afraid to move him."

Kent reached for his medical bag, not bothering with his hat and coat. "You were wise not to disturb your friend," he said. "He may have internal injuries, from the sound of the accident you describe. Take me to him."

"Thanks, Doc," the second man said fervently. "I don't know what we'd do if ol' Red was to up an' die on us."

"Well, I'll certainly do whatever I can for him," Kent said as the two men led him out of the office.

They hurried down Grenville Avenue, Kent studying his companions as they moved along the street. Both men looked like cowboys. He didn't know them, but there was nothing unusual about that. Grub-line riders drifted in and out of the area all the time, finding work on the Diamond S, the Latch Hook, and the other ranches that had been established around Wind River. Kent knew only a few of them well, such as Lon Rogers and Frenchy LeDoux from Kermit Sawyer's spread.

Dusk had settled down over the settlement, and shadows were thick in the alley down which the two cowboys led Kent. "Red's right back here," one of the men said, gesturing toward the rear of the building.

"Your friend was kicked by a horse, you said?"

"That's right, Doc. It was the damnedest thing. We were takin' a shortcut through the alleys back yonder when Red got down to check a shoe on his hoss. That critter had hauled off and kicked him 'fore any of us knew what was happenin'."

"How unfortunate," Kent muttered. He had seen men kicked by horses before, and he knew the injuries suffered in such an accident could be quite serious. Men had died from such a kick.

They reached the rear of the building and rounded the corner. The two cowboys stopped short, and Kent came to a halt as well, expecting to see a man curled up on the ground in pain. Instead there was nothing back here but some empty barrels, not even the horse that had supposedly kicked "ol' Red."

"Where is your friend?" Kent asked. "Surely he didn't get up and wander off, not if he was hurt as badly as you said."

"I don't reckon his health is what you ought to be concerned about right now, Doc," the taller of the two men said.

"What do you mean by that?" demanded Kent. He was beginning to get worried about this situation.

"We mean it's goin' to be mighty tough for a feller like you to be mayor around here," the second man said. "You're plenty busy with doctorin'. You don't need to take on any other chores, not if you know what's good for you."

Kent drew himself up to his full height. He couldn't see the faces of the other men very well in the gathering gloom, but there was no mistaking the air of menace that had sprung up in the twilight. "Are you threatening me?" he asked angrily.

"Just givin' you some advice, Doc. For your own good, you'd better get up bright an' early in the mornin' and tell everybody you ain't runnin' for mayor no more."

"I'll do no such thing! Hank Parker sent you to intimidate me, didn't he? The man is despicable!"

"Nobody sent us," the second man said. "We're just a couple o' public-spirited citizens, I guess you'd say. Just tryin' to help you, Doc. You goin' to listen to reason or not?"

"What I'm going to do," Kent snapped, "is find the marshal and report this outrage! You lied to me and threatened me, and I won't have it!" He started to push past the men.

One of them grabbed his shoulder. "Thought you was smarter'n that, Doc. Get him!"

The other man, the shorter of the pair, suddenly slammed a punch into Kent's back, just above the waist. Kent gasped in pain from the blow and would have staggered forward except for the painfully tight grip on his shoulder. The first man jerked him around. Kent sensed the punch coming more than he saw it. He flung his arm up to block the attack.

That hand was the one holding the medical bag, and the black leather satchel happened to hit the taller man in the jaw, throwing off his aim. The punch he had thrown glanced off Kent's shoulder. The second man hit the doctor in the back again before Kent could catch his balance. This time Kent did stumble forward a couple of steps.

"We'll teach you a lesson, you son of a bitch!" grated the taller of the pair. He sank a fist in Kent's unprotected midsection.

Kent doubled over, the breath knocked out of him, and tried to drag air back into his lungs. Fists struck him on the back of the neck, driving him to his knees. A booted foot crashed into his side and sent him sprawling.

"We'll stomp you good, you bastard!"

And they would do it, too, Kent knew. They would beat him within an inch of his life, perhaps even kill him, all because he had had the audacity to run for mayor against Hank Parker. Kent had no doubt Parker was behind this attack. The saloonkeeper hadn't been able to resort to open violence as long as he was running against a woman, but now that he was opposed by a man, everything was different. Parker would stop at nothing to get what he wanted, not even murder.

Those thoughts flashed through Kent's mind in an instant, in less time than it took for the shorter man to draw back his foot for another kick. When the man's leg flashed forward again, Kent twisted, snapped his arm up, and with a flick of his wrist threw his medical bag in the face of the taller man, then grabbed the ankle of the other one. With a strength born of desperation, he heaved upward. He was no brawler, but damned if he was going to let these roughnecks assault him without fighting back!

The man let out a surprised yelp as he found himself flying backward. He fell heavily to the ground and rolled over. Now he was the one gasping for air. Kent was scrambling in the other direction, putting a little distance between himself and the taller of the two assailants. Kent was able to get to his feet in time to meet the man's charge.

For a moment they stood there, slugging back and forth, and Kent realized with a savage exultation that he was giving as good as he got. It didn't last, though. One of the man's roundhouse punches connected with Kent's jaw, driving the doctor back against the wall of the building. Stunned, Kent was unable to block the next two punches, a wicked left-right combination that whistled into his belly and his solar plexus. Pain washed over him, and he was unsteady on his feet. The only thing holding him up was the wall. He felt himself starting to slip down it. Once he fell, the fight would be over. He had already done the best he could against these bruisers.

This time, he thought grimly, when he went down he would likely *stay* down—maybe forever.

Cole and Casebolt were on the boardwalk in front of the marshal's office when Cole spotted Brenda Durand and Margaret Palmer coming along the street toward them. Casebolt saw them, too, and muttered, "Uh-oh."

"Miss Durand doesn't look too happy," Cole agreed.

"I ain't talkin' about the girl. It's that old lady who's got me buffaloed." Casebolt glanced over at Cole, his lean, grizzled features wearing a solemn expression. "She's got her cap set for me, you know."

Cole tried not to grin. He knew Billy was right. Margaret did seem to be pursuing him, although for the life of him he couldn't see why a sophisticated Eastern woman like Mrs. Palmer would be interested in a codger like Casebolt. Billy had to have an appeal that Cole had never seen. Cole said, "If you want to, go through the jail and slip out the back. I reckon you can get a head start on her that way."

"Thanks, Marshal," Casebolt said fervently. He disappeared inside the building, and a moment later Cole heard the rear door slam.

Brenda and Margaret reached the marshal's office a

couple of minutes later, and the older woman said, "Good evening, Marshal. How are you?"

"Oh, just fine, I reckon," Cole replied. "And you ladies?"

"We're fine," Brenda said impatiently. "I want to talk to you."

"Go right ahead," Cole told her.

Before Brenda could proceed, Margaret said, "I thought I noticed Deputy Casebolt out here with you just a moment ago."

"Billy went inside," Cole said, jerking a thumb toward the door. "You're welcome to see if he's still in there, Mrs. Palmer. There's no prisoners locked up right now, so you don't have to worry about that."

"That's what I want to talk to you about, Marshal," Brenda said. "Do you think it's wise letting Simone McKay go like that? After all, she's been accused of murder!"

"I'll just step inside and see if the deputy is there," Margaret said as she moved past Cole.

"I didn't let Simone go," Cole said to Brenda. "She's locked up in her suite at the hotel, under house arrest. Or hotel arrest, I reckon you could say."

"But that's not the same as being in jail!" protested Brenda. "Mrs. McKay's suite at the Territorial House can't compare to a . . . a cell!"

"Begging your pardon, Miss Durand, but what business is that of yours?" Cole asked coolly. "As long as Simone is in custody until the circuit judge gets here and conducts a trial, what does anything else matter?"

"I just don't want her running away and trying to escape justice. I'm a citizen of this town now. I have a right to worry about such things."

Cole shrugged. "Maybe you do. You've voiced your concern, Miss Durand, and I'll take note of it. Now, if you'll excuse me, I've got a few things to do."

Brenda glared at him. It was obvious she was just being spiteful, Cole thought. She had *enjoyed* the idea of Simone being behind bars. If for no other reason, Cole was glad now that he'd had Casebolt take Simone over to the hotel earlier, simply because this spoiled little brat was irritated by it. Annoying Brenda Durand was worth something by itself.

Margaret Palmer came out of the marshal's office. "Deputy Casebolt doesn't seem to be in there," she said. "I looked all over."

Cole raised his eyebrows and said, "Fancy that. He must've left out the back door. No telling where he's got off to, I suppose. If I see him, you want me to tell him you were looking for him?"

"Oh, no, that's not necessary." Although it was difficult to tell for sure in the fading twilight, Cole thought Margaret might be blushing as she went on, "I'm sure I'll encounter him again soon enough."

"Yes, ma'am."

Brenda spoke up again. "When that judge gets here, I intend to tell him how you gave special treatment to Mrs. McKay."

"You tell him anything you want to, miss." Cole had reached the end of his patience. "Good evening to you." He strode away down the boardwalk.

He wasn't going anyplace in particular, just away from Brenda. As he walked down Grenville Avenue habit made him check the doors of the businesses that had already closed down for the night. He passed the hardware store and stepped down off the boardwalk to cross the mouth of an alley beside the building.

A noise made Cole stop in his tracks.

His mind flashed back to the night before, when a soft-voiced call had made him stop in front of another alley. That had been an attempt on his life. This was something completely different.

It sounded like somebody else was in danger tonight.

Cole heard the distinctive thud of fists against human flesh, the grunts of effort as punches were thrown, the rasp of air in a man's throat as he struggled to catch his breath. There was a fight going on back there in the near-darkness, Cole realized—or an outright beating, from the sound of it. Whoever was on the receiving end of those blows wasn't putting up much resistance.

And he was facing at least two opponents, too, because in the next moment Cole heard a harsh voice say, "Hold him up! He ain't learned enough yet!"

Cole had heard enough, though. He broke into a run down the alley.

16

Despite the haste with which he went down the alley, Cole moved quietly, so the two men beating up a third one were completely surprised when the marshal shouted, "Hold it, damn you! I'll shoot the next man who moves!" He had his revolver cocked and leveled to back up the threat.

The two cowboys froze, just as Cole had ordered. The taller one had been holding the arms of their victim while the shorter one pounded punches into the man's belly. The taller one let go, and the victim slumped to his knees. He almost fell forward onto his face, but he caught himself as he swayed back and forth.

The light was bad, but there was still enough brightness in the sky for Cole to recognize the bearded face of Dr. Judson Kent. The physician's face was bloody and swollen from the battering he had received.

"Judson!" Cole exclaimed. "What the hell—!"

Kent staggered to his feet and stumbled forward. "M-Marshal . . . ," he mumbled.

"No, Judson, stay back!" Cole said urgently as he realized that Kent was getting between him and the two men.

It was too late. The taller man planted a hand in Kent's back and gave him a hard shove that sent him careening straight at Cole. Then both cowboys slapped leather.

Cole couldn't fire with Kent right in front of him. His left hand darted out and closed over the doctor's right arm. Cole threw himself to the side, dragging Kent with him. Both of them went down, falling heavily to the dirt floor of the alley, as the two attackers opened fire. Slugs ripped viciously through the space where Cole and Kent had been only an instant earlier.

The barrel of Cole's revolver was lifting even as he fell, and he was squeezing the trigger as he hit the ground. The impact threw his aim off and sent his bullet whining past the two would-be killers. He thumbed back the hammer of the .44 and fired again, squinting against the dust that had been kicked up in his eyes by a bullet plowing into the ground not far from his head. He didn't know if he had hit anything or not, but evidently his shots had come close enough to discourage the two cowboys. They turned tail and ran.

Cole came up on hands and knees next to Kent, who was lying face down. He put a hand on the doctor's shoulder and rolled him over. "Judson! Are you hit?"

"No, I . . . I'm all right," Kent choked out. "Go . . . go after those bounders!"

"I'd call 'em something a mite stronger, but that's what I intend to do," Cole said. He got to his feet and helped Kent into a sitting position. "Billy ought to be here in a minute or two. He'll come a-running when he hears those shots. You'll be all right until then?"

Kent waved a hand urgently. "I'm all right now. Just go! Catch those men!"

Cole nodded and broke into a run again. He could still faintly hear the scurrying footsteps of the fleeing men.

He spotted them a moment later as they darted around the corner of a building up ahead and cut through another alley toward Grenville Avenue. The boots the men wore weren't made for running. Cole's boots had lower heels, and he had always been a fast runner, ever since he was a kid. He reached the alley in time to see them emerging from the other end. They swung east onto Grenville Avenue.

Cole was less than half a block behind them when he reached the main street. He was vaguely aware that some of the bystanders were yelling questions at him, but he ignored them. His attention was focused instead on his quarry, and that was a good thing because the two men suddenly stopped and snapped a couple of shots at him. Cole threw himself against the front of a building to let the slugs whine past him. Somewhere a woman screamed, and Cole hoped one of the stray bullets hadn't hit her. He returned the fire of the gunmen, sending a couple of shots at them but aiming low to cut down on the chances of a tragic accident. The lawman's bullets chewed splinters from the planks of the boardwalk at the feet of the two cowboys and sent them sprinting on down the street. Cole ran after them, aware that only one chamber in the cylinder of his .44 was loaded now. Nor was there time to reload.

One bullet . . . two gunmen. That could make for an interesting confrontation, Cole thought grimly. He would deal with the problem when he caught up to it.

Several men got out of the way of the fleeing cowboys. Cole had hoped that somebody would pitch in and lend him a hand, but he couldn't blame the townspeople for not wanting to tangle with a couple of wild-eyed, gun-waving hombres like that. The two men suddenly angled toward one of the buildings, and Cole realized with a shock that they were heading for the Pronghorn Saloon.

Maybe that was a stroke of luck, he thought. Maybe those rannies were going to lead him straight to the man who had hired them to beat up Judson Kent. From the moment Cole had seen whom the men were assaulting back in that alley, he had known who had to be behind the attack.

Hank Parker.

One of the men slapped the batwings aside and pounded on into the Pronghorn, but the other one, the taller of the pair, stopped on the boardwalk in front of the saloon. He swung around toward Cole again and lifted his gun, yelling curses as he did so. Cole was only about fifty feet away now, a good target with the lights from the other buildings behind him. He flung himself forward.

As he went down onto the boardwalk he resisted the impulse to pull the trigger of his Colt. He had only one shot, so it had to be a good one. The tall cowboy was silhouetted, too, by the lights of the saloon spilling out the entrance behind him. Cole skidded to a halt, his belly pressed against the boardwalk, and lined his sights on the gunman. He did his best to ignore the lead whipping through the air above his head as he eared back the hammer of the .44 and pressed the trigger.

The revolver roared, and the cowboy doubled over as if he had been kicked in the belly by a mule. The gun in his hand exploded one last time as his finger clenched convulsively on the trigger. The slug smacked into the boards at his feet. The man fell to the side, rolling off the boardwalk and falling into the street. He was still curled up around the spot where the marshal's bullet had bored into his body.

Cole surged to his feet and ran the rest of the way to the door of the saloon, well aware that the gun in his hand was empty now but unwilling to give up the pursuit. He paused a second at the entrance, just long enough for his gaze to flick around the big room. The shooting had caused everyone in the Pronghorn to dive under the tables or behind the bar for cover. The only people still on their feet were the remaining gunman and one of the percentage girls, who had been too slow about getting out of his way. The cowboy had one arm wrapped around her waist, holding her tightly to him, and his other hand held a gun with the barrel pressed against the young woman's head. He maneuvered both himself and his terrified hostage back against the bar.

"You better back off, Marshal!" the gunman shouted shakily as he spotted Cole at the entrance. "I'll kill this here calico cat if you don't!"

"Take it easy, mister," Cole said, trying to sound calmer than he felt. He kept the gun in his hand leveled and ready, just as if it were still loaded. The gunman didn't have to know that it wasn't. "You haven't killed anybody yet. No call to make this into a hanging matter."

"You want me to surrender?" The cowboy laughed, the sound like the rasp of a dull saw against hardwood. "I'll be damned if I'll do that."

"How about a trade?" suggested Cole. "Tell me who hired you to beat up Judson Kent, and things'll go a lot easier for you."

For an instant Cole thought he saw a flicker of hope in the man's eyes. He was ready to make a deal, Cole sensed that.

But then Hank Parker rose from behind the bar, a sawed-off shotgun gripped tightly in his hand, and said, "Hey!" as he thrust out the weapon.

The gunman twisted his head involuntarily, and the barrel of the pistol in his hand wavered away from the percentage girl. Cole could have shot him then—if his gun had been loaded, and if he had wanted the man dead, which he didn't.

Hank Parker's greener was loaded, though, and the muzzles of the twin barrels were about three inches away from the startled face of the cowboy. Cole opened his mouth to shout "No!" but before the word could leave his mouth, Parker had tripped both of the shotgun's triggers.

The roar of the greener was deafening. The gunman's head practically disappeared in a grisly spray of blood, bone, and brain matter as he took the double charge of buckshot point-blank in the face. The young woman began shrieking in a raw, ragged voice as she was pelted by the crimson gore, but she was otherwise unhurt. The gunman's body flopped away from her, falling on the sawdust-littered floor to twitch grotesquely.

Cole slowly lowered his gun, swallowing the sour taste that rose in his throat. He had seen some awful things in his life, but this was one of the worst. He looked across the bar at Parker and said angrily, "What the hell did you do that for?"

"Why, to save your life and the life of my girl here," Parker replied in a surprised voice. "Why else would I have done it?"

"Oh, I don't know . . . to keep that cowboy from admitting that you hired him and his partner to beat up Judson Kent?"

"Something happened to Kent?" asked Parker, still sounding surprised. "I didn't know a thing about it, Marshal."

The percentage girl had screamed herself hoarse, so that the only sound she could make now was a pathetic little squeak. She did that a time or two, then her eyes rolled up in her head and she collapsed, fainting dead away. Some of the other women who worked in the saloon were starting to emerge from underneath the tables now that the shooting was over, and they went to her side to help her. They stepped carefully around the pool of blood spreading from the dead man's body as they did so.

Cole reloaded five of the six chambers in his revolver, letting the hammer rest on the empty chamber as he holstered the weapon. He stepped across the room, studying Parker's face as he came closer to the bar. Parker was wearing what he intended to be an innocent expression, but Cole didn't believe it for a second.

Parker broke the scattergun open and shucked the empty shells from it. He reached underneath the bar for fresh loads and replaced the weapon on the shelf down there. "Are you all right, Marshal? I heard more shooting outside."

"I'm fine," Cole grunted, knowing that Parker didn't really give a damn about his health. "The other fella's outside in the street."

"Dead?" asked Parker.

"I'd say so. That's what I figured to do." With only one shot left, Cole had known he couldn't take chances. That was why he had gone for the man's belly. Even if the bullet hadn't killed the cowboy right away, the shock of the wound had been sure to knock him out. Chances were the man was dead now, either way. Cole jerked a thumb at the corpse in here and asked, "Did you ever see this gent before?"

Parker shook his head. "Never saw him in my life. All I know is that he came running in here, and there were shots right outside. Everybody hit the floor. I grabbed that greener and waited for the right time."

Maybe in more ways than one, Cole thought. Parker might have waited until he could no longer afford the risk of the gunman double-crossing him.

And yet there was no way to prove that. Everybody in the saloon had seen what happened. Parker could stick by his story about trying to help Cole from now until doomsday, and no one could claim otherwise.

"I guess I ought to be grateful," Cole said tightly.

Parker shrugged. "Doesn't matter to me either way, Marshal. The main thing I wanted to do was save Lettie there. She's one of my best girls."

Cole turned as somebody slapped the batwings open behind him. Billy Casebolt strode into the saloon, his Griswold & Gunnison revolver gripped in his hand, ready for use. "You all right, Marshal?" he asked.

"I'm fine," Cole told him. "What about that feller in the street outside? Did you check his body?"

Casebolt nodded. "Sure did, but there wasn't any need. He's sure enough dead. I already sent word to the undertaker." The deputy looked at the body on the floor and made a face. "See you got another 'un in here."

"Yeah. What about Judson?"

"The doc looks like he's going to be all right. He's beat up pretty bad, but nothing serious."

Cole turned back to the saloonkeeper. "Guess this plan didn't work, either, Parker. Maybe you'd better just give up."

Parker shook his head and said blandly, "I don't know what you're talking about, Tyler, but I'll tell you one thing: Hank Parker doesn't give up when he wants something, no matter what."

"We'll see," Cole snapped. "Tomorrow's Election Day. The people of Wind River are going to have the final word."

"And that's fine with me. I'll abide by the will of the people. All I want to do is serve."

Cole frowned. Parker was the only man he knew of who could stand there with a dead man at his feet and make a campaign speech out of it. He shook his head in disgust, turned to Casebolt, and said, "Get some of the boys to haul this carcass out of here. I need some fresh air, but I don't reckon I'll get it in here."

From the window of her suite on the second floor of the Territorial House, Simone McKay had heard the gunshots. Such noises didn't disturb the tranquility of Wind River as much now as they had during the early days of the settlement, but they still occurred all too often for Simone's taste.

She wondered if anyone had gotten killed tonight.

Turning away from the window, Simone went to a comfortable armchair and sank down into it. She sighed. While this suite in the hotel was much more comfortable than that jail cell, of course, she was still very aware that she was a prisoner. She didn't like the feeling, either. It was bad enough to be locked up, but to be locked up for something she hadn't even done . . .

Some instinct made her look up, and her breath caught in her throat. He was there, standing on the other side of the room next to the large four-poster bed. Once again he wore that solemn expression on his face as he stood there silently staring at her.

The shock Simone had felt the first time she saw her husband's ghost had faded considerably over the past few days. She was still somewhat surprised to see Andrew standing there in her hotel room, but more than anything else, she was annoyed.

"What are you doing here, Andrew?" she snapped. "You haven't come to whine about me finding your killer again, have you? In case you haven't noticed, I have some problems of my own. I've been accused of murder, for God's sake!" Simone's eyes narrowed. She went on, "And it's your fault, Andrew. If you hadn't been carrying on with that whore, none of this would have happened. She never would have come back here to blackmail me, and I never would have been accused of killing her. It's your fault!"

Without even realizing what she was doing, Simone came up out of the chair and strode toward the apparition, which didn't budge from its place beside the bed.

"Why did you do it, Andrew?" she hissed. "Why did you go from my bed to hers? Wasn't I good enough for you? I was good enough to give you advice about your business, but you preferred to take your pleasure with some pathetic little drab! How do you think that made me feel, Andrew?"

She stopped suddenly as she realized she was practically shouting. The ghost still said nothing, but it lifted an arm and extended a hand toward her, becoming more insubstantial in the process. Simone jerked back and turned away, lifting her own hands to her face. She wasn't sure if she was laughing or crying or a little of both as her shoulders shook.

A featherlight touch brushed against her, sending an icy chill all the way through her body.

She let out a strangled cry and flinched away from that touch. As she did she heard a man's voice shout, "Simone! Simone, are you all right?" There was the sound of a key in the lock of the door to the suite.

Simone turned toward the door in time to see it swing open. There was no sign of Andrew anywhere in the room. He must have vanished in an instant this time, instead of fading away slowly. A flesh-and-blood Cole Tyler was there, however, rushing into the room with an alarmed expression on his face.

The marshal put his hands on her shoulders and said urgently, "What is it? I heard you cry out when I was coming down the hall."

"I . . . I'm all right," Simone managed to gasp out. "I was sitting in the chair, and I . . . I must have dozed off. I was dreaming. . . ." The lie was easier than telling him the truth.

But then, lies had always been easier, hadn't they?

Simone took a deep breath and tried to pull herself together as Cole said, "I reckon if anybody around here has a right to a nightmare or two, it's you, Simone."

"Perhaps. But I'm all right now." She forced a smile onto her face, then grew more serious as she asked, "I heard some shooting earlier. Was anybody hurt?"

Cole nodded grimly. "There's been some trouble. Judson Kent was beaten up earlier by a couple of men who decoyed him out of his office."

"Oh, no! Is he all right?"

"He will be," Cole said. "He's got plenty of bumps and bruises, but that appears to be all. I took a hand in the game before it went any further. Chased the men down to the Pronghorn and had to kill one of them. Parker got the other one."

"Parker?" repeated Simone, surprised that the saloon-keeper would help Cole under any circumstances these days. She frowned and continued, "And why would the men who attacked Judson go to the Pronghorn?"

"Good questions, and I reckon the answers are all tied together. I figure Parker hired them, and when things didn't go the way they had planned, they ran back to him for help. One of them didn't quite get there, though, and the one who did made a fatal mistake. He put himself where Parker could get rid of him, rather than having him testify."

Simone nodded slowly, her keen brain following Cole's reasoning. "He killed the man so he couldn't admit that he'd been hired by Parker."

"That's the way I see it. Unfortunately, there's no way to prove it. Both of the hombres who jumped Judson are dead."

Simone sat down in her chair again. "My God, will there never be an end to all this? It seemed like such a simple idea to have an election."

"Politics is never simple," Cole said, "and it seems to me that it brings out the worst in most people. But it *will* be over soon. By this time tomorrow, Wind River will have a mayor."

"Yes, but will it be Judson or Parker?"

Cole shook his head. "I reckon we'll just have to wait and see, like everybody else."

17

Election Day dawned bright and clear in Wind River. There was no breeze, and the warmth that was already in the air promised a sultry heat before the day was over.

One of the vacant buildings had been set up as the polling place. Three citizens had been chosen as election judges: Nathan Smollett, the manager of the bank; Abel Warfield, a clerk at the Union Pacific depot; and Ben Calhoun, a bartender at one of the smaller saloons. As Cole watched the three men take their places at the table that had been set up inside the building, he thought it was a pretty fair selection. Smollett, Warfield, and Calhoun were a good cross section of the citizens of Wind River. On the table in front of them were stacks of paper ballots, dozens of pencils from the general store, and the locked metal box with a slot cut in its top where the ballots would be deposited once they had been marked. Cole had one of the keys to that box, and he was looking for somebody neutral to hold the other one.

Billy Casebolt ambled up and pulled a fat turnip

watch from his pocket. He flipped open the case and studied the hands of the timepiece. "Almost eight o'clock," he commented.

Cole nodded. "It's just about that time, all right." He looked along the street. There were a lot of folks out and about on Grenville Avenue, and many of them were drifting toward the building where the election would take place. The polls would be open from eight in the morning until four o'clock in the afternoon, to give everyone plenty of time to vote. Then the counting of the ballots would begin, and Cole figured the results would be official by nightfall.

"Reckon there's goin' to be any trouble?" Casebolt asked quietly.

"You mean from Parker and his supporters?" Cole shook his head. "I don't know. He's tried every underhanded trick you could think of so far to influence this election. Maybe he realizes it's too late now to do anything except sit back and wait to see what the people want."

"Hope you're right," said Casebolt, "but I ain't goin' to count on it."

"Neither am I, Billy," Cole said. "Neither am I."

The two lawmen stood on the boardwalk, waiting for the last few minutes to pass before the polls opened. After a moment, Casebolt nudged Cole with an elbow and said, "Would you look at that? I didn't 'spect to see them today."

Cole looked in the direction the deputy had indicated with a nod and saw a group of riders coming down the street. In the lead was an impressive-looking, white-haired, middle-aged man dressed in black range clothes. The dozen or so men with him were all cowboys. Cole frowned.

"What are they doing here? The Diamond S isn't within the town limits. Sawyer and his boys can't vote."

Kermit Sawyer, the Texas cattleman who had come up the trail from the Lone Star State with a herd of longhorns to establish the Diamond S, swung his mount toward the hitch rack in front of a nearby saloon. He was flanked by his foreman, Frenchy LeDoux, and young Lon Rogers, both of whom followed his example. All of the Diamond S riders dismounted and tied their horses to the rail. Sawyer stepped up onto the boardwalk and strode toward Cole, trailed by his men.

Cole stepped out to meet him. "Morning, Sawyer," he said tightly. The marshal and the cattleman had never gotten along very well, despite the grudging mutual respect they held for each other. "Hope you and your boys haven't come to vote. You're not eligible."

Sawyer hooked his thumbs in his gunbelt. "Hell, no," he grunted. "You townies can elect anybody you damned well please. We just came in to watch the show. Ain't that right, boys?"

Frenchy grinned. "Down in Texas we ain't had an election in a long time that didn't have at least a little gunplay involved. Thought this one might be just as interestin'."

"I wouldn't count on it," Cole said sharply. "Everything's going to be done nice and legal-like."

That brought a few hoots of laughter from the Texans. Cole's jaw tightened, but he didn't say anything else.

"I reckon we'll see," Sawyer said. "Anyway, that's why we're here, just to watch the goin's on. When do the polls open?"

Casebolt consulted his watch again. "In about three minutes."

Sawyer nodded. "Good enough. We'll get us some coffee in one of these saloons and watch from the porch."

"All right, just don't try to horn in," Cole warned. An idea occurred to him, and he went on. "How'd you like to give me a hand in something, Sawyer?"

The cattleman looked surprised that Cole would ask for his help in anything, and to tell the truth, it was an uncommon situation. Sawyer's curiosity must have gotten the best of him, because he said, "All right. What is it, Marshal?"

Cole withdrew a key from the pocket of his denim pants. "This is one of the keys to the ballot box. I've got the other one. I want you to hang on to this one for me, Sawyer. You don't have any stake in this election, so nobody figures you'd try anything funny with the ballots."

For a moment Sawyer made no reply; then he nodded and put out his hand for the key. "Sure, I'll hold it for you. Nobody else will get their hands on it."

"That's what I figured," Cole said. He gave Sawyer the key and watched the Texan tuck it away in the breast pocket of his black shirt.

While the Diamond S crew made their way toward the saloon in front of which their horses were hitched, Casebolt snapped shut the watch in his hand. "It's time," he announced.

Cole nodded and stepped to the open door of the building. The three election judges were in place. "You boys all ready?" he asked.

Nathan Smollett nodded and answered for himself and his companions. "Indeed we are, Marshal."

"Here they come, then. The polls are open."

People were already starting to line up outside. Cole turned and looked at them. He recognized just about all of them, which was a good thing. One of his concerns was that people who didn't actually live in Wind River would try to vote. That could cause a problem before the day was over, which was one reason either he or Casebolt would try to be on hand until the polls were closed.

Cole lifted his hands and raised his voice as he said, "All right, folks, the polls are open. Stay in line, and there'll be no pushing or shoving or arguing with the election judges. There's no drinking and no speechmaking, and you've got to leave your guns at the door and reclaim them on your way out. This is Wind River's first election, and we want everything about it to be proper." He stepped aside and waved the first voter into the building. "Go ahead and cast your ballots, folks."

Michael Hatfield stood on the boardwalk nearby, paper and pencil in hand. He watched the voters proceed into the building in an orderly fashion and said to Cole, "Can I get a statement for the *Sentinel*, Marshal?"

"What do you want to know, Michael?"

The young journalist grinned. "How about a prediction on the outcome of the election?"

Cole snorted and shook his head. "I'm not in the predicting business," he said. "I'll leave that to you newspaper fellers. I'm just here to make sure everything's done in a legal, orderly fashion."

"Are you expecting any trouble?"

"I'm not *expecting* trouble—but we'll sure be ready for it if it happens."

Michael jerked a thumb toward the nearby saloon where Kermit Sawyer and his men were arranged along the boardwalk, drinking coffee since according to territorial statutes it was illegal to serve alcohol while the polls were open. "What's the crew from the Diamond S doing in town?"

"Those crazy Texans have got the idea that an election is some sort of entertainment," replied Cole. "I reckon they'll be pretty bored before the day's over."

"Thanks, Marshal," Michael said as he scribbled on his pad. "Have you seen Dr. Kent this morning?"

Cole shook his head. "No, but I reckon he'll come by to vote sooner or later."

"What about you? Have you voted?"

With a frown, Cole realized that he had forgotten to cast his own ballot. So far he had been too concerned about making it safe and legal for everyone else to do so. "I'll get around to it," he said. "You can count on that."

"So will I," Michael said. "It's easy to forget, isn't it?"

Cole nodded, wishing Michael hadn't even brought up the subject.

Michael didn't press the issue, however, because the next moment he said excitedly, "Here comes Dr. Kent!"

There was a stir among the people lined up to vote. Dr. Judson Kent was indeed approaching along the boardwalk, accompanied by Jeremiah Newton. The doctor wore his best suit and held his head high and defiant, although he was moving somewhat stiffly from the beating he had received the night before. His features were bruised and puffy, but his expression was one of solemn dignity. He nodded to Cole as he and Jeremiah came up to the lawman and the newspaper editor.

"Good morning, Marshal. Hello, Michael. A fine morning, isn't it?"

"Already a little warm for my taste," Cole said dryly. "Come to vote, Judson?"

"Indeed I did."

The man who was about to enter the building next spoke up, saying, "Here, Doc, you can take my place in line."

Kent smiled and shook his head. "No, thank you, my friend. I'll wait my turn, just like everyone else."

Already turning into a politician, Cole thought a little cynically as Kent and Jeremiah made their way to the end of the line. Michael trailed along with them, getting a statement from the physician.

Cole looked across the doorway at Billy Casebolt and saw the weary acceptance in the deputy's eyes.

It was going to be a long day, and Cole just hoped that at the end of it, the outcome would be worthwhile. . . .

From the window of her suite, Simone could watch the voting. She wondered if she ought to send for Cole and have him escort her over there so that she could cast her own ballot. True, she had been accused of a crime, but she hadn't been found guilty yet. She ought to still have the right to vote, like all the other women who had recently been enfranchised by the Territory of Wyoming.

She shook her head and moved away from the window, deciding against the idea. Such a thing would just draw a lot of attention, and she didn't want that. She knew she must have already been the subject of a great deal of gossip during the past few days. By now she was probably the laughingstock of the settlement, and she couldn't stand the thought of that.

As she went over to the armchair and sat down, Simone glanced at the ghost of her husband. Andrew stood near the foot of the bed, his features seemingly locked in that same sad expression. He had been there when Simone woke up this morning, and he hadn't budged since, even when Billy Casebolt brought in her breakfast tray. It had taken Simone only a moment to realize that the deputy couldn't see Andrew, even though the ghost was in plain sight to her. She had been about to conclude that it was only further proof she had lost her mind, when Casebolt had shivered and said, "It's a mite cold in here, ain't it? Strange, since it's already pretty warm outside."

He had been sensing Andrew's presence, Simone thought. Andrew chose to reveal himself only to his wife, but that didn't mean he wasn't really there. The thought was oddly comforting. After that, she had tried to talk to the apparition, but Andrew was stubbornly silent. Finally she had said in exasperation, "Oh, all right. Be like that if you want to," and she had ignored him ever since. If he wanted to lurk around like a doomed spirit, that was his business. Simone had other things to worry about.

Like the election.

What if Hank Parker won? she asked herself now. With Parker as the mayor of Wind River, true reform would be difficult, if not impossible. The saloons and the gambling dens and the bordellos would continue to operate. In fact, they would probably thrive under Parker's administration. Every night there would be more robberies and killings, and Wind River would become known throughout the territory as a haven for lawlessness of all sorts. Eventually the good people would begin to leave—and then the town would be doomed.

She had never opposed Parker out of some moral high-mindedness, Simone told herself. Jeremiah Newton might rant and rave about sin, but Simone was too practical to get all worked up about it. She knew that a town *needed* a little sin; it was good for business. But Parker would allow it to run rampant, unchecked, as it had been in the early days of the settlement before Cole Tyler had put a dent in the hellishness.

Cole . . . What would he do if Parker was elected? Surely he wouldn't stay on as marshal and attempt to work with Parker. The two of them couldn't stand each other. Even if Cole had been willing, Parker wouldn't allow it.

The thought that Cole might leave Wind River sent a pang of emotion through Simone. She had sensed for a long time that he was interested in her. She had tried to encourage that without ever allowing him to get too close. It always helped to have the local law be sympathetic; Andrew had taught her that. But she realized now that she had grown genuinely fond of Cole Tyler. She would miss him if he was gone, and so would Wind River. Whatever toady Parker put into the office wouldn't be able to keep the peace as Cole had.

Simone took a deep breath. "I'm being foolish," she said aloud. "How could anyone in their right mind vote for Parker over Judson Kent? Judson will be elected, I'm sure of it."

Yet she wasn't really that certain, no matter how much she tried to convince herself otherwise. Judson had entered the race late, declaring himself a candidate only after Simone had dropped out. There hadn't been much time to spread the word that he was running. And Parker had almost unanimous support from the denizens of the red-light district.

Parker might win. It was possible, and Simone knew it.

Unless, somehow, she stopped him. Her hands tightened on the arms of the chair as the thought occurred to her. In the long run, the election of Hank Parker as mayor would be the death knell of Wind River. Simone couldn't allow that. Not after everything she had done to help build this town, not after all the sacrifices she had made so that Wind River could grow and prosper.

Her breath hissed between her teeth. She had to do it. She accepted that now.

She had to get out of here some way and make sure that Hank Parker would never be the mayor of Wind River.

And on the other side of the room, the ghost of Andrew McKay still looked on silently.

The election was proceeding more smoothly than Cole had ever expected it would. By the middle of the day, no one had tried to vote who wasn't a legal resident of Wind River. There had been no arguments, no fistfights in the line of voters even though supporters of Judson Kent and Hank Parker were often right next to each other. There was something almost ... majestic ... about the process, Cole thought. Election campaigns might bring out the worst in people, but the voting itself seemed to lift them up out of themselves and give them some added dignity. He supposed that was one reason those old boys back in colonial times had worked out this system.

During one of the lulls in the voting during the morning, Cole and Casebolt had both gone inside to vote. Cole had picked up one of the ballots, which had both Parker's name and Simone McKay's printed on them. Simone's name had been crossed out and replaced by Judson Kent's, a tedious job that had been carried out by hand by several volunteers. Cole used a stub of pencil to mark an *X* beside Kent's name, then folded the ballot and dropped it into the iron box.

This was the first time in his life he had voted on something, he realized. Always before he had been too busy to even be aware that it was Election Day, or else out in the middle of some godforsaken wilderness somewhere with the closest polling place hundreds of miles away. It was a good feeling.

When it came time for lunch, he and Casebolt swapped out, with Casebolt going first and bringing back from the cafe a burlap bag full of food for the election judges. Cole went to eat then, and as he passed the saloon where the Diamond S riders had been congregated, he saw that most of them were gone. Only Kermit Sawyer, Lon Rogers, and a couple of other men remained.

"Where's the rest of your crew, Sawyer?" Cole asked. "They get bored and go home?"

"Damn right," growled Sawyer. "You folks up here in Wyoming Territory just don't know how to hold an election. I sent Frenchy and most of the boys back to the ranch. Figured they might as well get some work done."

"I don't reckon the fact that they couldn't buy a drink while the polls are open had anything to do with it, did it?" Cole said with a grin.

The Texan snorted in disgust. "Like I said, you people up here just don't know how to hold an election."

Cole chuckled and moved on, heading for the Wind River Cafe.

The eating establishment was busy when he got there, with all of the tables occupied and most of the seats at the counter full. There was an empty stool next to Michael Hatfield, though, and the young newspaperman motioned for Cole to join him. Michael was drinking a cup of coffee and making notes on the pad that rested on the counter in front of him.

"How's the election going, Marshal?" Michael asked as Cole settled down on the stool next to him.

Cole nodded. "No problems so far. I've been very pleased."

"Is that an official reaction?"

"Sure." Cole shrugged. "But the election's not over yet. Won't be for—" He glanced at the banjo clock on the wall of the cafe. "—nearly three more hours. No telling what might happen between now and then."

"Have you heard any talk about who's leading?"

"Nope, and I don't want to. Some folks, you can tell who they're going to vote for while they're still standing in line outside the polls, but I haven't tried to keep a count of them either way. I'd rather just wait for the official results."

Michael nodded, scribbled a line or two on his pad, then pushed the paper away and put down his pencil. "You know, Marshal, I've been thinking—"

He was interrupted by the arrival of a harried-looking but still lovely Rose Foster, who came up on the other side of the counter and said, "Hello, Cole. What can I get for you? Monty's got some nice pork chops back there in the kitchen."

"Sounds fine," Cole told her. "I'll have potatoes with them and some of that deep-dish apple pie."

Rose smiled, nodded, and moved off to relay the order to Monty Riordan. Cole turned back to Michael and said, "Sorry about that. You were saying . . . ?"

"Well, I don't know if I ought to talk about it or not," Michael said hesitantly, "but I've been thinking about what happened up there at the church a couple of nights ago."

"When Becky Lewis was murdered," Cole said grimly.

"That's right. I've been racking my brain, trying to remember every detail about what I saw up there. I know that I'm prejudiced, but I just can't believe that Mrs. McKay killed that woman."

"Neither can I," Cole admitted. "But all the evidence says that she did."

"Maybe not," Michael said.

Cole leaned toward him. Michael's voice was pitched low, so that the other people in the cafe wouldn't overhear what he was saying. The young man went on, "I think I remember something that might support her story about finding the body just before I did."

"You're not imagining something just because you work for Mrs. McKay and like her, are you, Michael?" asked Cole, sounding a note of caution.

Michael shook his head firmly. "I'm sure of this, Marshal. When I saw those two figures struggling up there at the church, I'm certain that something about them struck me as odd. I really didn't think about it afterward because . . . well, like you said, all the evidence seemed to point toward Mrs. McKay as the killer. But yesterday and today, I've been trying to remember exactly what I saw that I might have noticed like that, and now I think I know what it was."

Michael hesitated again, and Cole said impatiently, "Go ahead. What did you see?"

"Well, I may be crazy, but . . . I could swear that one of the figures I saw had just one arm."

Cole stiffened. Hank Parker was the only one-armed man in Wind River, the only one in the whole area as far as Cole knew. And although Cole wasn't sure why Parker would have wanted Becky Lewis dead, there was a definite connection between the two of them. Cole couldn't prove that, but he was certain of it.

"You're sure about that, Michael?" he asked. "Maybe whoever you saw was turned so that you could only see one arm, but the other one was really there."

Michael shook his head and said, "I'm sure. I saw him turn around, and I saw both shoulders—but only one arm. It had to be Hank Parker! He must've killed that woman!"

"We'd both like to think so," Cole muttered. He looked intently at Michael and went on. "You'd be willing to swear to this in court?"

Michael drew in a deep breath. "Yes. Yes, I'd swear to it in court."

"All right. I'll think about it and try to figure out what to do."

"You're going to arrest Parker and let Mrs. McKay go, aren't you?" Michael asked with a frown.

Cole grimaced. "Well, no offense, Michael, but your word may not be enough to clear Simone. She *was* found with the body at her feet, and the knife in Becky Lewis's chest came from the Territorial House. With evidence like that, we may have to wait for Judge Sharp to get here and sort everything out."

"You can't mean that!" Michael exclaimed. "What about Parker?"

"May have to take him into custody, too. But he won't be going anywhere until after the election's over, so I'm going to wait until the polls are closed before I do anything."

Michael shook his head in disbelief, then shrugged. "Maybe you're right, Marshal. But you and I both know that Hank Parker is a much better suspect than Mrs. McKay. Why, she would never hurt anybody!"

"I'm inclined to agree with you," Cole said to him as Rose appeared with a platter of food. "But right now I'm going to eat my lunch and leave the law business until later."

There was one problem with that, he discovered as he dug into the pork chops and potatoes. It was damned hard for a fella to enjoy his food when his brain was all cluttered up with murder and the like.

Simone looked at the watch she wore as a cameo pinned to the front of her dress. Four o'clock. The polls were closing right about now. The election, for all intents and purposes, was over.

That meant she couldn't postpone her decision any longer.

All afternoon she had paced back and forth and looked out the front window, trying to figure out exactly how to proceed. She knew she had to stop Parker somehow. She couldn't allow even the possibility that he might win the election. That meant she had to get out of this hotel room, preferably without anyone knowing until it was too late that she had escaped.

This corner suite, fittingly enough the best accommodations in the Territorial House, had two windows for cross-ventilation, one on the front of the building, one on the side that overlooked the alley alongside the hotel. Simone went to that side window, which was raised a few inches to let air through. She slipped her fingers into the opening and raised the pane the rest of the way.

She had never had a fear of heights, and besides, this room was only on the second floor. She had told Cole Tyler how ridiculous it was to think of her clambering out through a window, and he had agreed with her. The whole idea was just too undignified to ever imagine Simone McKay doing such a thing.

But when she had to be, she was capable of a lot of things no one would ever imagine. She reminded herself of that fact as she took a deep breath and then hiked up her dress to stick a leg out through the window.

A glance back showed her Andrew's ghost, still standing silently on the other side of the room. She smiled at him, said quietly, "Goodbye, Andrew," and climbed out the window.

Grenville Avenue was only a few yards away, and there were nearly always people passing by on the street. But the alley was narrow and shadowy, and most of the time people just walked on past such places without ever glancing into them. Simone knew she was taking a chance by climbing out this window, but life was a risk. You had to seize your opportunities when and where you could. She had always lived by that credo.

She was wearing soft slippers, and they enabled her to find a grip with her toes against the wall when she had both feet out the window. Her hands held tightly to the sill as she lowered herself, taking as much of her weight as she could on those toeholds, which were small but sufficient. Finally, though, Simone had no choice but to let go with her toes and dangle full length from the window. She was sure she looked ludicrous, but she couldn't worry about that now. The pain in her fingers, arms, and shoulders was enough to make her bite her lip to keep from crying out. She hung there only for a couple of seconds, then let go of the window and dropped.

She tried to land as lightly as possible, but the momentum of her fall sent her tumbling off her feet. Simone rolled over a couple of times, aware that pain was shooting up her left leg from her ankle. It must have twisted under her when she landed, she realized.

She couldn't allow a little pain to stop her, she told herself.

She would pay no attention to it, would block it out just as she had blocked out everything else that threatened to keep her from what she wanted. Climbing quickly to her feet, she cast a glance toward Grenville Avenue. Pedestrians and riders passed by in front of the narrow alley's mouth, but no one seemed to have noticed her. The fact that she was wearing a simple, dark brown dress probably made it more difficult to see her back here. Quickly she moved even deeper into the shadows, toward the rear of the hotel.

Shards of pain lanced through her ankle and up her leg, but she paid them no heed. A slight limp was impossible to avoid, but Simone didn't let it slow her down. She breathed a little easier as she rounded the back corner of the hotel. Now she was completely out of sight from Grenville Avenue.

No one was back here at the moment. Luck was with her, Simone thought. She was meant to do this. Moving quickly to the rear door of the hotel, she opened it, and stepped silently into the building.

The hallway she was in led to the lobby, but before it got there the corridor passed the door of the private office she maintained here. Normally it was left unlocked during the day since there was nothing kept inside except papers pertaining to the hotel and a small safe for money and valuables belonging to the guests, which *was* locked. Simone knew the combination of that safe, of course. She tried the doorknob, found it unlocked, and heaved a sigh of relief. She opened the door and slipped into the office.

No one was there, which was just as it should have been. Fortune was still smiling on her. She closed the door and went to the safe, kneeling in front of it. It took her only a moment to twist the dial back and forth in the combination, and then she swung the door of the safe open. Her hand darted inside.

It came back out holding a small revolver.

Simone smiled as her fingers tightened around the butt of the gun.

Cole Tyler and Billy Casebolt stood inside the building that had been used as the polling place. Cole was by the table where the ballot box rested, and Casebolt was at the door. The deputy had his watch lying in his open palm, and as the hands of the timepiece moved to four and twelve, he looked up and said, "That's it, Marshal. It's four o'clock."

Cole nodded and said, "Close 'er up."

Casebolt snapped the watch shut and then closed the door of the building. He sighed. "Reckon the election's over."

"All that's left is counting the ballots," Cole said. He glanced at the three men sitting at the table. Nathan Smollett, Abel Warfield, and Ben Calhoun all looked tired, and their job wasn't over yet. Cole reached into the pocket of his buckskin shirt and withdrew the two keys that fit the lock on the iron box. He had reclaimed the second one from Kermit Sawyer a few minutes earlier. Cole dropped one of the keys on the table and fitted the other one into the lock.

"I'll call out the votes," Smollett said to his two fellow judges, "and each of you can keep a running count of them. When we get done, we'll compare the counts and see if the totals match."

"Sounds all right to me," Calhoun said, and Warfield nodded.

Cole twisted the key and lifted the lid of the box. It was filled almost to the top with the paper ballots, some of them flat, others folded once or twice or even more. He turned the box so that Smollett could reach easily into it.

Smollett plucked the first ballot from the box. "A vote

for Hank Parker," he said as he checked to see how the paper was marked. Warfield and Calhoun each made a mark on a sheet of paper in front of them. The banker picked up another ballot and said, "Another vote for Parker . . . one for Judson Kent . . . another for Kent . . . another for Kent . . . one for Parker . . . "

"We'll leave it with you," Cole said. "Ought to take you at least an hour to count all those ballots, and that's if your totals agree the first time."

Smollett nodded. "We'll be out to announce the results as soon as everything is confirmed, Marshal."

Cole and Casebolt stepped outside, closing the door firmly behind them. The deputy inclined his head toward the building and asked, "You reckon one of us ought to hang around here, just in case anybody tries anything funny with the ballots?"

"Nobody's going to do anything now, not with three men in there and all of them armed," Cole said. "Besides, if anything was to happen now, the election would just be declared invalid and we'd have to start all over. Parker wouldn't want that. His only real chance of beating Dr. Kent is having the election come so quickly after Judson got into the race. A delay would just work against Parker."

Casebolt nodded slowly. "I reckon you're right. Still, I might just pull up a chair here on the boardwalk and do some whittlin'—" The deputy stopped short and made a gulping noise. "An' maybe I won't," he went on hurriedly. He was staring wide-eyed down the street.

Cole followed Casebolt's gaze and saw Brenda Durand and Margaret Palmer coming toward them. A grin tugged at Cole's mouth, despite his weariness and tension. "I'm surprised you let a little lady like that buffalo you, Billy," he said.

"That little lady's got matrimony on her mind," snapped

Casebolt. "I still ain't figured out why she picked me, but I ain't of a mind to get myself hitched. I'll see you later, Marshal."

Casebolt moved off quickly down the boardwalk, casting nervous glances over his shoulder. A moment later Margaret Palmer swept past Cole, calling, "Excuse me! Deputy Casebolt!" Casebolt looked back again, and his gangling form almost broke into a run.

Brenda came up to Cole. "I take it the polls are closed?" she said.

He nodded. "As of a few minutes ago. The ballots are being counted now."

"Is Dr. Kent going to win?"

Cole shrugged. "I reckon we'll know in a little while, Miss Durand, like everybody else."

"My grandmother voted for him, and I would have, too, if I were old enough." Brenda sniffed. "It's not fair. I own property here in Wind River, a lot of it. I should have been allowed to vote."

"I don't make the laws," Cole told her. "I just enforce 'em."

She sighed. "I know. Well, I suppose I'll go back to the hotel and wait for the results."

Cole nodded politely to her and watched as she started back toward the Territorial House. His mind wasn't really on Brenda Durand, however.

Now that the polls were closed and the election was officially over, he could act on what Michael Hatfield had told him earlier in the day. Michael's testimony about seeing a one-armed man at the scene of Becky Lewis's murder was enough for Cole to justify the arrest of Hank Parker. Parker could sit in a jail cell for a couple of weeks until the circuit court judge arrived, and then it would be up to that esteemed jurist to untangle things.

Cole glanced over his shoulder at the closed door. Everything would be all right here, he thought. It was time for him to start moseying down to the Pronghorn— and the showdown with Hank Parker.

Brenda Durand walked briskly toward the hotel, wishing that Marshal Tyler hadn't been so stiff-necked. It wouldn't have hurt the lawman to at least give her a hint as to how he thought the election would come out. She had quite a stake in the results, after all. She owned a great deal of property in this town, and depending on what happened with the murder case against Simone McKay, she might own even more, or at least control more.

Simone couldn't run a business from a cell in the territorial prison. All the power she now possessed would soon rest firmly in the hands of Brenda Durand. That thought made a satisfied shiver run through Brenda's body.

Her mind was so full of such pleasant speculation that she almost didn't see the figure go hurrying past at the far end of the alley she was passing.

A split second later Brenda stopped short, and her breath caught in her throat as she realized what she had seen out of the corner of her eye. Unless she was badly mistaken, that had been Simone McKay back there, scurrying furtively along the lane that ran behind the buildings lining Grenville Avenue. Brenda took a step back and peered down the alley. There was nothing to be seen now, of course.

But she *hadn't* been imagining things. She was sure of that. She had seen Simone, who was supposed to be locked up in that suite on the second floor of the hotel.

Without really thinking about what she was doing, Brenda stepped into the alley and hurried along it to the rear of the buildings. She stuck her head past the corner and looked in both directions. She caught her breath again as she spotted the woman about a block to her right. It was Simone McKay, all right, and the older woman was still moving quickly but furtively, heading toward the east side of town.

And the most amazing thing of all, Brenda saw with widening eyes, was that Simone had a gun in her hand. "Oh, my God," Brenda whispered to herself. "What's she going to do?"

There was only one way to find out.

Brenda stepped out into the lane and hurried after Simone, moving as quietly as she possibly could.

19

Billy Casebolt leaned against the side of a building and lifted a hand to wipe sweat from his forehead. The day had turned hot and sultry, all right, but that wasn't why he was sweating.

Margaret had almost caught him.

He thought he had given her the slip, though. He knew the side streets of Wind River a lot better than she did. This reminded him of the time a Crow war party had chased him through the Bighorns. He had been damned lucky to get away with his hair that time.

And he'd be damned lucky to get away with his bachelorhood this time.

Not that Margaret Palmer would put a gun to his head and *force* him to get married. A lady like her wouldn't have to resort to such things. She had better weapons, such as a smile and trusting eyes, and a lower lip that could pout just a little bit and get a feller to do most anything she wanted.

Fresh beads of sweat broke out on Casebolt's forehead at the thought.

He sleeved them away and decided he needed something cool to drink. Maybe he'd stop by the Pronghorn, he decided. He didn't have any use for Hank Parker, but a gent didn't have to like a saloonkeeper to appreciate the other things the place offered. Yes, sir, a cold beer sounded mighty good right about now.

Casebolt looked warily up and down the street, checking for any sign of Margaret Palmer before he moved out of his place of concealment and scuttled toward the Pronghorn.

"Well, how do you feel now, Doctor?" asked Michael Hatfield.

Judson Kent sighed. "That's at least the tenth time you've asked me that question today, Michael. And I feel the same as I've felt all the other times: optimistic. I believe the voters of Wind River will place their faith in me, and if they do, I intend to do my utmost to serve them well as their mayor."

"I won't bother writing that down again," Michael said. "I suppose I ought to go get a statement from Parker."

They were sitting in Kent's office, waiting for the counting of the ballots to conclude, just like everyone else in Wind River. Jeremiah Newton was there, too, accompanying Kent as he had been doing all day. If anybody tried to attack the doctor again—an unlikely possibility—Jeremiah intended to be on hand to deal with the threat.

Michael stood up and said, "I'll go on over to the Pronghorn and talk to Parker." He smiled suddenly as an idea occurred to him. "Why don't you come with me, Doctor?"

"I hardly think that would be a good idea," Kent said. "Mr. Parker and I are not what one would call boon companions, are we?"

"Maybe not, but it would make a good story, having the two candidates together when the results of the election are announced. With any luck, it won't be too much longer now."

Kent frowned in thought. Michael's suggestion had taken him by surprise, but the idea of going over to the Pronghorn held a certain appeal now that he considered it. Kent had never thought of himself as a vindictive man, but after all the trouble Hank Parker had fomented over the past week or so because of this election, it might be nice to see the man's face when he found out he'd been defeated. Kent looked over at the big blacksmith and asked, "What do you think, Jeremiah?"

With a shrug of his massive shoulders, Jeremiah replied, "I've no fear of venturing into that den of iniquity, Brother Judson. And perhaps I could console Brother Parker with a Scripture or two when he realizes he's lost the election." There was a twinkle in Jeremiah's eyes as he spoke. It would do him good to see Parker experience defeat, too.

Kent nodded to the young editor and came to his feet as he said, "All right, Michael, we'll go with you. Perhaps you'll get a good story for the newspaper."

Michael Hatfield was practically rubbing his hands together in anticipation. "Maybe we ought to have elections more often," he said.

Kent just shook his head and tried not to roll his eyes as the three men left the doctor's office and headed toward the east side of the settlement.

Kermit Sawyer and Lon Rogers were about to go into the Wind River General Store when Cole stepped up onto the boardwalk in front of the emporium. The cattleman nodded to Cole and said, "Ballots bein' counted?"

"That's right," replied Cole. "Ought to have the results in a little while."

"Well, I'm disappointed," Sawyer said dryly. "I reckoned there'd be some fireworks 'fore the day was over. Looks like I was wrong. Lon and me are goin' to pick up a few supplies, then head back to the ranch."

"I'm surprised you're not going to have a drink, after waiting all day for the saloons to start serving liquor again," Cole commented.

Sawyer chuckled. "Oh, we might stop by the Pronghorn for a beer 'fore we hit the trail."

Cole nodded and started to move on past them, then stopped and looked more intently at the two men. The late afternoon sun was shining on the faces of the Texans, and Cole noticed something about them that he had never seen before. There was a certain resemblance between Sawyer and Lon, something about the eyes . . . In the right light, a person could almost take them for father and son.

But then they moved on into the building, and Cole grunted and shook his head. He had been imagining things, he told himself. He'd just chalk it up to the fact that Sawyer and Lon Rogers were both from Texas and carried themselves with that state's familiar air of self-confidence bordering on arrogance. That was all it was.

Besides, he had other things with which to concern himself now, such as arresting Hank Parker on suspicion of murder. He moved on down the street, forgetting all about Texans and resemblances and fathers and sons.

Trailing somebody without being seen wasn't something at which Brenda had much experience. Several times she had been forced to duck behind barrels or into alleys to avoid being seen by Simone when the older woman looked back. So far she thought she had been successful. Simone didn't act like somebody who knew she was being followed.

In fact, Simone didn't seem to be paying too much attention to anything that was going on around her, as if she was concentrating so much on what she was doing that there was no room in her mind for anything else. That was a little frightening, Brenda thought.

She wondered if Simone planned to kill somebody else.

Simone's heart was pounding so loudly she was surprised the entire town couldn't hear it. Her breath rasped in her throat. She forced herself to keep moving, to take one step and then another. Even though it was unladylike, her palm was sweating where it was wrapped around the butt of the little revolver.

She had no trouble finding where she was going. She knew these back alleys as well as anyone in town, although she had never frequented them. But why shouldn't she know them? she asked herself. After all, Wind River was *her* town. She had studied all the maps, and had walked every foot of the settlement in her mind. Even when the place had been only an idea in the heads of Andrew McKay and William Durand, Simone had been able to *see* it. She had worked behind the scenes, making a subtle suggestion here, asking a pointed question there. It was *her* vision that was responsible for the creation of Wind River, hers and hers alone.

And she wasn't going to let anyone cheat her of that. Hank Parker would never take away what was hers.

It would still be simple, even though her original plans for the election had been ruined. Once Judson Kent was the mayor, he would do anything she told him to. She would still be running Wind River, regardless of what Kent or anyone else thought. If he tried to cross her . . .

Well, she could deal with that, too.

She stopped at the back of a building and looked up at the door that sat at the top of three steps. That was the rear entrance of the Pronghorn, she knew. Not far on the other side of that door was the only man who stood in the way of her retaining her grip on this community.

Simone's fingers tightened on the gun. She went up the three steps, grasped the knob of the saloon's back door, turned it, and went in.

Cole spotted Judson Kent, Michael Hatfield, and Jeremiah Newton walking down Grenville Avenue ahead of him, and from the direction they were going, it seemed they might be bound for the Pronghorn, as unlikely as that was. Increasing his pace, Cole lifted a hand and called out to them.

The three men stopped and turned to greet him. Michael asked excitedly, "Have the ballots been counted?"

"Not that I know of," Cole replied. "Give it a little more time, Michael. Where are you fellas headed?"

"I'm going to the Pronghorn to get a statement from Parker," explained Michael. "Dr. Kent and Jeremiah agreed to come along."

Cole frowned. "Are you sure that's a good idea, Judson?" he asked the doctor. "Parker may not be very happy to see you."

"I expect he won't be," Kent said. "But I think it's appropriate that the two of us be together when the results of the election are announced, don't you?"

Cole thought about it for a moment. He had been planning to take Parker into custody, but if the arrest had waited this long, it could wait a little longer. There was something appealing about Michael's suggestion, all right. And since Cole had already decided to accompany the three of them to the Pronghorn, it wasn't very likely Parker would start any trouble.

Besides, Cole wanted to watch Parker's face when the saloonkeeper found out he had lost the election. Cole had a feeling that was going to be the case.

"All right," he said. "Let's go."

Walking side by side on the boardwalk, the four men had gone less than a block when Billy Casebolt appeared on the corner ahead of them, emerging from a side street. He grinned at them and said, "Howdy, fellers. You look like you're settin' out on some serious business. Anything wrong?"

"We're just going down to the Pronghorn to wait for the election results," Cole told the deputy. "You want to come along, Billy?"

"I had in mind headin' down there anyway, just to get a drink." Casebolt chuckled. "Looks like Parker's goin' to get even more business than he counted on today."

"He's going to be mighty surprised when he sees all of us come in," Michael said.

They were only a few doors away from the saloon now. They crossed one more alley mouth and stepped back up on the boardwalk.

A pair of gunshots cracked through the air, and Cole knew immediately that they came from inside the Pronghorn.

"Stay back!" Cole snapped at Kent, Michael, and Jeremiah. "Come on, Billy!" He was reaching for his gun as he broke into a trot.

Casebolt was right behind him. Cole had his revolver in one hand as he slapped the batwings aside with the other and hurried into the saloon. He stopped short at what he saw, and Casebolt almost plowed into his back, the deputy catching himself just in time. Curious about what was going on, the doctor, the editor, and the blacksmith disregarded Cole's orders and crowded into the doorway behind the two lawmen.

Some of the saloon's customers were rapidly diving for cover, while others sat at the tables and gaped up toward the balcony overlooking the big room, mouths open in shock. Cole could understand how they felt. He was looking at something he had never expected to see.

Simone McKay and Hank Parker stood on the balcony. Simone had a gun in her hand, and the barrel of the pistol was pointed straight at Parker's head. The muzzle didn't waver even a fraction of an inch as Simone held it rock steady. Parker stood about ten feet from her, his one arm half lifted in a gesture of surrender. "Hold on there, Mrs. McKay," he was saying nervously. "Why don't you just point that gun somewhere else?"

"Simone!" Cole exclaimed.

She didn't turn her head toward him, didn't give any indication that she had heard him. She stared over the barrel of the gun at Parker and said in a voice loud enough to be heard throughout the room, "You can't have Wind River. It's mine."

Parker swallowed hard and said, "Look, lady, just put down the gun. We'll talk about whatever's bothering you."

Behind Cole, Judson Kent said quietly, "Oh, my God, what's happened to her?"

Cole thought he knew. He had seen the same stiff expression Simone now wore, the same blazing-eyed stare, in men who had finally been pushed too far, men who were willing to go to any lengths to remove whatever was tormenting them. Simone was a little bit mad, he thought, and somehow she had gotten out of that hotel room and gotten her hands on a gun.

Then she had come here to kill Hank Parker. Cole was sure of it.

"Reckon we'd better do somethin', Marshal?" Casebolt asked nervously. "Miz McKay acts like she don't even know we're here."

"Maybe she doesn't," Cole said. Slowly he holstered his gun. "Let's all just take it easy. Maybe I can go up there and talk some sense into her." He started toward the foot of the stairs.

"You killed her!" Simone suddenly accused Parker. "You were trying to get rid of me, so you had Becky Lewis blackmail me just to give me a motive for murdering her! But *you're* the one who killed her, Parker. You knew I'd be blamed for it, and you knew I'd have to drop out of the election! It was you all along, it was you!"

Cole paused at the foot of the stairs. Simone might be out of her head, but what she was saying made sense. Maybe she wasn't crazy at all, he thought. Maybe she was just fed up with Parker getting away with the frame he had built around her.

Parker's face was pale, and he was still sweating. "That's a lie!" he said angrily. "I didn't kill anybody."

Cole glanced around. The saloon was just about deserted now, with the exception of Casebolt, Kent, Michael, and Jeremiah. And one of the bartenders, who stood practically cowering at the end of the bar. Cole caught the man's eye and asked, "What happened?"

"She's crazy, Marshal!" the man exclaimed. "She must've snuck in the back, because all of a sudden she was in here waving that gun around and demanding to see the boss. When he stepped out onto the balcony, she ran up the stairs and took a couple of shots at him. You'd better shoot her before she kills somebody, Marshal!"

"There's been enough killing," Cole snapped. He turned

his attention back to the tableau at the top of the stairs. "Simone, we'll handle this now," he said. "Why don't you just put the gun down and let me take care of Parker?"

For the first time, Simone seemed to hear him. She turned her head a little and said, "Cole . . . ?"

Parker tried to take advantage of her distraction and darted toward a nearby open doorway. Simone jerked the trigger of the pistol, and the gun cracked wickedly. The bullet struck Parker in the left shoulder and jerked him around. He stumbled to a halt and pressed his hand against the wound.

"If you move again, I'll kill you!" Simone screamed at him. "Now tell them the truth! Tell everyone the truth! I didn't kill Becky Lewis—you did!"

Down below, Kermit Sawyer and Lon Rogers came through the bat-winged entrance, and the middle-aged cattleman frowned and said, "What the hell—!"

Casebolt said, "Hush! Get out o' here if you can't be quiet."

Sawyer and Lon exchanged a glance and stayed where they were, silent and watchful now.

Cole had considered rushing up the stairs at Simone when she fired the shot, but he knew he couldn't reach her in time to keep her from pulling the trigger again. The little revolver probably had at least two rounds left in its cylinder. At this range, even the small-caliber gun could be fatal.

Instead he took one step and then paused, hoping he could keep Simone talking long enough to work his way closer to her. Making sure his voice was calm, he said to her, "Killing Parker won't help anything, Simone. I came here to arrest him. I've got a witness who says he was up at the church the night Becky Lewis was killed."

"That's a damn lie!" Parker said, still gritting his teeth

against the pain of his wounded shoulder. "I wasn't anywhere near the place."

Michael Hatfield spoke up. "Then why did you come to my office and make sure I'd be up there that night, Parker? You had to be certain there would be a witness on hand to implicate Mrs. McKay."

"I was just trying to help the Lewis girl," Parker said, an edge of desperation creeping into his voice. "After all she suffered at the hands of the McKays, she deserved whatever she could get!"

"I think you killed her," Michael shot back. "I'm the one who saw you up there. I saw a one-armed man fighting with Becky Lewis!"

"You're crazy, too!" growled Parker. "You've all been out to get me, ever since I came to Wind River!"

"All right," Cole said suddenly. "Maybe what we all ought to do is just clear out, Parker, and leave you here alone with Mrs. McKay. The two of you can settle this between yourselves."

"No!" Parker exclaimed. "You . . . you can't do that! She's a lunatic. Just look at her! She'll kill me like she killed her husband!"

Cole began, "That's just the lie Becky Lewis used—"

"No, it's the truth!" Parker broke in. "Becky convinced me. She was there on the platform that day! She saw Mrs. McKay shoot her husband."

"It's much more likely," Judson Kent put in, "that the Lewis woman herself was guilty of Andrew McKay's murder—"

"No," Simone whispered in a choked voice that made everyone else in the room fall silent. "No, that woman didn't shoot Andrew."

Cole wasn't sure what Simone meant by that, but it didn't matter right now. What was important was getting the truth out of Parker. "What about it, Parker?" he asked. "Do you tell us the truth, or do we leave you with Mrs. McKay?"

"You can't do that!" Parker protested. "You're the law!"

Cole started to back down the stairs.

"All right!" Parker cried raggedly. "I did it! I killed that little slut! She was worth more to me dead than alive. Are you satisfied, Tyler? Are all of you satisfied, damn it?"

Simone let out a long sigh, and the hand holding the gun suddenly drooped.

Parker's face wore a look of horror. He realized he had just confessed to Becky Lewis's murder, and he must have been seeing his dream of being the mayor of Wind River disappear like smoke. He must have been seeing himself standing on a gallows and then plummeting through the trap to wind up at the end of a hangrope. . . .

With an inarticulate shout of rage, he leaped toward Simone, his hand dropping away from his wounded shoulder and sweeping underneath his coat to pluck a gun from a hidden holster.

Cole saw the pistol emerge in Parker's hand and lunged up the remaining stairs toward Simone. "Get down!" he shouted, planting a hand in her back and shoving her roughly to the side as he went to one knee at the head of the stairs. The gun in Parker's hand blasted, and a slug whipped past Cole's head.

Then his own revolver was in his hand and bucking against his palm as it came level. More shots crashed against Cole's ears, and he saw dust leaping from the front of Parker's coat and vest as bullet after bullet thudded into the saloonkeeper's body. Cole triggered twice and saw both of his slugs drive into Parker's chest. The man did a jittering, grotesque little dance under the impact of the lead, then slumped against the wall. His gun slipped from his fingers and fell to the floor of the balcony. As the shooting stopped, Parker lurched away from the wall, leaving an ugly bloodstain behind. He careened across the balcony and hit the railing, which cracked and split apart under his burly body. Parker fell heavily, landing on a poker table, which splintered into kindling under him. He lay motionless in the debris.

Cole took a deep breath and looked toward the entrance to the saloon. Billy Casebolt and the others stood just inside the batwings where he had left them, and powder smoke drifted from the muzzle of the deputy's gun. But Kermit Sawyer and Lon Rogers were both holding smoking revolvers, too, and Cole knew they had taken part in the fusillade that had blown Hank Parker to hell.

The violence was over. Cole jammed his gun back in its holster and turned anxiously toward Simone.

Her ears rang deafeningly from the gunshots, but still she was able to hear the familiar voice that boomed out at her. *"You!"* it accused. "It was you! Now I know the truth!"

Simone was lying on the balcony, next to the wall where Cole Tyler had shoved her to get her out of the way of the murderous saloonkeeper's shots. Now she saw Andrew standing there in front of the broken railing, his hand lifted so that he could point a finger at her. His ghostly features were set in grim, angry lines.

"No, Andrew!" she cried. "It's a lie! He was lying! I never would have hurt you!"

"I know the truth," he repeated. "I didn't want to believe it, but they're all here now—William and Becky and Parker. They've told me the truth about you. You killed me, Simone. *You killed me!*"

"Noooo!" she screamed as she came to her feet and pointed the gun she still held at him.

"Simone!" Cole said urgently as he drew back, away from the barrel of the gun she was waving around wildly. "Simone, stop it! It's over now! Nobody's going to hurt you."

"Get away!" she cried, but she didn't seem to be talking to him. "Leave me alone, damn you! I never wanted to kill you! I just wanted you to appreciate me! There wouldn't have even been a town here without me, but you and William acted like it was all your doing! And then you went to that slut's bed . . . Damn you, Andrew! Damn you, damn you, damn you! I'm *glad* I killed you! Now go away and leave me alone!"

Cole and all the others in the saloon were staring at her, aghast and amazed at what they were hearing. The gun Simone held was shaking crazily now as she put both hands on it and tried to aim it at the empty air where the balcony railing had been. Cole edged toward her, slowly and carefully, thinking that maybe he could dive underneath the gun and tackle her. She had been out of her head before, but she was completely mad now, he sensed, and the knowledge made him feel hollow inside. But she was still his friend, and she needed help.

If he had to, he would risk his life to give her that help.

Andrew still stood there, mocking her with his presence and that accusing finger he was pointing at her. Simone didn't know where she was anymore, was not aware of anything except the face staring at her with that awful expression on it. In a voice like thunder rolling over the Wyoming plains, Andrew opened his mouth again and intoned, "*You . . . killed . . . me!*"

"Shut up!" Simone screamed, and the gun jumped in her hands as she jerked the trigger. She fired again and again, the hammer striking now on empty chambers as the cylinder whirled. Still Andrew stood there, the bullets having no effect on him. He started to speak again, but Simone couldn't bear to hear his voice. Shrieking out her rage, she flung the empty gun aside and threw herself at him, her hands reaching out for his throat, willing to do anything to silence the terrible truth that came from him.

Suddenly she felt cold, a deep, numbing cold, unlike anything she had ever experienced. And she seemed to be floating, taking the cold with her as she plunged into nothingness. Faintly she heard a cracking sound, and instantly, to her incredible relief, the cold was gone, replaced by warmth. Warmth, and a darkness that spread up around her, cradling her like a gentle hand, comforting her as it enveloped her and carried her away.

Simone went willingly. Andrew was finally gone, and that was all that mattered. She didn't care about anything else.

Until the warmth became heat, and it grew hotter and hotter until Simone began screaming again. Her skin blistered agonizingly, and everything inside her seemed to shrivel. But even that wasn't the worst of it.

She knew that when she got to where she was going, Andrew would be waiting for her. After all, she had found his killer at last. She had freed him.

And he would be there to greet her.

20

Judson Kent looked up from the body sprawled beside Hank Parker's and said, "She's dead." The doctor seemed to have aged ten years in the past few moments, like everyone else in the saloon.

Cole stood at the edge of the balcony, next to the broken railing. He clenched his hands into fists, closed his eyes, and said miserably, "Damn it! If I had just been a little faster . . ."

"The fall broke her neck," Kent went on, as if Cole hadn't spoken. "No doubt she died almost instantly."

Cole shook his head, turned away from the edge, and went slowly down the stairs.

To his surprise, a very pale and shaken Brenda Durand was waiting for him at the bottom. He frowned at her and asked, "Where did you come from?"

Brenda pointed toward the rear hallway that emerged near the base of the staircase. "I was hiding back there," she said. "I saw Mrs. McKay sneaking in here with a gun, and I followed her. What . . . what happened?"

Cole looked at the pair of bodies on the sawdust-littered floor of the saloon and said quietly, "Judgment day. I reckon it caught up to more than one of us today."

Michael Hatfield was as pale as Brenda as he came up to Cole. He had to swallow hard a couple of times before he was able to ask, "Do you . . . do you think she was telling the truth, Marshal? There at the end, I mean?"

"I don't know, Michael. She was saying what she *thought* was true." Cole sighed, struggling to accept all the implications of what had happened here. "I'd say there was a good chance she was telling the truth."

"But that would mean . . . that Mrs. McKay really killed . . . Oh, Lord!" Michael looked sick, but he was fighting against it.

Judson Kent stood up, took off his coat, and draped it over Simone's face and upper body. Just before her features disappeared underneath the garment, Cole was struck by how twisted and frightened they were.

As if Simone had found something even worse than death.

Jeremiah moved up and knelt beside the bodies. He began praying silently, his head back, and Cole wasn't sure if he was saying a prayer for Simone or for Hank Parker. Both of them probably could have used it, Cole thought. Right about now, everybody in here could use a prayer said for them.

Kermit Sawyer came across the room and said to Cole, "Hell of a note, ain't it? When I was complaining about there not being any fireworks around here, I sure didn't mean for something like this to happen."

"Not your fault, Sawyer," Cole said to the Texan. "I reckon the seeds for this were planted a long time ago."

He heard the sound of the batwings being pushed open and turned around to see Nathan Smollett standing in the entrance of the saloon. The banker looked at the bodies and gulped audibly. "My God," Smollett said in a hushed voice. "I . . . I never dreamed . . . I was told there was some trouble over here, but I never dreamed . . . "

"What is it, Mr. Smollett?" Cole asked, breaking into the man's horrified reverie.

Smollett gave a shake of his head and tore his gaze away from Simone and Parker. "I . . . I just thought you'd like to know, Marshal. The ballots have all been counted, and the figures match up." The banker swallowed again, looked at Kent, and went on, "Congratulations, Doctor. You're the first mayor of Wind River."

Cole Tyler stepped out onto the boardwalk in front of the marshal's office and took a deep breath. It was amazing, he thought, how everything could change, yet still look the same. A casual visitor to Wind River would never know how different things were now than they had been a week ago.

The distant sound of hammering floated to Cole's ears. Jeremiah and some of the townspeople who had volunteered to help him were up on the knoll rebuilding the church. Closer at hand, wagons rolled by in the street, riders made their way along Grenville Avenue, and pedestrians strolled on the boardwalks. Life went on.

But not for Simone McKay.

She had been buried six days earlier, Jeremiah presiding over the service as Simone was laid to rest beside her husband. Cole felt a little uneasy about that for some reason, but it had seemed like the proper thing to do. There was plenty of gossip around town about what had happened inside the Pronghorn, but only those who had been there knew what had been said and how Simone had really died. There was an unspoken pact among them to keep the facts to themselves. Even Michael Hatfield had resisted the temptation to print the true story in the newspaper. The *Sentinel* had belonged to Simone, and Michael had refused to dishonor her memory in its pages.

The problem with that, as Cole saw it, was that he wasn't sure if her memory deserved to be honored. She had been a cold-blooded killer; she had fooled everybody in town, including him, and had used all of them, manipulating them for her own purposes for over a year. Cole wasn't sure if he was ready to forgive and forget just yet.

He was brooding about that when the sound of a buggy coming to a stop in front of the marshal's office broke into his bleak thoughts and made him look up. A grin suddenly tugged at his mouth, the first genuine smile on his face in over a week.

Judge Burl Sharp had arrived.

The circuit court judge was a burly, middle-aged man with a salt-and-pepper beard. Cole had known him for a long time, since before Sharp had been a jurist. In fact, the man had started out as a wagon train guide, back in the forties. He had taught himself the law, practiced for years as an attorney, and then been appointed to the territorial court by the governor. Despite the rough edges he still possessed from his earlier days, Sharp had a keen legal mind, and that was a good thing, Cole thought. It would take a smart fella to figure out the mess that Simone's death had left behind.

Sharp lifted a hand in greeting and called out, "Hello, Cole! Good to see you again!" Beside the big man on the seat of the buggy was his adopted daughter, the half-breed

Indian girl known as Mockingbird, who traveled the circuit with him. The little girl, who was about eight years old, held out her arms to the marshal and said excitedly, "Uncle Cole!"

Cole stepped down off the boardwalk and moved to the side of the buggy, picking up Mockingbird and giving her a hug. He shook hands with Burl Sharp, then said, "I'm glad you're here, Judge. We've got a skillet full of snakes for you to untangle."

"That's what I'm here for," Sharp said heartily as he climbed down from the buggy. "Let's get to it."

The meeting took place inside the same building that had been used for the election. Chairs had been brought in so that all the people Judge Sharp had summoned could sit down while he announced his findings. This wasn't a formal session of the court, since there was no longer a murder trial for Sharp to preside over, but the people gathered here still had a solemn air about them.

Sharp sat at the table where the ballot box had been. He had a pair of reading glasses perched on the end of his nose and several pages of documents spread out in front of him. He looked up at the group and cleared his throat, obviously ready to begin.

Cole tried not to squirm in his chair. He hoped the judge didn't take too long about this. There were things he had to do.

"First of all," Sharp said in his booming voice, "I have decided not to reopen the matter of Andrew McKay's death. The case has been officially closed for more than a year, and I see no compelling reason to alter that."

Cole nodded, glad of the judge's decision. No matter what had happened in the past, McKay, Simone, Durand,

and Becky Lewis were all dead. Nothing was going to bring them back.

"The death of Hank Parker has been ruled self-defense by your local coroner, and I concur in that assessment," Sharp went on. "As for the tragic passing of Mrs. Simone McKay, a ruling of accidental death is unavoidable."

Cole agreed with that, too.

"Mr. Parker died intestate, so his holdings—primarily the establishment known as the Pronghorn Saloon—will be auctioned by the territory and sold to the highest bidder. Mrs. McKay, however, did leave a will, and the original partnership agreement between her husband and the late William Durand also comes into play." Sharp looked at Brenda Durand, who sat in the front row with her grandmother. "Miss Durand, I find that as the sole surviving heir of the original partners, ownership of the joint holdings of said partnership devolves to you. Congratulations, little lady. With a few exceptions, you own yourself a town."

Brenda blinked and tried to smile, but Cole thought she looked more scared than pleased. Quite a responsibility had just fallen on her young shoulders. He hoped she was up to the task. With her grandmother's help, maybe she would be.

Sharp went on, "There are a few codicils to this agreement that are rather irregular, but which I am going to allow anyway. Mrs. McKay wanted ownership of the properties on which the Wind River Cafe and the blacksmith shop stand to go to the operators of those businesses, Miss Rose Foster and Mr. Jeremiah Newton, respectively. Do you have any objection to that, Miss Durand?"

Brenda shook her head without hesitation, and Rose and Jeremiah, also seated in the front row, looked at each other and smiled.

"Now we come to the matter of Mrs. McKay's personal holdings, which are considerable. Mr. Hatfield?"

Michael looked up at the judge. He had been scribbling furiously on his pad of paper, trying to keep up with Sharp's rulings for the story he would write for the *Sentinel*. Michael had told Cole he wasn't sure what would happen to the paper, but he intended to keep publishing it until someone told him otherwise.

"Mr. Hatfield," Sharp continued, "Mrs. McKay's will specifies that you are the new owner of the *Wind River Sentinel*."

Michael gaped at the judge for a moment before finding his voice and saying, "Me? But . . . but I can't run the paper by myself. . . ."

"Mrs. McKay obviously believed you can," Sharp said dryly. "The newspaper is yours, Mr. Hatfield."

Cole leaned forward and clapped a hand on Michael's shoulder. "Don't worry, Michael," he said. "You'll do just fine."

Michael nodded but didn't look convinced of that.

Judge Sharp cleared his throat and said, "We've almost come to the conclusion."

Maybe so, Cole thought, but it wasn't soon enough to suit him. He had waited long enough. He stood up and said, "Begging your pardon, Judge, but since the mayor is here, can I conduct a little town business?"

Judson Kent was sitting a couple of chairs away from Cole. He looked up at the marshal with a frown of confusion and surprise on his face. Sharp didn't look pleased at the interruption, but he said, "Is this important, Marshal?"

"I think it is," Cole replied. He reached up and unpinned the badge from his buckskin shirt. "I'm resigning as the marshal of Wind River." He dropped the badge on the chair next to Kent.

Billy Casebolt had been standing at the back of the room, leaning against the wall beside the door with his arms crossed over his chest. Now he straightened abruptly, his eyes widening, and he exclaimed, "Resignin'! You can't do that, Marshal!" His cry was echoed by several of the other people in the room.

"The hell I can't," Cole snapped. "I never intended for the job to be permanent. I stayed on here a lot longer than I ever figured I would. But now it's time to move on." He turned toward the doorway. Ulysses was at the hitch rack just outside, saddled up and ready to go.

"Wait just a moment," Kent said crisply. He stood up, the marshal's badge in his hand, and moved so that he was facing Cole squarely. "As the mayor of this community, Cole, I refuse to accept your resignation." His voice softened a little as he went on, "The town needs you, and I think you need Wind River. You've made a life here. Your friends are here."

Cole shook his head stubbornly. "Doesn't matter whether you accept my resignation or not. I'm leaving either way."

Judge Sharp spoke up, saying with a chuckle, "Well, it's not quite that simple, Cole."

Cole frowned and looked over his shoulder at the judge. "What do you mean? I don't reckon you've got any say in this, Judge."

"No, but the late Mrs. McKay does. She left you the hotel, the land development company, her house, and all the rest of her estate except the newspaper." Sharp chuckled again. "You're the first lawman I've ever seen who owned such a sizable chunk of the settlement he worked for."

Cole was thunderstruck. He couldn't have been more surprised if the heavens had fallen on him. He stared at

Judge Sharp for a long moment, then finally said, "I . . . I never owned much in my life. . . ."

"Well, you do now, my friend."

Judson Kent pressed the badge back into Cole's hand and smiled as he said, "You see, you can't quit. You can't just ride away from Wind River, Cole. It's *your* town, too."

Rose Foster stood up, moved to Cole's side, and put a hand on his arm. "It always has been, right from the first," she said quietly. "Please stay, Cole."

Billy Casebolt said, "I ain't deputyin' for anybody else, Marshal. If you ride off, I'll just have to go with you, and then Wind River'll be without any law at all."

"And I figure as long as you're around, Marshal, I'll have something to write about in the paper," Michael Hatfield put in.

Jeremiah reached out with a long arm and put his huge hand on Cole's shoulder. "I'll trust in the Lord that you'll make the right decision, Brother Cole."

Cole looked around at them, the people who had come to mean so much to him. Simone was gone, but they were still here. His friends . . . Even Brenda Durand caught his eye, smiled at him, and nodded.

For a long moment Cole was silent. Then he drew a deep breath and said, "Oh, hell—"

Before he could go on, there was a patter of footsteps on the boardwalk outside, and one of the townsmen stuck his head in the door. "Better come quick, Marshal!" the man said urgently. "Some of those boys from the Diamond S and the Latch Hook spread rode in at the same time, and I think there's going to be a gunfight!"

Cole reached out, plucked the marshal's badge out of Kent's hand, and pinned it on. "Looks like I'll be here for a while longer," he said as he turned toward the door. "Come on, Billy."

"Yes, sir!" Casebolt responded with a grin that threatened to split his grizzled face in half. The two men hurried out of the building, and Cole was grinning, too, even as he made sure his revolver was riding easy in its holster.

He was still the law in Wind River.

James Reasoner lives in Azle, Texas.

#5 DARK TRAIL

No one is laying out the welcome mat for the latest visitors to Wind River. These revenge-seeking New Orleans natives send bullets flying in a deadly showdown that could change the face of Wind River forever.

#6 JUDGMENT DAY

Not everyone is glad to see the railroad coming to Wind River. Caught in the middle of those for and those against, Marshal Cole Tyler must keep the peace even as events force him to choose sides in the battle for the future of the town.

Order 4 or more and postage & handling is FREE!

For Fans of the Traditional Western: